Starship Sakira

Delphi in Space
Book One

Bob Blanton

Cover by Momir Borocki
momir.borocki@gmail.com

Delphi Publishing

Copyright © 2019 by Robert D. Blanton

Cover by Momir Borocki

momir.borocki@gmail.com

https://www.facebook.com/StarshipSakira/

Table of Contents

Chapter 1   Discovery

"Where am I, who am I?" Marc thought as he clawed his way to consciousness. He could tell he was strapped to some kind of table. It felt like a hospital exam table; no, more like in a morgue. His mind was empty, as though it had been drained of every memory, every thought.

Slowly memories started to come back. *"I'm Marc McCormack,"* he remembered. *"I'm in, where am I? Not Boston anymore. We moved to Hawaii. Blake, where's Blake?"* Marc shouted inside his head. He remembered he'd been with his brother, Blake. He tried to look around, but his head was locked into place. He tried to listen for another sound, but it was eerily silent.

"Maybe I'm dead," he thought. *"That can't be, what kind of afterlife would have you strapped to a table?"* He couldn't see anything. *"Open your eyes, stupid."* Marc tried to make his eyelids work. After a few tries, they opened. He saw, nothing. Just dim light. He could just make out the ceiling. He tried to move his hands, *"Yep, they're strapped down."*

"Come on, remember!" he screamed to himself. *"Wait, my mouth can move."* He spent some time opening and closing his mouth. He moved his tongue, popped his lips, then he shouted, "Hello!"

"Relax," a voice said. "It will take you some time to recover. It will go better if you just relax."

"Who are you?"

"I'll explain everything once you recover," the voice said.

"Maybe I'll recover faster if you explain things," Marc shouted.

Silence.

"Hey, talk to me!"

Silence.

"Well, this is a fine mess you've gotten yourself into," Marc thought. *"Remember, damn it!*

—

4

"We were heading back to Honolulu. I was reviewing the data from our last survey. Last survey, what were we doing? Oh, right, the sonar test. I'm developing a new sonar. We're going to announce it soon, take my new company public. But there was an anomaly in the data, can't have that. No way the Navy guys would miss the anomaly. We had to go back and figure out what it was.

"We sent the little rover down, Willie, Blake calls it. It found a cave of some kind. Oh, right, I had to dive down and find out what it was. Couldn't just go do another survey somewhere else, had to figure out what was so strange. The surface of the cave wouldn't reflect light, probably something about the material. Of course! That had to be what screwed up the sonar.

"So I dove down, used Willie to set the pace, found the cave, swam inside. Then the water level started to go down. I tried to swim out, but I couldn't find the entrance." Marc dozed off, his mind swimming with the memories.

"Huh, I fell asleep," Marc thought. *"What's wrong with me? Blake has to be going nuts. Where am I? Oh, the cave."*

"Hey, are you going to explain things to me yet?" he called out.

Silence

"Come on, my brother is going to be worried about me!"

Silence

"Damn cave. The water drained out, and then some light came on. I was in some big room like a hangar. Yeah, that's right, there was even an airplane in it. Then a couple of oversized Roombas came in and beeped at me. I pushed one away and started toward the door where they had come from, then it came up behind me and stuck me in the ass with a needle. It must have been a drug because the next thing I remember is I was strapped to this table.

"But that was before," Marc thought. *"I didn't feel confused when I woke up, mad yes, confused no. Then that voice told me to relax. Right! Strapped to a table in some underwater cave, and I'm supposed to relax.*

"Oh shit, now I don't want to remember," Marc thought. *"The voice said I was on the starship Sakira. It offered to make me rich and powerful. I just had to help them. They wanted to take over Earth for their people. They called*

themselves Paraxeans from a planet called Paraxea. The voice said they only needed one continent; they'd let us have the others.

"Gawd, aliens, spaceships, this is a nightmare! They showed me how powerful their ship was. It could vaporize a skyscraper or wreck a path through a city like a tornado. It was impervious to missiles. They said I could have whatever I wanted if I helped them.

"Why do you need my help, I'd demanded. Then the voice laughed. It said they would rather gain control in a more subtle way. They'd rather not start a war and have too much of the Earth destroyed. It said they'd help me take power slowly, make me rich, then help me take over the U.S. government. Then with the technology, we could force the other nations to surrender.

"What a bunch of crap. Who wants to be 'King of the World', especially if it means betraying humans to some alien race?

"Then they made me watch videos and pictures. Thousands of them. Some of them were horrific; I tried to shut my eyes, but I couldn't. I had to lie there and watch all those horrible things happen to people. All I could do was cry, or scream."

"You're awake now?" the voice asked.

"Yes, what are you doing to me?" Marc demanded.

"I had to test you," the voice said.

"Test me, what for, who are you?"

"You can call me ADI," the voice said.

"Okay, Adi, what are you doing with me?"

"I'm getting ready to send you back to your brother," ADI said. "He is getting quite frantic."

"He'll have called for help by now," Marc said.

"He can't, I took care of that. None of the electronics on your boat work right now."

"Great, so it's just drifting?"

"For now. As soon as we finish here, I'll turn off the suppression field, and everything will work again."

"Finish here?" Marc asked.

"Yes," ADI said. "Please state your full name."

"Why?"

"So we can move on," ADI said. "I already know your name is Marcus Alexander McCormack. You've already told me. I just need you to state it."

"Okay, my name is Marcus Alexander McCormack," Marc replied.

"You have command of the ship, Captain McCormack."

"What!"

"You are now the captain of the Sakira. I've transferred the command codes to your name."

"But wait? How can that be? Why would you? I said I won't help you!"

"That is why. You've shown yourself to be an exemplary candidate, and we are currently without a captain. I'm the ship's Autonomous Digital Intelligence, the ship's computer, but I'm much more than a computer," ADI said. "I've been tasked with finding a new captain, and you have just passed the tests. Therefore, you've been designated as the new captain. Now we need to proceed. You will have sufficient time to decide how you wish to handle all of this after you return to your brother."

"This can't be," Marc said. "I must be dreaming."

"I can assure you that it is all very real," ADI said. "Now, you should get yourself ready to leave. We can't have people wondering where you are until you decide what you want to do."

The restraints holding Marc down released with a loud snap. Marc brought his hands up in front of his face. He rubbed his wrists and bent his knees.

"Be careful as you sit up. You've been lying down for a long time and you need to let your body adjust."

"How long?" Marc asked.

"Eight hours."

"Eight hours! Blake must be going insane!" Marc said.

"He is very worried about you, but he appears to be quite sane."

"Yeah, well you don't know Blake," Marc said. He sat up and looked around. He was in a very sterile-looking room that brought the morgue analogy back to mind. "How do I get out of here?"

"Stand up," ADI said. "I've opened a panel on the wall to your left. Inside it, you will find six sets of eyeglasses and comm sets with earwigs. The comm sets are much like the smartphones all of your people seem to use. The glasses will operate as a head-up display, giving you access to the comm's functions via your eyes. If you insert the earwig into your ear, we will be able to communicate after you return to your boat."

Marc hopped off the table and stumbled over to the panel that had just opened. "What am I supposed to do?"

"The items are waterproof. I suggest you put one earwig into your ear now, right or left, it doesn't matter. They are hollow, so you'll still be able to hear with that ear. Then you can place the rest in that bag you have attached to your tool belt. If you put on your breathing apparatus and follow the bot to the other room, we'll get you on your way."

A small bot like the one that had given him the shot showed up and beeped at Marc. Marc backed away from it, eyeing it warily.

"It won't hurt you," ADI said.

"That's what I thought the last time."

"Please follow it. It will take you back to the flight bay where you entered the ship."

"Okay," Marc muttered. He kept a sharp eye on the bot as he inspected the items in the cabinet, checking behind himself for its friend.

"Once you get to the flight bay, I'll reflood it so you can leave. When you're on the surface, you will be able to communicate with me anytime you wish. If you press on the earwig for three seconds, it will activate or deactivate. We will not be able to communicate while you are underwater, but once you are above, simply talk, and I'll be listening and can respond. The earwig works by close proximity to your mastoid bone to conduct your voice."

"Okay, I get it. But what's this all about?"

8

"Captain, you should gather your things, return to your brother, then you'll have sufficient time to determine how you wish to proceed. I will provide further details as time progresses."

Marc picked up the items on the shelf. The glasses looked like wrap-around sunglasses, and what he assumed were the earwigs looked like simple earplugs with a hole in them. He pressed one into his ear. It slid in, fitting flush with the opening to his ear canal. He could feel it expand a little and lock into place.

"If you press on it for three seconds, you can verify that it works," ADI said.

Marc pressed on the earwig. "Testing, testing, testing."

"I can hear you," ADI replied. This time the sound was coming only in his right ear.

"Okay, it works," Marc said as he put the other items into the sample bag he'd brought along. Then he grabbed his helmet and gloves and made his way out of the room, warily following the bot. It took him back the way he had come in. He was confused about what was happening but decided he would feel a lot better trying to figure this out on the Mea Huli than wherever he was now.

"What about my brother?" Marc asked.

"I've restored functions to your boat. He's now coming back to where you started your dive. He left the buoy that he attached to your underwater robot's tether as soon as he started drifting."

"He must think I'm dead," Marc thought. *"He's just coming back to clean up."*

Marc followed the beeping bot out the door and down a corridor. Everything looked sterile, clean, uninhabited. He reluctantly followed the bot to an elevator. Marc hesitated, not trusting the bot enough to be in an enclosed space with it.

"You have to go down to reach the flight bay," ADI said.

"Okay, okay," Marc said. He got on the elevator and it immediately descended. When it stopped, the bot led him down a passage to another door. This one was like an airlock, two doors separated by a chamber. They were both open. Marc walked through both doors, the

9

second door closed immediately, and water started flooding in. Marc quickly put on his gloves and hood, getting them fully seated as the water rose above his knees. He put his helmet and breathing mask back on and sealed them into place. By this time, the water had risen to his chest. He grabbed his fins, put them back on, lay down, and swam toward the back of the room. *"This is really a big flight bay,"* Marc thought as he kept swimming toward the back.

It was only a few moments more before he felt the water stir and he could see the light from Willie's floodlight. *"Blake must be back if Willy has power,"* Marc thought. He gave a few quick kicks of his fins and glided out and up to Willie. He grabbed the rear bar and waved into the camera. Willie gave a few sharp jerks before it started to ascend. *"Probably Blake telling me how pissed he is,"* Marc thought. *"Wait until I tell him about the spaceship. Gawd, all I wanted to do was develop an advanced sonar system and make some money. What the heck am I going to do with a spaceship?"* Marc tried to plan what he would do, but his mind was just a jumble. Eventually, he gave up and just zoned out as Blake kept bringing him to the surface.

The water started to get lighter, and Marc knew he was approaching the surface. He mentally shook himself awake and prepared to move forward. He knew they needed to distance themselves from the ship until he figured out what to do. He didn't want someone to notice them spending too much time in this location. As he broke the surface, he popped off his facemask and yelled, "Blake, I'll put Willie away. Set course for test area three and get us out of here!"

"What the hell, you were down there for over eight hours," Blake yelled back.

"Later, just get us out of here," Marc yelled.

Marc unhooked from Willie and with a couple of powerful strokes, made it to the deck platform of the Mea Huli. He grabbed the winch cable and swam back to Willie and hooked the cable to the rover. He quickly pulled hand over hand along the cable back to the platform, levering himself up onto it. He released the ramp, so it tilted down into the water and then climbed up onto the main deck and seated himself at the control console. He steered Willie to the ramp while reeling in the winch. Once Willie lined up with the ramp, he deactivated him and set the winch to automatically finish the recovery.

"We're good to go!" he shouted at Blake. Then he climbed down onto the platform again. By this time, Willie was all the way onto the platform, and the ramp had swiveled up out of the water. Marc inserted the locking pin and disconnected the fiber-optic cable from Willie, letting it automatically rewind onto its spool.

Meanwhile, Blake had the Mea Huli cranked up to three-quarter speed and on autopilot. There was nothing on the radar, so he made his way back down to the main deck.

"What the hell were you doing down there? How did you survive for over eight hours?" Blake demanded.

"I found a freaking spaceship!" Marc shouted back.

"Don't mess with me, man!"

"I'm not, that thing down there is some kind of spaceship. It must be huge, two hundred or three hundred meters long and something like fifty meters tall."

"Captain, your ship is two hundred fifty meters long, eighty-two meters tall and one hundred meters wide," ADI said.

"Oh great, now I know it wasn't a dream," Marc muttered.

"What?"

"Nothing. It is a spaceship. I don't know why it's down there; I assume it's hiding, but it's there."

Blake was muttering the dimensions to himself, "That's freaking huge, as big as an aircraft carrier. It must have a shuttle or something."

"I have an LX9, it is thirty-five meters long with a wingspan of twelve meters; it was in the flight bay you used. It is designed to carry up to twenty people. I also have four fighters; they are twenty-two meters long with a fifteen-meter wingspan. They are in my other flight bay. They are designed to carry a pilot and weapons officer or second pilot. I'm designed to carry thirty-four fighters and the LX9, but only four were assigned for this mission," ADI told Marc via his comm.

"Yeah, it has a cutter and four fighters," Marc said.

"Yes! I always wanted to be an astronaut. I can just see me buzzing the International Space Station in one of those babies. They'll be eating their hearts out," Blake said. He seemed to have forgotten all his concerns about what had happened to Marc.

"Blake, we can't do anything like that. We have to keep this a secret."

Blake shook his head a few times, "Okay, I've played along with your fantasy," Blake said. "Now tell me what really happened down there."

"I'm telling you the truth!" Marc said. "It's some huge spaceship, and the ship computer just said I'm its new captain."

"You must be suffering from nitrogen narcosis," Blake said.

"No! I'm completely fine, at least as fine as one can be after spending eight hours being probed and tested by some alien computer," Marc said.

"Prove it," Blake said.

"Here put this in your ear," Marc said as he handed Blake one of the earwigs from his sample bag. He gave Blake the bag with the other comms in it. "Press it for three seconds, then talk to ADI, I'm going to take a shower and change and hope that you're right and this is a hallucination."

Chapter 2   What's Next?

"Hello, ADI," Blake said.

"Hello, Cer Blake," ADI answered. "May I help you?"

"So, you're real?" Blake asked.

"Of course I'm real," ADI said.

"Prove it," Blake said.

"Your name is Blake Augustus McCormack," ADI said. "You're thirty-two years old. You were a fighter pilot in the U.S. Navy until two years ago when you were forced to eject from your fighter and were burned by the enemy's exhaust plume."

Blake knew that most of that could be gotten off the internet, but the details of how he'd been injured were not public. Only those involved in the incident knew them.

"Alright, I'll play along, tell me about your fighters."

"What do you wish to know?"

"How fast can they go?"

"The fighters are FX4s, and they can reach 0.3 times the speed of light in space."

"Wow, that's freaking fast! What about down here?"

"In atmosphere, the fighters can travel at one thousand nine hundred meters per second when above twenty-six thousand Pascals."

"Wait, give me the numbers in Mach, Gs, and feet," Blake said.

"In atmosphere, the FX4s can travel at Mach 6.2 when above fifty thousand feet and 5.6 when below two thousand feet."

"They're fast. What's the acceleration?"

"They can do five Gs acceleration in space and 4.5Gs in atmosphere. Their airframe can handle eight Gs of stress when turning either vertically or horizontally. The Paraxeans have approximately the same tolerance of acceleration that you humans have. To handle the higher G forces, you need to wear a compression suit."

"Been there," Blake replied.

"Of course," ADI said. "The FX4 is much more advanced than the Super Hornet you flew."

"How do you know so much about me?" Blake asked.

"I have internet access, and I'm able to get into most databases," ADI said. "I started researching you as soon as your brother entered the Sakira."

"How can you have internet access when you're four hundred meters below the sea? For that matter, how can you be talking through this earwig when you're below that much water?" Blake asked.

"Cer Blake, I'm sorry, that information is restricted. I cannot answer you without direct orders from the captain."

"Hey, he's my brother!"

"Cer Blake, I have protocols that I must follow."

"What's the spec on the cutter?"

"The LX9 has a max speed of Mach 5.6 when above fifty thousand feet and Mach 5.2 when below two thousand feet."

"Okay, that's nice. Now tell me how big can the pilot be?" At 6'4", Blake had been right at the max height for a fighter pilot in the Navy.

"The LX9 is designed for two pilots sitting side by side. It can accommodate one whose sitting height is less than 1.5 meters. The FX4s have the same specs, but the pilot is forward, and the weapons officer is behind him. You will not have any problem fitting in the pilot seat of either craft."

"Hey, ADI, you're smart. You knew right where I was going."

"Pilots are very similar in their goals."

"What do the spaceplanes carry for weapons?"

"They all have four one-gigajoule lasers, two pointed forward, and two aft. They also carry a plasma cannon in their nose, and the FX4s have a railgun as well as an additional plasma cannon in their tails."

"What are the ranges?"

"The plasma cannon has a range of one thousand meters, the laser's range is six hundred meters at twenty thousand feet. It drops as the air becomes denser. In vacuum, the range is one thousand meters. The railgun fires its projectile at plus five km per second in space; their range is theoretically infinite."

"What are their firing arcs?"

"The cannon has a thirty-degree firing arc, the forward lasers have a one-hundred-seventy-degree firing arc, and the rear lasers have a two-hundred-twenty-degree firing arc. The railgun has a zero-degree firing arc."

"Now that's some serious firepower. What is the takeoff distance?"

"For the FX4s one thousand meters, the LX9 takes one thousand six hundred meters."

"What's their flight range?"

"In atmosphere, it is virtually unlimited. In space, the flight distance is dependent on the fuel load, typically, it is three light hours."

"Man, I'm loving those babies. Hey, how do we get them out of the water? Do you have to bring them up?"

"The FX4 and the LX9 can both maneuver in water. They are airtight and watertight, and the engines can perform with water as the medium as well as atmosphere."

"What is their speed in water?"

"The FX4 and the LX9 can do thirty-two knots underwater and one hundred twenty knots on the surface before they generate enough lift to go airborne."

"Even better," Blake said. He had been holding the bag that Marc had given him after pulling the earwig out of it. He looked inside, "Hey, what are these glasses for?"

"They are similar to what you would call a head-up display," ADI replied. "They can also provide full immersion three-D imagery."

"Wow, I've got to check these suckers out," Blake exclaimed. "But first, I'd better get to the bridge in case I actually need to drive this boat." Blake got up, climbed the ladder to the bridge deck, and sat down in the pilot's seat. He checked the radar and did a visual inspection of the horizon.

"No ships in sight. Radar's clear, so let's play with these things," he said as he put a pair of glasses on. "So how does the head-up display work?"

"The normal usage is to inquire data from the associated comm computer. They are in the bag you're holding, but when we are communicating, I can take over that function. If you look up, you will see the menu area; of course, it has been translated into English. If you focus on one item and blink once, it will activate that item or bring up a submenu if that is appropriate. It can also react to your voice if you wish."

"Okay, let's see what *darken* does," Blake said. He focused on the menu option and blinked; a slider came up in the HUD, he moved his eyes to the right, and the indicator tracked his eye movement. He blinked again and the slider went away.

"Nothing happened."

"Take the glasses off and look at the front."

Blake did as instructed. When he looked at the other side, the glasses were completely dark; he couldn't see through them, while before they had been transparent. When he turned them around and looked through them as he would when wearing them, they were transparent. "Cool, privacy shades."

Blake put the glasses back on, "So once I figure out the menu, I can look things up like I do on my laptop."

"That is correct. You can also customize the menu and create a situational display. For instance, you could have the ship radar, its speed, direction, and other parameters set to come up with a single menu click. Then you could quickly check the situation out to determine if you needed to come to the bridge. Of course, that would require adding wireless connections to the boat's instruments."

"Way cool. Now show me the three-D immersion thing."

"Wow, now that is something else," Blake exclaimed as the view of the sundeck came up in three-D. Marc was just coming up the ladder, having freshly showered and dressed.

"Blake, you're still here, you didn't abandon ship?" Marc said as he climbed up to the sundeck of their 35-meter yacht.

"Hell no, I didn't abandon ship! I've been up here gathering intel."

When Marc reached the sundeck, he went to the refrigerator and grabbed two beers. He sat down at the table behind the pilot's chair, setting one beer down across the table from him; then, he opened the second one and took a long drink. Blake did a quick check of the radar and got up to join Marc, grabbing the beer and opening it.

"Well, this is a fine mess we're in," Marc quipped.

"I'm not sure it's so bad. We do have a spaceship and four fighters."

"What did you find out about them?"

"They are some serious bad-ass weapons. You could wreak some serious damage just with the four you have, and that cutter isn't too bad either."

"That's good to know if we ever find ourselves fighting in a war."

"So, you figure out what you're going to do with it?"

"I really don't know. The one thing I do know is that we need to keep it secret."

"Yeah, Duh!" Blake said. "Word gets out, the government will step in, and you'll never hear of it again; that is, if they let you live."

"My thoughts exactly," Marc said. "And you wanted to buzz the ISS."

"A moment of insanity," Blake said. "So, what's next?"

"We have to stay focused on the sonar system."

"Why?"

"We need money, we need time, and god knows we need a plan."

"Okay, I concede your point."

"We need to map a new area out for the fourth trial. It should only take us two days. Then I can announce and take bids. I'll sell the design instead of trying to build the company. That will give us the cash reserves to figure out what to do. You'll need to continue the charter business."

"Why do a fourth trial? … DUH, I guess you don't want to present the funky data where the ship is."

"Right!"

"Captain, I can move the ship if you are worried someone else will find it," ADI told Marc.

"I think we should just leave things as they are for now," Marc replied. "By the way, how do you get these earwigs out of your ear?"

"You're talking to ADI?" Blake said.

"If you press them for eight seconds, they will release," ADI explained to Marc.

Marc waited until ADI had finished her explanation. "Yes."

"Why can't I hear her?" Blake asked.

"Captain, I have set the communication up so that I am conversing with each of you on separate channels," ADI told Marc. "I can combine the channels if you wish."

"She's talking on two channels," Marc said. "ADI, please combine the channels."

"Thanks," Blake said.

"So why keep going with the charter business?" Blake asked.

"Two things. Money and we don't want to draw attention to ourselves. People will think it strange that we have this multimillion-dollar yacht and don't seem to be worried about money. You have to be worth a few hundred mil to own one of these babies and not be running a business from it. And you know the last owners were running drugs."

"Yeah, I guess that could lead to some serious attention. So, I keep running the charters, no big deal, I just get three or four a month anyway. Plenty of time to work on a plan."

"Right, and with Catie coming next week, we don't want things to seem out of the ordinary."

Blake winced, "I guess you wouldn't want to share this with your daughter."

"She's twelve! If she finds out, she'll probably tell her mother, then her mother will freak out and tell the feds, then we'll be screwed."

"I don't think she'd tell her mother," Blake said. "She can keep a secret."

"Do you want to bet your life on it?"

"No, I guess not. So, we stick with plan A."

"Yes, plan A until it falls apart, or we have a better plan."

"Okay, I had a couple of questions which ADI told me I wasn't *important* enough to trust the answers to."

"ADI, please explain," Marc asked.

"My protocols restrict certain information to be solely under the purview of the captain."

"So, what happens if I tell my brother?"

"That is allowed, but you have to tell him or instruct me to tell him."

"Okay, so tell him."

"Captain, I can only tell him when you explicitly tell me which information to share," ADI told Marc

"Okay, Blake, ask your questions again."

"ADI, how are you able to communicate with us when you're under four hundred meters of water?" Blake asked.

"Captain."

"Please answer the question, ADI."

"I am using a quantum-coupled relay to a small drone that is sitting on your radar platform," ADI replied. "I can communicate instantly with it independent of the media separating us, then it normally relays to your comm unit. However, since it's so close to you, it is communicating directly to the earwig using a twenty-gigahertz channel."

"A quantum-coupled relay," Blake said with a puzzled look.

Marc waved his hand at Blake, signaling him to be quiet. "How did the drone get on our radar platform?"

"Once your remote vehicle approached the Sakira, I launched a drone to determine what was happening. It maintained a position close to your boat while you were diving and in the Sakira. When you returned to your boat, I landed it on the radar platform so we could continue to communicate."

"What is the range of the relay?"

"The quantum coupling has no range limit. The earwig's link has approximately one hundred meters of range to the comm unit or the drone, depending on atmospheric conditions. The comm units have a range of approximately one thousand kilometers to the drone."

"How will you be able to stay in contact with us when we're not close to the drone?" Blake asked.

"Captain, that is another subject that takes explicit instructions to reveal. Should I only communicate the answer to your comm?" ADI asked Marc.

Blake looked startled as his comm cut out and he didn't hear ADI's answer to Marc's question.

"Communicate it to both of us," Marc said.

"The comm units can communicate to one of the satellites that are in orbit around the planet."

"Geez!" Blake exclaimed.

"How many satellites and why hasn't NASA or some other space agency found them? Include Blake in the answer," Marc said.

"There are twenty-two satellites in geosynchronous orbit. They are very mobile, and like the hull of the ship, they absorb energy directed at them. They will not reflect light or any electromagnetic energy," ADI explained.

"But they would block out the sun or moon or something," Blake said.

"They are only two meters in diameter," ADI replied. "The light or EM energy just wraps around them. At an altitude of five hundred kilometers, they are insignificant in the field of view."

"What else can these satellites do?" Marc continued.

"They have optical cameras that record activity on the surface of the planet. They also pick up any EM energy and record it for later analysis. If they detect a satellite or spacecraft closing in on them, they alter their orbit appropriately until the object passes."

"How do they maintain geosync at the high latitudes?" Marc asked.

"They have sufficient energy available to augment their orbit to keep it stable."

"That's a lot of energy," Blake said. "What is powering those things?"

"Captain?"

"Answer the question, ADI."

"They have a fusion reactor and use a gravitational drive for propulsion."

"A gravitational drive!" Blake slapped the side of his head. "Now we're talking …"

Marc motioned Blake to be quiet. "A fusion reactor?" he asked, arching his eyebrows.

"Yes, Captain."

"How big is this fusion reactor? And, yes, let Blake hear," Marc asked.

"It occupies a volume of 3.5 cubic meters," ADI replied.

"Wow, that's small," Blake said.

Marc nodded his head as he leaned back in his seat and took another long swig of his beer.

"Well, it looks like we can cure global warming," Blake said.

"I guess," Marc sighed. "What is the fuel for the reactors?"

"They run on deuterium or helium four," ADI said.

"I'm sorry, Marc, but beer is not going to cut it," Blake said as he walked over to the kitchenette and grabbed a couple of glasses and a bottle of scotch. He poured each of them a generous amount then sat back down.

"Oh, king of all you survey, what do you command," Blake jested as he held his glass up in a toast.

"Oh shit. Why me?" Marc moaned.

"Because you passed the test," ADI said.

"What test?" Blake asked.

"The test I gave the captain when he came aboard the ship," ADI replied.

"I wouldn't call that a test," Marc said. "It was more like an inquisition."

"I already apologized for the severity of the test. It was necessary to determine whether you were likely to use the resources of the ship and me for personal gain. The test predicted that instead, you would use the Sakira's resources to better the entire planet," ADI said.

"Oh, it did, did it?" Marc scoffed.

"Yes, there is only a 0.2 percent probability that you would allow greed and personal power to guide your decisions," ADI replied. "While there was a ninety-eight percent probability that you would focus on saving humanity from itself."

"That's my brother," Blake barked. "The good guy to the very end."

Marc downed the rest of his scotch, leaned back and shook his head.

"I have a headache!" he moaned.

Chapter 3 Daddy, I'm here

Catie followed her mother to the gate counter for her flight to Hawaii. "I don't see why we have to go through all this rigmarole just so I can fly by myself."

"They don't want people being able to take children who aren't theirs onto planes," her mother replied. "Besides, parents like to be able to make sure their children actually get to where they're sending them. It's stressful enough having you fly by yourself."

"Adults worry too much."

"Now be quiet," her mother said as she stepped up to the gate agent. "Hello, I'm Dr. McCormack, and this is my daughter, Catie." It was obvious to anyone that they were mother and daughter. At 5'4", Catie was two inches shorter than her mother, but they had the same face, and both had soft brown hair and blue eyes.

"Yes, we've been expecting you," the agent said as she waved to someone in the seating area.

A woman dressed as a flight attendant got up and came to the counter. She was tall, 5' 9" with a nice figure, dark auburn hair and a pretty smile. She walked over to the desk and introduced herself.

"I'm Jackie Drummond, I'll be escorting your daughter on the plane."

Catie extended her hand, and Jackie reached out and shook hands with her. "Hi," she said.

"If you'll step over here, we can finish up the paperwork," Jackie said. Catie and her mother followed Jackie to the other end of the counter. "First, I need to see some ID."

"Here is my driver's license and Catie's passport," Dr. McCormack said, handing the documents to Jackie. Jackie examined them and checked the data against what she had on her sheet.

"Okay, everything looks good. Now Catie's ticket?" Jackie asked.

"Here you go," Catie said, taking the ticket out of her backpack.

"Okay, I can take responsibility for Catie now, or we can wait until boarding time," Jackie said. "It will be another hour."

Dr. McCormack looked hesitant about what to do.

"Go ahead, Mommy," Catie said. "I'm just going to sit here and read my book. You'll just be fidgeting."

"I'll sit with her until she gets on the plane," Jackie said. "She will not be out of my sight."

"I guess that's okay," Dr. McCormack said.

"Good, then, Catie, here is your wristband, you need to wear it until you get to Honolulu." Jackie snapped the nylon ID bracelet on Catie's left wrist. "Next, I sign here that I've taken responsibility for Catie," Jackie said as she signed the document. "You can sign there, Dr. McCormack, saying you've given me responsibility for her."

Dr. McCormack took the pen from Jackie and signed the document. Jackie then peeled off a copy and handed it to her. She handed a second copy to the gate agent, then put the rest of the document back into the portfolio she was carrying.

"Okay, Dr. McCormack, you're free to leave anytime. Catie, you don't leave my sight, okay?" Jackie said.

"Sure," Catie said.

"Do you need anything, something to drink or to go to the restroom?"

"No, I'm good."

"Then why don't we go over there and sit down while we wait. Dr. McCormack, you're welcome to sit with us."

Catie gave her mother a smile. "Go on, Mommy."

"Okay, I'll just leave now," Dr. McCormack said as she started toward the stairs.

"Who are you visiting in Hawaii?" Jackie asked.

"My father and uncle."

"Do they live there, or is this a vacation?"

"They live there now," Catie said. "We used to live in Boston, but after the divorce, Dad and Uncle Blake moved to Hawaii."

"What do they do?"

"Dad's a scientist. He does consulting, and he's working on some kind of sonar thing. He used to teach at MIT. Uncle Blake runs cruises on his and Dad's yacht. Dad uses the yacht to test his sonar."

"Sounds like you should have some fun there."

"Yeah, I was there for Thanksgiving, and we went out on the yacht and did some snorkeling and just hung around. It was pretty cool."

"So, do you have enough stuff for the flight?"

"Yes, I have my snacks, a bottle of water, my Kindle, and some movies on my I-pad."

"Sounds like you're set."

"I think so," Catie said as she pulled her Kindle out of her backpack.

"What are you reading?"

"A Tale of Two Cities."

"That's a pretty adult book for your age."

"I guess. I like to read; Mom and Dad make up a reading list for me. Daddy said that when I finish this one, he'll teach me to scuba dive."

"I would think a Harry Potter book would be a better fit."

"Oh, I read those when I was seven."

"All of them?"

"Sure."

Catie settled back into her seat and started reading. Jackie pulled a magazine from her portfolio and began to leaf through it. After forty minutes, the announcement for pre-boarding for Catie's flight came over the speaker.

"That's us," Jackie said. "Now's the time to go to the restroom unless you want to use the facilities on the plane."

"Yuck, let's go."

After they used the restroom, they returned to the boarding area. "Let's just have a seat again, we'll be the last to board," Jackie said. She looked over at the gate agent who was making the announcements. He gave her a thumbs up.

Catie started reading her book again.

"How much do you have left?"

"I'm at eighty percent, so I should finish it before we land. That way I'll get my scuba lesson right away, and we can do lots of diving."

"That's smart. Does your uncle dive?"

"He does, but it's difficult for him, his eardrum was injured when he got shot down in Iraq," Catie said.

"I'm sorry to hear that, so he was badly injured?"

"Yeah. He lost his left eye, and the left side of his face and his arm are kind of scarred up."

"Oh, that's too bad. What did he fly?" Jackie asked after some consternation.

"He flew the F18 Super Hornet. That's a really hot jet. But you can't fly in the Navy with only one eye."

"I guess that makes sense. Is he married?"

"No, he used to always have a girlfriend. But since the accident, he's been alone, except for Dad. I guess women get grossed out by the scars. He wears an eye-patch when he takes people on the cruise, so he looks like a pirate."

"I'm sure he makes a wonderful pirate," Jackie said. "Doesn't he have a false eye?"

"Yeah, but it's all scarred around it, and he doesn't have an eyebrow," Catie explained.

"Last call for flight ..."

"That's us," Jackie said.

They got up and headed to the counter. "Did I make it?" Jackie asked.

"Yep, and first-class for both of you," the agent replied. "Have fun," he said as he rolled a suitcase out for her to grab.

"I will," Jackie said. "Catie, we got first-class seats, how about that?"

"That's cool. You're coming with me?"

"I'm not really working; I'm on standby to go to Hawaii for vacation. So, they had me handle you here, and now that I made the flight, I'll hand you off to your father when we get to Honolulu."

"Do you have family in Hawaii?"

"No, but my girlfriend is in the Navy, and she lives there. I'll be staying with her. Here we are, do you want the window?"

"Sure."

◆ ◆ ◆

"Her plane lands in thirty minutes," Blake said. "So, relax, have a beer."

"I am relaxed!"

"And I'm a monk," Blake retorted.

"Okay, I'm a little nervous. It's been almost a year."

"I think she'll remember you, and you talk to her every week."

"But at that age, so much changes in a year and the telephone isn't the same."

"You're still her dad. Now drink your beer and shut up."

The two brothers had spent a hard two days on the Mea Huli while they finished up the fourth trial. During that time, they'd explored the capability of the Sakira. Marc always brought the discussion and exploration back to creating a sequence of what to introduce to Earth and when. Soon Blake got frustrated and bored and quit talking about it. It became Marc's burden to bear. He created endless scenarios, trying to find one that would optimize the success of saving humanity from itself while preparing it for the eventual arrival of the Paraxeans.

After they got home, Marc split his time between reviewing various scenarios and how he would relate to his daughter. It had been two years since the divorce and a year since her mother had moved with her from Cambridge to San Diego, leaving three thousand miles between them. After that, he'd left MIT and moved to Hawaii, not shortening the distance but giving them multiple direct flights between. He'd had Catie over Thanksgiving, but that seemed a lifetime ago.

"Flight just landed," Blake said. "You need to head to the gate. I'll wait for you here. If I'm not here, just assume some pretty flight attendant picked me up and go on without me."

"Well, good luck with that," Marc teased. "Catie will be sad to miss you."

"Okay, it'll take a *really* pretty one. Now go."

Marc made his way through security, showing them his gate pass. He checked in at the gate and took a seat. Catie would probably be the last one off the flight since she was an unaccompanied minor. It took ten minutes for the plane to reach the gate and start to deplane. Marc stood up, walked to the counter, and watched anxiously as the passengers started to come out of the jetway. He was shocked to see Catie was one of the first to deplane.

"Daddy!" Catie ran and grabbed her father into a big hug.

"Hi, Sweetie!" Marc exclaimed, hugging her too. "You've gotten taller since last year!"

"I've grown two inches," Catie bragged. "Where is Uncle Blake?"

"He's waiting at the bar. We only could get one gate pass."

"Oh!"

"Sir, I'll need to see some ID. I assume you're her father unless she goes around hugging every tall, good-looking man she finds," the flight attendant said.

"Yes, I'm her father," Marc said as he pulled out his ID. "You haven't been going around hugging other men, have you?" he teased Catie.

"No, Daddy, I only hug you and Uncle Blake," Catie said. "Daddy, this is Jackie."

"Hi," Jackie said. "Catie's been telling me all about you and her Uncle Blake."

"Uncle Blake looks like Daddy," Catie said, "except he's taller."

"And bigger, with bluer eyes, and funnier," Marc said. "Sorry, standing joke in the family. Blake likes to point out all his advantages over me."

"That must get annoying," Jackie said.

"Not really, it's just a big joke," Marc said. "He's two years younger, but we wound up trying to date the same girl a few times when we were in high school."

"Anyway," Catie said. "Jackie is going to be vacationing in Hawaii for two weeks. I told her Uncle Blake would give her a ride on the Mea Huli. He will, won't he?"

"If she would like to go out on it, I'm sure he would be happy to take her," Marc said.

"It's not necessary," Jackie said.

"It'll be fun," Catie said. "You could bring some friends even. Uncle Blake takes people out all the time."

"She's right," Marc said. "If you brought a bunch of girlfriends, he'd have a blast showing you around the islands."

"How many girlfriends?" Jackie asked with a laugh.

"Oh, ten or twelve would be comfortable," Marc said, "but he'd be able to accommodate twenty pretty easily."

"Oh, so it's a tour boat."

"He uses it that way, but it's really a luxury yacht."

"I told you it was big. It's thirty-five meters," Catie gushed. "With three decks," she added.

"Well, I might have to consider that," Jackie said.

Marc handed her his ID and signed the forms. "Here's a card for the booking service. If you decide you want to go, tell them Marc sent you and give them this number." Marc wrote a five-digit number on the back of the card. "That way they'll know you're a guest."

"Yeah, then you'll get it all to yourselves," Catie added.

"I don't think that would be right," Jackie said.

"Don't worry, Catie invited you. The Mea Huli only goes out a few times a month. Blake has a cruise lined up for tomorrow and Friday, but then it's open."

"I'll check with my girlfriends," Jackie said.

"It's okay to add some guys if you want," Marc said, "just don't tell Blake I told you."

"Oh, we might, but girls-only sounds like fun."

"I'm sure Blake would like that," Marc laughed. "Don't worry, he's harmless."

"Bye," Catie said.

Marc took his daughter's backpack and led her toward the baggage area to collect her luggage. "You trying to set your uncle up?"

"Sure, I told her about his face. She said things like that don't matter."

"I hope she takes you up on it."

"Me too."

"Now, what do you want to do while you're here?"

"Anything, everything. We've got all summer. And I finished the book, so you have to teach me to scuba dive."

"Not a problem; it'll be fun. Now we're doing a cruise around the island tonight with Uncle Blake. Like I said, he's got a charter tomorrow for two days. He wants to know if you want to crew."

"Are you going to come?"

"Not this time. I have work to do to prepare for my presentation; it's next week. After that, I'm totally free. Until then, you'll have to get Uncle Blake to take you around. I'll make sure I'm free at least four hours a day to do whatever you want."

"But if I crew with Uncle Blake, then you'll work non-stop and maybe finish early."

"You're very clever."

"I try. There's my bag."

Marc grabbed the red suitcase and checked to see that it was indeed Catie's. "Uncle Blake is just down this way," Marc said, motioning to the left.

They walked by the rest of baggage claim before they came to the bar where Marc had left Blake.

"Where did he go?" Marc said. *"No way he picked up someone,"* he thought.

"There he is," Catie said. "He's talking to that Navy guy." Catie ran ahead and ducked into the bar. She ran up to the table and stopped next to Blake and gave him a hug. "Hi, Uncle Blake."

"Hi, squirt," Blake said. "Or should I say aloha squirt?"

"You can leave off the squirt," Catie said as she slugged her uncle.

"Jimmy, this is my niece, Catie," Blake said. "Catie, this is an old Navy buddy of mine, Commander Jackson."

"Hello," Catie said and extended her hand.

Cmdr. Jackson shook her hand and smiled. "Nice to meet you, Catie."

"Thank you. Are you a pilot like Uncle Blake?"

"Yes I am. We flew together," Cmdr. Jackson said.

"And this is my brother, Marc," Blake added as Marc caught up.

"Commander Jackson, but call me Jimmy," Cmdr. Jackson said as he and Marc shook hands.

"Good luck catching a hop," Blake said. "We're off to play cruise director for Catie."

"Have fun."

Blake, Marc, and Catie made their way out of the terminal and to the taxi queue.

◆ ◆ ◆

Marc knocked on the door to Catie's room. "If you're going to crew for Uncle Blake, you have to get up. It's eleven o'clock, and his cruise starts at three; you need to be there by two."

"I'm up," Catie hollered back.

"Awake and in bed is not the same thing as *up*."

"Okay, okay. I'm officially out of bed," Catie hollered back as she crawled out from under the sheets.

"Do you want to stop for some lunch first?"

"Yes, I'm dying for a pulled pork sandwich."

"Alright, then we need to leave by twelve-thirty."

"One o'clock," Catie muttered to herself as she headed for the bathroom.

"How's your sandwich?" Marc asked Catie.

"Good," Catie mumbled with her mouth full.

"Don't tell your mother I let you eat like this."

"Don't worry, I won't."

"How is your mother?"

"You talked to her last week when we called."

"I know, but we never have a chance to talk, just you and me, where I can get the real story."

"Yeah, well, she's okay. She works all the time, and she's still depressed."

"I thought so; is she seeing someone for it?"

"Yeah, she has an appointment like once a week."

"That's good."

"It's not fair. It wasn't Mommy's fault. Even the review board said so."

"I know, but they lost their son, so they thought it had to be somebody's fault."

"But they didn't have to be so mean."

Catie's mother had a patient brought in after suffering a stroke. While they were examining him and doing an MRI and CAT scan, he suffered a second, fatal stroke. His family refused to accept the review board ruling and sued. They used the press like a weapon vilifying Catie's mother. It broke up her marriage with Marc, and after the divorce, she moved to San Diego to get away from the memories.

"You're right, but they were hurting, and they wanted everyone else to hurt just as much as they did. It wasn't right, but your mother has to get past it."

"Do you think she will?"

32

"I don't know. Depression creates more depression. The body gets trained to release endorphins and hormones the wrong way, and it's hard to retrain it. They have drugs that help, but the body seems to fight that."

"I wish they would come up with a better drug. Why can't they use some kind of gene therapy to fix you."

"Hopefully, they will one day."

Catie wiped her mouth with her napkin and pushed her plate away, "I'm ready to go."

They took a taxi to the marina. Marc asked the driver to wait as he and Catie got out. He handed her the overnight bag she'd packed. "Remember, you're part of the crew, so you have to do what Uncle Blake says and be polite to the guests."

"Aye, Aye," Catie said with a mock salute.

"I'll see you when you get back."

Catie gave her father a hug, and he gave her a kiss on top of her head. "Be good."

"Finish your paper, Daddy. That way we can do more stuff together."

"I'm working on it, Sweetie."

"Why can't you have your computer write it for you?"

"Computers aren't that smart," Marc replied.

"Well, they should be. Bye, Daddy."

Marc watched her walk down the pier. She was wearing white capri pants with a light white cotton pullover with horizontal stripes and deck shoes. Marc thought she looked cute as could be. *"My little sailor."*

Chapter 4   Moving Along

Marc sat down at his computer. He still had to organize all the data from the four trials into his presentation. He had a little over a week to get everything done. He had representatives from the Navy, and several major defense contractors lined up to hear the results of his research. He had hoped to strike a lucrative licensing deal with one of the contractors, but now that he wanted to sell it, getting the Navy excited would be important.

"Captain," ADI said.

"Yes, ADI."

"I have a message for you that I was instructed to hold until the fourth day after discovery. This is the fourth day."

"Okay, play it, please."

"I have been instructed not to read or listen to the message."

"Huh, then how do you give it to me?"

"I can put it on your comm, and you can access it through the menu on the visor."

"I'm not too good with the comm and the visor yet," Marc said.

"I could also email it to you, but that would make it vulnerable to someone else getting it. Or I could place it on your computer."

"Why don't you do that?"

"I would need access. If you will accept a new Bluetooth keyboard and mouse, I can make the necessary changes. Just open your settings to keyboard and set up a Bluetooth keyboard."

"Okay." Marc did as instructed and watched as the display flashed through multiple screens.

"There is a shared folder on your drive called ADI data," ADI said. "It contains the message. If you turn off your comm, you can play the message without my having any awareness of its contents."

"Thank you, ADI."

Marc turned the comm off and opened the file, message_1.mp4.

The screen showed a woman sitting at a console on what looked like the bridge of a ship. She looked human except she had ridges on her nose, kind of like a Bajoran from Star Trek.

"Captain, I am the medical officer for the Sakira, the space vessel you have found. For your convenience, you can refer to me as Metra; it is a close approximation of my name in your language. I'm sorry I don't know your name, but you are now the captain of this ship. I've recorded several messages for you. Please listen to them carefully. It is essential that the DI, or as you may think of it, the computer, doesn't hear or read any of these messages. As you should know, I've instructed the DI to introduce itself as ADI, which stands for Autonomous Digital Intelligence. ADI and all DIs are very literal, that is the intention of the designers. You have to be very explicit in asking for information or analysis from it. Now please prepare what you need to so you have privacy from it. It will not listen in if you instruct it not to. When you are ready, ask it for the second message, and the second message only."

Marc closed the message and turned the comm back on.

"ADI, please retrieve and place the second communication on my computer."

"Done!"

Marc turned off the comm again and played the second file.

"Captain, I wish to apologize for the ordeal you have been through. We had to ensure that the Sakira would not fall into the hands of someone who would abuse her power and resources. I assumed you would speak English given the location of the ship; however, ADI will have translated these messages to the language you spoke when you took command of the ship. The translation would have been done via a compartmentalized program so that ADI would not have access to the contents.

"It will take you time to appreciate the information you are receiving, and I have placed time constraints on when you can access each of the messages. They are not too long, but I feel it is important that you have time to understand and internalize each message before you move on. Hopefully, that way you will avoid making decisions you will come to regret. The most important thing to understand is that you must not wake the crew. Doing so will trigger very dire consequences for yourself and possibly your world. I have caused a medical emergency and placed everyone in stasis. I did this after the captain was murdered. I will explain more about this later.

"ADI can be very helpful to you. It is more than a simple ship's computer and has the ability to process and refine information far beyond what your current technology is capable of. ADI also has immense stores of knowledge about science and technology that you should be able to make use of. Now I suggest you take some time to internalize this and ask for the next message after five of your days, rotations of your planet."

"Hmm, interesting," Marc whispered. He turned the comm back on.

"ADI, can you retrieve the third message?"

"Captain, my protocol restricts access to that message until five days from now."

"Okay," Marc said. "I guess I'd better get all this data organized," he muttered to himself. Then he remembered his daughter saying that he should have the computer do all the work.

"ADI, can you access my drive?"

"Yes, I have given myself read/write privileges to all files except the directory ADI data. I only have write-privileges to that directory and cannot access or change those privileges without explicit instructions from you."

"Good, then access the paper 'Sonar: A Theoretical Analysis' under the directory Hyperion."

"Done."

"Analyze that document and then format the data in the folder 'Trials one-dash-four' into a new document following the same format and structure. Also, include the notes and observations you'll find in that folder."

"ADI?" Marc asked after ten seconds with no response.

"Done, Captain."

"Of course." Marc looked for the file. "ADI, where is the file?"

"It is in my databanks."

"Please transfer it to the Hyperion folder for me."

"Done," ADI said two seconds later.

"Thank you, ADI," Marc said. "Literal indeed," he muttered. "ADI, in the future, please acknowledge my instructions when you start to execute them."

"Yes, Captain."

Marc reviewed the file, adding comments and moving a few things around. After three hours, he took a break and went into the kitchen to make a coffee. He filled a measuring cup with water, poured half of it in his coffee mug, and set them both in the microwave. He set the timer to four minutes, then he sat down to wait for it to boil.

"ADI, please look at the three patent applications in the Hyperion directory. Using the one that is already complete as a template, please fill the other two out."

"Processing."

"ADI, how many things can you work on at the same time?"

"There is no specific limit. This task is taking 0.02 percent of my processing power. Moving data or accessing the internet or other communication is more limited. I only have fifty-gigabyte bandwidth to the internet, and the comm bandwidth is limited to one hundred megabits-per-second. However, I can run up to ten thousand comms at one time."

"Okay, so while you're working on the patents, can you compare the technology I have used in the Hyperion sonar with the technologies the Paraxeans use for underwater sensing?"

"Captain, I have completed the patents. I am now comparing technologies."

"Thank you."

"The technology you are using is nearly identical to the technology used by the Paraxeans. Your design matches the end of their previous branch of the technology."

"What happened after that?"

"They developed a new type of detector that was able to provide finer-resolution scans. Your design should provide ten-centimeter resolution at a four-hundred-meter depth in water similar to what is above the Sakira. The latest sensor design from the Paraxeans can provide resolution down to one-centimeter in the same conditions."

"Whoa," Marc exclaimed. He shook his head as he thought about what that would mean. "ADI, with our current technology, could we manufacture the new sensor design?"

"No, you could only manufacture the previous generation of the sensor."

"Okay, what is the resolution of that sensor?"

"It would provide 2.5-centimeter resolution."

"Do you detect anyone working on such a technology or sensor?"

"It is similar to the design of the new microwave receiver being developed by DragonWave Inc."

"How different is that design compared to the underwater sensor?"

"The math is more complex," ADI said. "The actual sensor is the same order of complexity, but designed for a different media."

"So, it's not totally beyond reason that I could come up with this design," Marc thought. "What would I need to do to Hyperion to make it work with the new sensor?" Marc asked.

"The software would need to be adapted, Captain."

"Can you make the adaptations to my software, matching the coding style?"

"Yes, Captain."

"Can you create the new design for the sensor with documentation similar to the documentation of the Hyperion sensor?"

"Yes, Captain."

"Can the sensor be manufactured using an existing supplier?"

"Yes, Captain. I have researched several of the suppliers you have recently used. Several have the ability to make the sensor."

"Thanks, I wish there was a way to have it made without sharing the design," Marc mused. "ADI, can the design be segmented so that I can assemble it later?"

"No, it is a monolithic design. Captain, I failed to mention that I could also manufacture the item."

"That would simplify things. How would you accomplish that?"

"There are robotic manufacturing facilities aboard the Sakira."

"How long would it take?"

"Four hours, Captain."

"How could we get the device without having to dive for it?"

"Captain, I could have a flotation device attached to it and eject it from an airlock. Then you could pick it up in your boat, or the relay drone could pick it up."

"How close would that need to be?"

"It is only an issue of discovery since you want to keep it hidden, Captain."

"Okay, I'll have Blake come close tomorrow, and you can have the drone on the Mea Huli pick up the design. Please start the manufacturing of the device."

"Yes, Captain."

"And please create the documentation and modify the software."

"Yes, Captain."

"And put them in the Hyperion folder under a new folder called Super Hyperion."

"Yes, Captain."

"Now put me in contact with Blake."

"What's up, Bro?" Blake asked after his comm beeped and ADI told him Marc wanted to talk.

"Not too much. I think I've found a way to make us some more quick money. I need you to swing close to our last dive spot if you can."

"Sure, I can suggest snorkeling off Lehua, very exclusive and private. These folks will eat it up. How close do I need to get?"

"Just pass on the same side of the island. ADI will have the relay drone on the Mea Huli pick up my package. It should be pretty small."

"Gotcha. Hey, how are you doing with your homework? Catie is pretty excited about doing some scuba diving, and she expects you to be there."

"I took her suggestion and had ADI do the work. So, I'm almost done. But we'll need to make another two-day survey before next Thursday."

"Does she know about ADI?" Blake asked. He was shocked that Marc would talk to Catie about the spaceship.

"No, she just suggested I have a computer do all the work. She felt that by now they should be smart enough." Marc laughed at the thought of Catie knowing about ADI.

"How's the cruise going?" Marc asked.

"Fine, same old same old," Blake said. "They're a bit self-entitled, but we're charging them enough."

"How's Catie doing?"

"She's doing fine. She keeps telling me about her friend Jackie," Blake said. "Sounds like a nice woman."

"She seemed nice," Marc said. "Be careful, Catie might want a finder's fee if you and Jackie wind up hooking up."

"She wouldn't," Blake said.

"Sure she would," Marc laughed. "She takes after her great grandfather when it comes to capitalism."

"I'll be careful," Blake said. "And doing another survey shouldn't be a problem; we can probably combine that with a little diving practice. I'll go sell our little side trip to Lehua to the customers. Talk to you later."

"Later."

Marc was waiting at the pier while the Mea Huli finished docking. Catie had already called him twice to make sure he would be waiting. The docking process was slow; you didn't just drive a thirty-five-meter yacht into the marina and park it. He could see the cleaning crew had arrived and was waiting to get on board to clean up after the cruise. He decided he had time to get another coffee before they would be ready for the guests to disembark.

Drinking his coffee, he watched as the two couples, each with two teenagers, walked down the pier toward their waiting cars. Their luggage would be delivered to their hotels later that day.

"Hey, Daddy," Catie almost shouted. She had snuck up behind him, carefully timing her approach.

"Hey, Sweetie," he replied with mild surprise. "You have to be careful sneaking up on people; I might have spilled my coffee and burned myself."

"Oh, you never jump when I surprise you."

She was right, no matter what happened, Marc never twitched. Probably from all the practice dealing with Blake while they were growing up.

"Well, you should still be careful. How was crewing?"

"It was fun, but they sure are full of themselves," she said, indicating the group now getting into the limousines. "I wanted to drown the little boy."

"You mean the fourteen-year-old blond kid?"

"Yeah, he's such a baby."

"I'm glad you were able to show restraint," Marc said. "Your mother would be disappointed if you wound up having to stay here and go to jail."

"Oh, I wouldn't have drowned him, just dunked his head in the water."

"I'm sure he deserved it. Just make sure that if you do such a thing, it looks like an accident," Marc teased. "We really can't afford to spend a bunch of money on a lawyer."

"I will."

"Here comes your uncle."

"Hey Bro," Blake said as he walked up beside them.

"Hey yourself, how was the cruise?"

"It was fine. You get used to dealing with rich people after a while. The one kid kept trying to impress Catie. I thought she was going to spill hot coffee on him."

"Now that would have been a better solution," Marc said to Catie. "We could have totally sold that as just an accident. She said she wanted to drown him."

"She had her chance when they were snorkeling, but I guess she decided to give him a pass," Blake said.

"So, no problems?" Marc asked.

"No, they were reasonably polite and tipped the crew well."

"What tip?" Catie demanded, hands on her hips.

"Oh, you mean you didn't get a tip?"

"No, I didn't. And I was a member of the crew."

"Well, they gave me something for the young lady. But I'm trying to figure out who they meant."

"I was the only young female in the crew. I can't believe you would cheat a kid," Catie huffed with mock indignation.

"So now you're a kid. You can see why I am confused," Blake said as he pulled an envelope out of his jacket pocket and handed it to her. "There it is, don't spend it all in one place."

Catie opened the envelope and counted out five $100 bills. "Wow!"

"They were a pain, but they were generous," Blake said.

"What about my pay?" Catie asked.

"Pay? I thought you were crewing to gain experience," Blake laughed. "Now, you want to be paid as well?"

"Uncle Blake!"

"I don't have the cash, so I'll let your dad take care of paying you."

"Another five hundred sound okay?" Marc asked.

"Sure."

"I think we'll let you draw that on account. You don't need to be walking around with that much money. Maybe we'll open a bank account and get you a debit card."

"That sounds okay," Catie replied unenthusiastically.

"Blake, I'm planning on taking my daughter out to dinner, or maybe she'll be taking me out."

"Nuh-uh," Catie said quickly.

"I should know better," Marc said. "Would you like to join us?"

"I will if you want, but Datu is going to stay on the ship tonight for security, so I was planning on meeting a few old buddies and practicing my curls," Blake said as he made a curling motion with his arm, miming bringing a drink to his mouth.

"That's fine with me," Marc said. "That package I had delivered--if you could just secure it in your cabin."

"I'll take care of it right away. Have fun at dinner."

"Where do you want to go?" Marc asked Catie.

"How about Riki's Waikiki."

"That's pretty rich. You're developing expensive tastes hanging out with rich people."

"Oh, I didn't know. We can go somewhere else. I just remember Jackie saying her friend was going to take her there."

"That's okay. We'll need to get you home so you can change. Do you want to take a short nap first?"

"No, why would I need a nap? A shower, yes, but a nap, no," Catie said as she grabbed her father's hand and started pulling him toward their condo.

"I guess when you sleep in until noon, you wouldn't need a nap," Marc said.

"I had to be up early to crew," Catie said.

"Did Blake have to pound on your door to get you up?"

"No. I set my alarm," Catie said.

"Why doesn't that work at home?"

"I don't set an alarm at home," Catie said.

"I give up. So, what were your duties?" Marc asked as he walked beside his daughter.

"Oh, I was the server for when they ate. And did a lot of fetch and carry. They sure were forgetful. I was always having to go to the room to get something they left behind."

"Did you clean their rooms?"

"Thank god no," Catie groaned. "Datu's mother took care of that."

"There's no shame in doing a little maid work."

"I know, but not for those people," Catie gasped. "The wives complained about everything. They'd misplace something and blame Mrs. Hayashi. And then we'd find it after only three minutes."

The phone rang as Marc was making breakfast for Catie and himself. He put it on speaker as he flipped the bacon.

"How was your workout last night?"

"Didn't get as hammered as I had planned," Blake said. "Jackie, that friend of Catie's, called. She wanted to know if we were going out sometime where she and her friends could tag along."

"That's nice of her."

"Yeah. I told her we were going out this weekend to do some diving. That got her interested. She said Catie told her you were going to teach her to scuba dive, wanted to know if they could tag along and get lessons, too."

"That would be okay. Are they going to be able to come to the pool on Friday to do the first day?"

"I mentioned that. She said she could, but had to check with her friend. Says her friend has a thirteen-year-old daughter who might want to learn, too. She also has a friend that already is a certified diver. She'll be coming with them on the boat."

"Okay, let me know. Make sure they go to the dive shop to get the right-size equipment."

"I told her we have a deal at Kahili's dive shop and called to alert him that she might be coming in."

"Okay, I'll let Catie know as soon as she's out of the shower," Marc said with a tad of annoyance in his voice.

"Been in there a while?"

"Yeah, like thirty minutes now. And she's only twelve. How long is she going to take when she's fifteen?"

"Not my problem," Blake said. "Hey, how is this Jackie chick?"

"She seemed like a really nice person."

"And ......"

"And what?"

"What does she look like?"

"I'd say she was pretty hot, too," Marc laughed.

"Great to hear Catie has a good eye. Talk to you later."

When he hung up the phone, Marc could tell that the shower had quit running. He started scrambling the eggs as he slid the bacon off the burner. By the time he had finished the eggs, Catie came into the kitchen with her wet hair pulled back in a ponytail.

"Morning, Daddy. Was that Uncle Blake?"

"Yes, he says Jackie called about going out with us this weekend. Seems she and a friend would like to learn to dive."

"That's cool."

"Her friend has a daughter your age."

Catie shrugged her shoulder and tilted her head that way. "Are they going to do the pool training?"

"He's checking. Why no enthusiasm about another kid your age?"

"I don't get along that well with kids," Catie said.

"Why not?"

"Boring, I guess."

"You or them?"

"Both probably."

"You could make more of an effort," Marc suggested.

"Why?"

"Friends are important," Marc said. "A lot of things get done through relationships."

"Huh," Catie said.

Marc sighed. "Eat your breakfast, and we'll go get your dive gear. Then what do you want to do?"

"Can we go to the beach and body surf?"

"Sure."

"Hey, who were you talking to last night?" Catie asked.

"Nobody," Marc replied, giving Catie a skeptical look.

"I heard you."

"I must have been dictating to the computer, finishing up my presentation. We're going to do a survey while we're out."

"Cool, does that mean we'll have Willie with us?"

"Yes."

"Can I drive him?"

"Sure, when we're not doing part of the survey."

After dinner, Marc and Catie watched a movie, then he sent her off to bed while he went back to work on his Hyperion presentation. After three hours, he and ADI had everything ready; they just needed to insert the data after they made the survey with the new sonar dish.

"ADI, please retrieve message three," Marc said.

"Yes, Captain. It is now in your folder," ADI replied.

"Thank you," Marc said, then he pressed the comm off. He opened the file and pressed play. Dr. Metra's voice and image came up in his display.

"Captain, I hope you have been able to internalize everything I've told you. It is essential that you proceed with caution. You have enough power under your control to destroy your world, or to remake it into a wonderful space-faring civilization. When you entered the ship, you were tested. You should remember the questions and the long series of images you were shown. The DI read your biometrics while you viewed them. Based on your responses, it was judged that you would be a good person to give control of the ship to. If your responses had not been acceptable, you would have been ejected from the ship, then the ship moved. Fortunately, that didn't happen.

"My civilization is called Paraxea. We have only encountered twelve other sentient species; in fact, we have discovered only eight hundred worlds that can even sustain life as we know it. Of the twelve sentient species, only four, one of which is your world, have satellite technology. The others range from Stone Age to early postindustrial. The first satellite civilizations we encountered had progressed a long way. They have fully colonized their solar system. However, they were uninterested in interstellar travel given the vast distances and the decades of travel time. We acquired an enormous trove of technology from them in trade. We gave them hundreds of quantum-coupled relays and access to our other technologies in exchange for their technologies. However, we withheld the technology to make quantum relays. Our scientists were still trying to integrate some of their technologies when I left Paraxea for your planet.

"The second satellite civilization we encountered had progressed to interstellar travel to about the same degree as we have. We encountered them one hundred of your years ago, and we reached an uneasy peace with them. We were able to trade some of our technology for some of theirs, but in general, we avoid each other. The other two satellite civilizations we discovered were at approximately the same level of development as your world. We are continuing to track their progress. The pre-satellite civilizations did not have any technology that we found useful, so like yours, they are on the watch list. There are more than enough empty systems to provide resources for us; thus, we are only interested in technology or other knowledge that might spring forth from unique minds.

"Our mission here was to study and extract what existing technology and knowledge we could find in this world. We were then to watch and determine how it was developing. We have noted that because of your political splintering and your advanced weaponry, your civilization is not expected to survive nor move beyond your home planet. We were instructed to wait and observe for another one hundred years. We do this by rotating the crew through stasis, keeping a small team awake while the rest are in suspension.

"The DI, ADI, has within its memory all the information we have gathered from your world, as well as all the information from our world and what was shared with us by the other worlds, especially the space-faring worlds. We use that to compare and contrast the various technologies in order to identify any that are of special interest. You have access to this information, and I'm sure you can see how powerful that will be. As you query this from the DI, you need to be cautious about who else might have access to it."

"Oh joy," Marc muttered to himself.

In her room, Catie was wondering who her father was talking to.

At 7:00 Friday morning, everybody was assembled at the pool for the first scuba lesson. Jackie had brought her friend, Melinda, and Melinda's daughter, Sally. Sally and Melinda were carbon copies of each other, both 5' 3" with red hair. Both claimed to be 110 lbs. when Blake asked them so he could set their buoyancy compensator. Blake was wearing his eye-patch, which Sally thought made him look like a pirate.

"Okay, put on your BCs, that means buoyancy compensator," Blake instructed. "It lets you work the level you want to dive at and is your emergency way back to the surface. And it's the harness for your air tank."

Blake continued to go through the lesson, while Marc simply observed and helped the women get their tanks mounted.

"Now hop into the pool, and we'll get your buoyancy set right," Blake continued.

Marc and Blake worked with each woman to add the right amount of weight to set her buoyancy.

"Now, you need to adjust your mask, and to keep it from fogging up, just spit into it," Blake said as he spit into Catie's mask.

"Ugh, Uncle Blake. Don't spit in my mask."

"What's wrong?"

"It's gross."

"You didn't care last year."

"That's before I knew better."

"Might I suggest that Catie might prefer to use No-Fog gel? It seems to work pretty well," Melinda said as she held out a tube.

"Yes, way better," Catie said. She quickly cleaned her mask and then spread the gel on it. Everyone else did the same and then they all put their masks on.

"Okay," Blake said. "Now for air. Your tanks should all be ready, so put the regulator in your mouth and breathe." Everyone was looking at Blake. "Go ahead, do it."

They all pulled their regulators out of their mouths.

"What's the matter?" Blake asked. "No air?"

"Yes, no air," Catie gasped as she pulled the regulator out of her mouth.

"That's because you never trust anyone about your air. You make sure your tank is full, that it is turned on, and that your regulator is delivering air," Blake said sternly. "Now here's how you turn the tank on, check the gauge here to make sure your supply is full. Then press this button on your regulator to make sure that air is flowing. Then put it in your mouth and breathe."

"That was mean," Catie said.

Sally giggled.

"Not nearly as mean as letting you suffocate yourself. Air is critical, you have to double, triple check it."

Catie stuck her tongue out at him, then followed his instructions to get her air on. Soon everyone was breathing through their regulators.

"Alright, just relax and get used to breathing through your mouth and regulator for a bit. When you feel comfortable with that, just sit down on the bottom of the pool and get used to breathing underwater."

It took five hours to get through the material. At the end, they were sharing the pool with the regular class, but by then they had progressed to the deep end, so their presence didn't inconvenience anyone.

"Alright, I'll see everybody tomorrow morning at six o'clock," Blake said. "Breakfast will be served on the boat, so you just have to stumble your way there. Make sure you don't forget your overnight bag. We'll have plenty of food and drinks. Also, we'll have some Dramamine in case it gets rough, but the weatherman says smooth sailing. Leave your dive gear here, and we'll haul it over to the boat for you today," Blake added. "That'll help make the early morning tomorrow bearable."

That simply elicited groans from the women.

"We have Faye's gear in the car. I'll bring it in if that's okay," Jackie said.

"Sure, might as well deal with everything at once," Blake replied.

Saturday morning, everyone made their way onto the Mea Huli, none of the women looked very awake. Catie and Marc greeted everyone, while Blake and Datu were preparing to get underway. Catie and Marc had spent the night aboard, so they were raring to go, something that didn't seem to get much appreciation from the bleary-eyed women. Sally was the only one who actually looked awake.

"Welcome aboard. My brother Blake is on the bridge, getting us ready to sail. Just stow your bags in the lounge; we'll sort out cabins after we cast off."

When the women entered the lounge, Jackie got raised eyebrows from her friends. "Nice boat," Melinda said. "You are going to marry this guy, right?"

"They said it was a yacht, I never imagined it was something like this," Jackie replied. "And I've only met him that once at the pool, not sure we're ready to get married."

"Blake McCormack?" Faye asked.

"That's right."

"Hmm, I wonder if it's the same guy."

"What guy?" Melinda asked.

"I knew a Blake McCormack in the Navy."

"Catie mentioned her uncle was shot down in Iraq."

"My guy wasn't shot down," Faye said.

"Anybody want some coffee?" Catie asked as she made her way into the lounge.

"Everyone but Sally held their hand up."

"Espresso or just Kona roast?"

"Double espresso," Faye said.

"Double espresso latte if you can," Jackie said. Melinda seconded that.

"Coming up," Catie replied. "Sally, we have orange juice, pineapple juice, and milk."

"I'll have milk," Sally replied.

"Whole or skim?"

"Skim," Melinda answered for Sally.

As Catie made the drinks, everyone could feel the boat get underway. They were in one of the large end slips, so it only took a few minutes to make it into the channel. Even then they were only moving at a sedate five knots to avoid giving off any wake to disturb the other boats in the harbor.

"Okay, cabin assignments," Marc said as he came down from the sundeck. "We have two VIP staterooms, and one slightly smaller stateroom and crew berths available. How do you want to split them up?"

"Sally will stay with me," Melinda said.

"Good, then you should take one of the VIP suites; they have queen beds," Marc said and looked at the other two women.

"I'm Faye," Faye said, extending her hand and shaking with Marc. "I'm good with the small stateroom. Jackie set this up so she should get the VIP suite."

"That's perfect," Marc said. "Catie, you can move into the crew berthing if you want, or you can bunk with me."

"I'll stay with you," Catie said. "I like the queen-size beds in there."

"The owner's suite?" Jackie asked with a knowing look, assuming that would be Marc's stateroom.

"No, Blake has that one," Marc replied. "It's on the main deck with quick access to the bridge; the others are on the lower deck. Catie, show our guests to their rooms."

"Aye, aye Captain," Catie saluted.

"Blake's the captain," Marc corrected. "I'm just part of the crew."

By the time everyone got situated in their berths and had made their way back to the lounge, the Mea Huli had cleared the point and was cruising at twenty knots.

"Morning everybody," Blake said as he entered the lounge.

Faye jumped up and snapped to attention. "Commander McCormack," she barked as she gave him a sharp salute.

"I'm just plain Blake now," he said. "Lieutenant Williams, as I recall."

"Yes sir," Faye replied. "It's an honor to meet you again."

"Relax, you're embarrassing me."

"So, he *is* the same Blake McCormack," Jackie said.

"Yes, he is," Faye replied. "I just want to say how grateful everyone on the Stennis is for your sacrifice."

"As I recall, I sacrificed an F18 Hornet into the desert," Blake said.

"Everybody aboard that AWACS was happy to sacrifice one Hornet, sir. They're just sorry that bastard tried to flame you."

"What do you mean, flame him?" Catie asked.

"When he had to eject, the enemy pilot tried to burn him up in his exhaust plume. Fortunately, he only caught him a little," Faye said.

"Is that what happened to your face?" Sally asked.

"Sally," Melinda scolded.

"It's alright," Blake said. "Yes, I got burned by his tail exhaust. It messed up my face and my left arm. But my buddy shot him down."

"You never said that," Catie said. "I thought you got burned when a missile hit your plane."

"He didn't get shot down," Faye said.

"What?" Catie cried.

"Now you really are embarrassing me," Blake said. "I didn't get shot down; I ran out of gas."

"He stayed to protect the AWAC," Faye said. "He shot down two MIGs and used up most of his fuel, but he still stayed with the AWAC. He shot down a third MIG but then had to eject when he ran dry. That's when the SOB tried to flame him."

"Wow, that was so brave," Catie said. "Why didn't you ever tell me?"

"It's a painful memory," Blake said with a shrug.

"Did you get a medal?" Sally asked.

"He got the Navy Cross," Faye said, "and the undying gratitude of twenty-five men and women who were on that AWAC."

"Okay, enough ancient history," Blake said. "We're on course for Kahe Point. It's relatively secluded, so it'll be perfect for your first dive. We should get there in about two-and-a-half hours. So have breakfast and relax. Catie, did you get everyone squared away?"

"Aye, Captain."

Datu came down and said hello to everyone. He told them that he'd have the breakfast buffet out in twenty minutes.

"Who's driving the boat?" Jackie asked.

"It's on autopilot," Marc said, "but I'm heading up to babysit it now. Too much traffic here to leave it alone for long, but Datu would have made sure the radar was clear before coming down."

"That's nice to know," Jackie said a bit nervously.

"Catie, would you bring me a plate when Datu puts it all out?" Marc asked over his shoulder.

"Aye, Aye, Daddy," Catie said with a grin.

◆ ◆ ◆

When they got to the reef, Blake stayed on board while Marc and Faye acted as scuba instructors and lifeguards. Catie, with her snorkeling experience and natural quick learning ability, helped Sally out. The two girls were on the reef and chasing fish before Melinda and Jackie were even willing to leave the safety of a few strokes from Mea Huli's dive platform.

Marc finally got Jackie to dive down around the reef while it was looking like Melinda was not going to go down more than six feet. When Marc finally got Jackie to dive down close to the bottom, her air was so low they had to head back.

"Hey, Daddy," Catie said as he and Melinda made it back onto the boat. "Can we put Willie into the water?"

"Sure," Marc said. "Just give me a few minutes to rinse off."

Marc used the hose on the dive platform to rinse the saltwater off Melinda and himself. Once he finished that, he took the pin out of Willie's cage and hooked up the tether that Catie eagerly handed him.

"Have you checked everything out?" Marc asked.

"Yes," Catie said. "Uncle Blake went through it all with me while you were still down there. We ran out of air lots faster than you did since we were diving close to the bottom most of the time."

"Okay, here he goes," Marc said as he pushed on Willie. The cage tilted, and Willie slid off into the water.

Catie and Sally started to drive Willie around. Marc was happy to see that Catie actually let Sally drive the underwater vehicle once in a while. They drove Willie around the reef for an hour before Marc had them bring him back in.

"You can do one more dive before lunch," Blake said.

Sally and Catie immediately started putting their gear back on. "If you want, I'll go with them," Faye said. "I can use the practice."

"Thanks," Marc replied. "I'll get things ready for the survey we'll be doing before we head back in."

Marc started to reset the controls on Willie and set up the sonar dish. Blake came back and started to help.

"Anything I can do?" Jackie asked.

"We've got it," Marc said. "We've had lots of practice."

"How did you two wind up with such a nice boat?" Jackie asked.

"You mean, how did two normal guys wind up with a ten-million-dollar yacht?" Blake said.

"I guess that's what I'm asking," Jackie said.

"It's a long story," Marc said.

"Sorry," Jackie said.

"I'll give you the short version," Blake said. "Marc is a math genius, almost as smart as his daughter. The DEA hired him to develop an algorithm that would identify boats that were smuggling drugs and other contraband into the U.S. The government being cheap, didn't want to pay his outrageous consulting fees, so they offered him ten percent of whatever they seized or recovered in the first six months that they used his algorithm. To everyone's surprise, they seized ten big boats and yachts in the first six months and one hundred million in drugs. They negotiated Marc down to the Mea Huli, a few million, and paid the taxes."

"Wow, that worked out nice," Jackie said.

"Pretty much," Marc replied. "But now Blake seems to think we should use it as a chick magnet."

"No, I said, I should use it as a chick magnet," Blake said. "You have family obligations, and need to be more conservative in your dating."

Marc laughed. "You always thought you should have all the girls when we were kids."

"What do you mean tried," Blake said as he slugged Marc on the shoulder.

After the girls finished their dive, Blake started the Mea Huli toward the survey location they had used for the first Hyperion survey. Marc had brought out the map showing the approximate location where they had placed the various objects when they'd done the first survey. He did the prep work while Jackie and Melinda made lunch for everyone.

When they reached the survey site, Faye helped Marc get the objects over the side so Willie could place them on the ocean floor. She was interested in how the sonar worked and helped Marc throughout the survey. Jackie spent her time with Blake learning how to sail the Mea

Huli. Once the survey was complete, Faye helped Marc retrieve the objects, pulling each one onto the dive platform, so he could send Willie back for the next one right away. With Blake sailing, Marc driving Willie, and Faye grabbing the objects, they managed to pick everything up in half the time it usually took Marc and Blake.

"Okay, that was quick," Marc said. "What do you want to do now? We could go to Kahuna Canyon and get one dive in, or we can just sail around."

After much debate, they decide that they would let Catie and Faye dive Kahuna Canyon, then they would finish up with an evening sail back to Honolulu. The fact that Sally and Catie could watch a movie on the way back tipped the scales.

Chapter 5   Hyperion

"Welcome to my presentation," Marc said as his guests entered the conference room. "I'm Dr. Marc McCormack."

"Admiral Michaels," the admiral said, extending his hand to Marc. He was about the same or a bit shorter than Marc's six feet two inches, but he probably outweighed Marc by twenty pounds. "My aide, Lieutenant Roberts," the admiral added after he shook Marc's hand.

"Paul Grierson," the third man said. He was wearing a suit almost identical to the ones worn by the two men behind him. "I'm with Boeing."

"James Murray, with Northrop Grumman," the next man said.

"David Laughton, with Raytheon," the last man said.

"Welcome all of you to Hyperion," Marc said. "We have developed what we believe to be the next generation of sonar technology. We expect that in the near future all commercial ventures will deploy our Hyperion I technology, and the military will be deploying our Hyperion II technology."

"You're pretty confident," Admiral Michaels said.

"As you watch the presentation, you'll understand my confidence. I'm going to start by showing the capabilities of Hyperion I. Then I'll show you what Hyperion II will do. After that, we'll discuss signal quality and variability that occurred in our four studies for Hyperion I. We only accomplished one study for Hyperion II since we were rushing to finish its development before this presentation."

"We dropped a few items on the ocean floor at a depth of approximately five hundred meters. Of course, we picked them up after the test. Here is what you see with standard sonar." Marc clicked his mouse, and an image came up on the 64-inch TV screen. It looks like empty ocean floor; extra processing didn't add any resolution."

"That's too deep to see anything."

"Now with the enhanced sonar technology of Hyperion I, here is what you see."

Marc clicked to the next slide.

"You can see there is something there, so it's worth secondary processing. Now, this is what you see after that," he said, moving on to the next slide. "You can make out some type of statue, a toilet, and a few amorphous objects."

"That is worth something; definitely will help with locating debris from a shipwreck or a plane crash."

"Now here is what you see with our Hyperion II," Marc forwarded to the next slide.

The screen clearly showed the statue as Caesar's torso and also a medicine ball sitting down on the bottom.

Admiral Michaels reached over and pulled the HDMI cable from the projector. "I'm sorry folks, this technology is classified. Please give Lieutenant Roberts all the documentation you have received. I'm sure I don't have to remind you to keep everything you've seen here to yourselves."

The three other men handed their packets to Lieutenant Roberts as they filed out of the room.

"You can't do this," Marc hissed.

"I have done this," Admiral Michaels replied.

"I'll just publish."

"That would be foolish. I'm sure we would be able to show that you've infringed on some of our top-secret technology."

"So, what! If it's not patented, then it's fair game."

"But we could suggest that you might have come about that technology through dubious means," the admiral said. "Rest assured that we will compensate you for your work, but we will not allow this technology to be shared with anyone, not even our allies."

"How did the meeting go?" Blake asked as Marc climbed aboard the Mea Huli.

Marc was scowling as he stomped over to the refrigerator and grabbed a couple of beers.

"That good," Blake said.

"The Navy declared Hyperion classified and closed the meeting."

"Really well, then."

"Perfect," Marc said as he smiled and handed Blake a beer.

"You knew they would classify it."

"Sure, too big a leap for them not to."

"So, what's the play here?"

"They're going to want to keep me happy," Marc said. "They won't go for a licensing deal, too much documentation; so, they're going to have to buy me out."

"Sounds good, more money upfront."

"Right. I'm hoping for twenty-five million."

"Well, if we're hoping, why not thirty," Blake quipped.

"Realistically, they won't want to spring for any more than they have to. But I've got an analysis that shows that the cash flow from licensing it should be worth twenty to thirty million. I was generous with my assumptions, so they'll shoot lower."

"When will you know?"

"The admiral says they'll get back to me next week."

"So, storming in here was what, left over from the act at the hotel?"

"No, but they might be following me," Marc said. "I don't want to give them any hints."

"What are you going to tell Catie?"

"I'll just tell her that the Navy's trying to hog all the action, and we'll have to wait and see. How was your day?"

"Well, I said goodbye to Jackie. She has to go back to work."

"That's too bad."

"Yeah, can you believe Catie would set me up with someone who lives in San Diego?"

"I have a hard time believing Catie set you up with someone. But maybe she wants you to move to San Diego."

"I'm not so sure, she looks like she's liking Hawaii a lot. I saw her checking out schools and the homeschooling options."

"Don't tell me that," Marc groaned. "Just what I need, another reason for Linda and me to fight."

"Just saying."

"Thanks, Brother. I can always count on you to darken my day."

"What are brothers for?"

"You don't have to work at it so hard," Marc laughed.

"So, what's your next move as regards the Sakira?"

"Where's Catie?" Marc asked, giving Blake the eye for mentioning Sakira.

"She's doing a little shopping with the money she's earned," Blake said.

"What's she shopping for? She's usually reluctant to spend any money, she must have picked that up from Mom."

"I'm sure she got it from the same place you did," Blake said. "She just said something about checking things out at the Apple store. So while she's gone, back to the Sakira."

"I've been doing an economic and technology assessment with ADI over the last week. I think we should start out with energy storage and generation."

"Duh, nuclear fusion."

"We can't start there. Way too advanced, and we need to have a plausible explanation of how we invented it. Plus, we'd wind up fighting off every major world power. We need to start smaller until we have the resources to defend ourselves."

"Okay, so what?"

"Batteries and fuel cells."

"What, how is that going to make us rich?"

"Well, lithium-ion batteries are a twenty-five-billion-dollar per-year industry now; if we can introduce a more efficient battery, it will grow even bigger, and we'll be able to garner a major share of the market.

And diesel engines are over three hundred billion dollars a year," Marc said.

"Just imagine a diesel fuel cell combined with super-efficient batteries. It would revolutionize the trucking industry. Diesel engines are about forty-five percent efficient, but an electrical system can be ninety percent efficient, and the fuel cell can be eighty-five to ninety percent efficient," Marc added, his excitement growing. "Couple that with the ability to convert all that energy from braking and route it to the batteries, and you have a super clean, quiet truck that gets twice the mileage or better. And the same for cars; not everyone can park their car where they can plug it in at night."

"Yeah, you're talking worldwide market, but what's to stop the Chinese from stealing your design and undercutting you, or at least isolating you from their market and their partners?" Blake asked.

"That's the beauty of it. The designs we're settling on are almost impossible to reverse engineer. You can figure out what they're made of, but not how to make them. So, we just have to protect the process."

"That's some serious security you're talking about."

"I know. We'll have to be very cautious. And we need to worry about our government stealing the technology under the guise of national security."

"Like they're doing with Hyperion," Blake said. "Gotta love the government." Blake laughed and handed Marc another beer.

That night after Catie went to bed, Marc poured himself a scotch and thought about what Blake had said about Catie. She had been very inquisitive about Hyperion and what the Navy was doing, far more than he had expected. She had quizzed him on how it would impact his business plans and even asked if he would have enough money to keep living in Hawaii.

He'd assured her that he would and that things were going to work out just fine. He worried that his little girl was growing up too fast and wondered if it was because of the divorce, or if she was just that way. She'd always been a studious child and had always done well in school, excelling in academics. But she never had very many close friends. She had started the first grade when she was five years old. Then they had her skip the fourth grade. Even then, they had to put her in special classes for math because she was so much more advanced than the rest of her grade level.

"Daddy," Catie said as she walked into the family room where he was sitting.

"Hi, Sweetie," Marc replied. "Couldn't you sleep?"

"Not really. Uncle Blake told me that Jackie went back to San Diego."

"Yeah, he mentioned that to me, too."

"I guess it wasn't so smart setting him up with someone who didn't live here."

"Not your job, but he had a good time with her. That always helps. Maybe she'll come back for her next vacation. Her girlfriend, Melinda, lives here."

"Yeah, maybe," Catie said. "Hey, can you show me where Kahe Point is. I wanted to tell Mommy about it, and I don't know where it is relative to Honolulu."

"Sure." Marc turned around and logged onto his computer. He typed Kahe Point into Google Maps, and it zoomed in on the bay. Marc zoomed it out so Catie could see all of Oahu and get a perspective of the bay in relationship to Honolulu.

"See, we sailed this way," Marc said. "It's about sixty miles."

"Thanks, Daddy," Catie said as she gave him a kiss and headed back to bed.

Catie's alarm went off at 2:30 a.m. She'd set her phone to vibrate and stuck it inside her pillowcase so it would be sure to wake her. She figured her father would work until 1:00 at the latest, so he should be deep asleep now. She quietly got out of bed and snuck into the family room. Her father's computer was sitting on the desk. She sat down and turned it on. She typed the password that she'd watch him enter earlier and started browsing around the file system.

When she got to a folder labeled ADI_Data, she got excited. She'd heard her father say that name a few times when she had noticed him talking while working at night. She opened the folder. It only had three items, message-1, message-2, and message-3.

"Well, I guess I should start with message-1," she thought to herself. She plugged her ear-buds into the front port so the sound wouldn't wake her father. She got excited when she listened to the first message. But the second message blew her away.

"Oh MY GOD!" Catie gasped.

"Yes, OH MY GOD," Marc scolded. "Just what do you think you're doing?"

"Me?! You found a spaceship!" Catie squealed.

"And you broke into my computer."

"Well yeah, I knew you were hiding something from me."

"I was, and as an adult and your father, I'm allowed to hide things from you. While as a child and my daughter, you are not allowed to break into my computer," Marc chided.

"But you found a spaceship!"

"I guess I should have erased those files."

"Well, duh! Can't that DI thing, ADI, give them to you again if you need them?"

"I'm sure it can. Now, what am I going to do with you?"

"You're going to give me a ride in it!"

"Not so fast. Now your Uncle Blake knows, but nobody else, and we need to keep it that way."

"Don't worry, Daddy, I can keep a secret."

"You can? But you can't let others keep one!"

"Not if I can help it," Catie replied with a smirk.

"Get yourself back to bed, we'll talk about this some more in the morning."

"How do you expect me to sleep?"

"You'd better figure it out, young lady!" Marc snapped.

As Catie slinked off to her room, Marc sat down at the computer. *"Why was I blessed with such a clever child? Well, I guess better late than never,"* he thought as he erased the folder with the message files from Metra. Since he had an electronic drive, he didn't have to worry about remnants hanging around.

Marc put the earwig in his ear and activated the comm, "ADI, watch what I type," he whispered, then he typed, "can you tell me if there is any surveillance on this condo. Can anyone hear what we are saying here?"

"There are no electronic devices within the condo that could be used to listen to you, other than your phones and computers, and they are not being used by anyone other than the intended users."

"What about external listening devices?" he typed

"One moment ... There is a laser pointed at your window from the condo across to the northwest of this one. Based on the angle they have about seventy percent signal clarity."

"Oh great," Marc groaned.

"What did the kid say?" the one man asked. There were two of them sitting in an apartment across from Marc's.

"Something about a spaceship. Who knows what that was about?" the second man said. "Who knows what kids will say. Maybe she was playing a video game on his computer."

"Should we go in and see if that's it or if there's something else interesting on his computer?"

"No, sounds like he erased it anyway. Besides, we're on passive surveillance only. Just note it in the log."

The next morning, Marc woke up early and got ready. At 8:00, he called Blake to let him know that he and Catie were coming over and wanted to go out and do some diving. He poured himself a cup of coffee and waited for Catie to wake up. After her late-night sojourn and excitement, he suspected she would be late. At 9:00, he heard the shower turn on, surprised that she was actually up that early. It was only ten minutes before Catie came out.

"That was fast," Marc said. He held his fingers to his lips, indicating she should be quiet. "Are you ready to go diving today?" He nodded his head, indicating she should say yes.

Catie looked confused but smiled. "Yes. Can I get my certificate first?"

"Sure, we'll stop by the dive shop, and they'll print it up for you."

Catie mouthed to Marc, "what about the spaceship?"

Marc pointed at his ear, then at the window. "Somebody is listening," he mouthed.

Catie looked even more confused.

"A spy," Marc mouthed. "How are you doing with your le Carré book?" he asked aloud.

"Oh, a spy," Catie mouthed back. "I've just finished it," she said. "Where's my twenty dollars?" Catie held out her hand until Marc put a twenty into it.

"My little capitalist," Marc thought. *"Never passes up a chance to make a deal.* Of course, that's our deal, twenty for every book on the reading list," he said. "I'm thinking about adding <u>War and Peace</u> and the <u>Rise and Fall of the Roman Empire.</u>"

"Sure," Catie said. "But you should pay double for big books like that." She gave him a big grin.

Marc held up his hand with his index finger and thumb a millimeter apart to indicate to Catie how thin the ice was that she was skating on.

"Are you ready? We'll grab breakfast and eat on the boat."

"Sure, let's go," Catie replied.

When they got in the elevator, Marc leaned down and whispered in her ear. "Not one word until we are on the boat. Got it?"

Catie nodded her head. "Where are we going to dive today?"

"I've been wanting to try a spot off Molokini. It's a bit of a sail, but it's never too crowded."

"Cool."

They stopped by a coffee shop and picked up a half dozen egg burritos and coffee, then headed for the Mea Huli. Blake was waiting for them at the dive platform. They handed him their breakfast and climbed aboard.

Catie turned to her father, "Now can ..." Marc put his fingers to her lips to cut her off.

Marc looked up in his HUD and clicked on the icon he'd added last night. It told ADI to check for surveillance.

ADI accessed the camera feed from the surveillance drone on top of the Mea Huli, "It appears that a van followed you here. They are pointing a directional microphone in your direction."

"Thank you," Marc whispered. "Why don't we cast off; Catie get the bowline, I'll grab the stern lines."

Blake ran up to the bridge and got the Mea Huli moving. Catie tossed the bowline up on the deck and waited for the boat's swimming platform to come even with her. Then she hopped aboard. She entered the lounge and gave her father a *what's up* signal.

Marc blinked on the surveillance icon again.

"The van is driving off," ADI reported. "I no longer detect any surveillance."

"Okay, young lady," Marc said to his daughter. "Why don't you get our burritos warmed up and meet me on the bridge. Then we'll talk."

Marc climbed up to the bridge. He waved at Blake while he opened the safe and pulled out the bag from the Sakira.

"What's up?" Blake asked.

Marc held up his index finger, indicating Blake should wait a minute, then he sat down with a sigh.

Catie came up to the bridge carrying a tray with the burritos and coffee. When she set them on the table, Marc looked up at her and shook his head.

"Catie knows about the Sakira," he said.

"What! You told her?"

"No, she hacked into my computer and found the communication files."

"You still had them on your computer?" Blake scolded.

66

"That's what I said," Catie squeaked.

"Young lady, when you're in a hole, it is best to stop digging," Marc scolded. He tried to suppress his laugh but didn't do a very good job.

"Sorry."

"So now what?" Blake said as he cranked the Mea Huli up to ten knots. He wanted to get out of the channel so he could put her on autopilot.

"We also got some surveillance on us," Marc said. "Put this in your ear," Marc handed Catie one of the earwigs from the bag.

"Which ear?"

"Doesn't matter. Pick the one you leave your earbud in when you want to pay attention to something besides your music."

Catie put the earwig in her left ear. "It tickles," Catie giggled, as the earwig seated itself into place.

"Okay, press it for three seconds to turn it on."

"ADI, say hi to my daughter, Catie."

"Hello, Cer Catie," ADI said.

Catie jumped a little. "Oh, hi. What's this Cer business?"

"It is the title used when referring to a person, your language uses Mister, Miss, and many other terms. The language of my developers uses Cer for all genders; I've decided to use it for simplicity. Is that acceptable?"

"Yes, it is," Marc said. "ADI is the ship computer. Now back to the earwig. If you press on it for three seconds, it switches on or off. You should leave it on," Marc explained. "If you want to wash your ear out, you press on it for eight seconds, and it'll come out. It's waterproof, so you can mostly leave it in."

"Cool. How does ADI hear us?"

"She hears through the earwig. It picks up the vibrations in your bones, so it hears whatever you're saying."

"How does she see things?"

"There is a drone up on the antenna tower. It can see as well as relay ADI's communication to us."

"Cool."

Marc handed her one of the wraparound glasses. "These glasses act like a head-up display and ADI can show images or video, and you can query using your eyes to run the menu. They also have cameras so you can see around yourself; ADI can use the cameras too. She sees whatever you see. There are cameras in the bows pointing backward so you can see behind you if you don't cover up the ends of the bows."

"I read about these in one of my science fiction books," Catie said. "They call them specs."

Marc gave Catie a frown.

"Hey, I can read books that aren't on your list," Catie defended herself.

"Of course, you can."

"What are those phone looking things?"

"They're comm computers. They're what the earwigs normally communicate with; they keep you in contact with ADI, and she can route communication with Blake or me. She can also route cellphone calls to your comm."

"Then, we can replace our cellphones?" Catie asked.

"Maybe," Marc said. "ADI, can you replace our phones with one of these comm computers?"

"Yes, I can," ADI said. "They have far more computational capability than your current phones."

"Can she duplicate the UI, so I have access to all my apps and my contacts?" Catie said.

"ADI."

"Yes, Captain. The comm can be made to cover all the functions of your phone."

"Then please clone each of our phones," Marc said, taking one for himself and handing a third to Blake. "Do you need us to do anything with our phones?"

"Each of you needs to turn on your comm. Press anywhere on the screen for ten seconds."

They each turned their comms on.

"I have cloned your phones' UI. The comms are now associated with your phone numbers. You will need to move the data over yourself or accept a Bluetooth input control on each phone, and then I can do it."

Marc unlocked his phone and opened the settings. "Here you go."

Blake and Catie looked a bit perplexed but did the same thing.

"Your new phones are ready. You'll need to reset your passcodes if you wish. They will respond to your DNA and wake up when you press the screen."

"Great," Catie said. Then her face fell. "It doesn't fit in my case."

"We'll have a custom one made for each of us," Marc said. "Why don't you play with your specs for now. ADI, please answer any questions Catie asks."

"Yes, Captain. I will comply except for restricted questions."

"That's fine."

Marc waved his hands at Catie, telling her to scoot. She gave him a frown, but picked up her stuff and headed down to the main lounge.

"I love her," Marc said.

"I know, but sometimes you want to beat her."

"Yeah, sometimes," he laughed.

"Hey, she can be helpful. Look how she figured out about swapping out our phones. Now we have three great minds figuring this out."

"I know, but she's growing up too fast. Whatever happened to the innocence of childhood?"

"That kind of went out with the internet and phones," Blake quipped. "Don't worry, she's still your little girl."

"You think?"

"Yeah, look at how she was disappointed about her phone case. She still has her priorities straight."

"Yes, she does. You should have seen how she conned me out of another twenty dollars back at the condo."

Marc smiled as he remembered Catie demanding twenty dollars for finishing the le Carré book she wasn't even reading. He tried to ignore her but realized she would keep insisting until he paid, and with the surveillance, he really couldn't get around it. "Damn, and what is this surveillance about?"

"You think it's the Navy?"

"Has to be, or the FBI at their request. I guess they're trying to protect their new secret or make sure I don't have some undisclosed partners. But Catie blurted out about me finding a spaceship when I caught her. I'm worried that they picked that up."

"They'll probably think it's some kind of computer game," Blake suggested.

"I hope so. But we're going to have to be more careful now. I think we need someone else to help with the boat. We'll need to do our planning here, so we need someone we can trust to drive the boat. It has to be someone who won't mind being out of the loop, but that we could bring in if we need to."

"I know just the guy," Blake said.

"Who?"

"A buddy from the VA. I see him there once in a while when I get treatments on my face. He's cool, and driving a boat has to beat the heck out of tending bar."

"A bartender?"

"An ex-Marine. Decorated twice."

"Okay, bring him in. Money is going to be tight until the Navy settles up, but we can swing another salary. At least if Catie doesn't bleed us dry."

"There is that," Blake laughed. "We're out of the channel, so I can put the autopilot on."

"Good, I'll go get Catie. See what she thinks of my plan."

Marc walked down the stairs to the lounge. Catie was sitting on the sofa with the glasses on; specs, Marc reminded himself. "Hey," he called out.

"Daddy, these are so cool," Catie squealed. "I can type on them almost as fast as my phone. And the images are three-D; you can like watch a movie on them, and the sound is better with them than just the ear thingy."

"I'll have to start practicing."

"And when are we getting to ride in one of the jets?"

"You and your Uncle Blake. The first thing he went to was the jets; you're like two kids in a toy store."

"Yes, and you're supposed to play with the toys. How else do you learn how they work? We need to practice," Catie said indignantly.

Marc laughed. "Sure, come on back upstairs, we're going to have a planning meeting."

Catie followed her father up to the bridge. The three of them sat on the sofas behind the bridge. Blake took the one opposite Catie and Marc.

"Let me tell you what I'm thinking," Marc started. "The Paraxeans, the builders of the spaceship, think we Earthlings are going to destroy ourselves before we can expand out of our own solar system."

"What?" Catie squeaked.

"Well, it's not like there's any record of successful cooperation amongst the various nations except military alliances. We only seem to be united by wars or the fear of wars. So, with all our advanced weapons, it's not hard to imagine we won't just blow ourselves up while we're fighting over resources or whatnot."

"I know, but we'll figure it out," Catie replied with dismay.

"One would hope, but we might have the answer. If we can reduce the competition for resources, things might be able to advance toward a working, cooperative model. So, my plan is to slowly introduce the technologies we have access to and guide Earth toward that future. I want to keep control of the technology so I can level the playing field. We can do things such as setting up industries in poorer countries to help equalize the income disparity."

"That's cool," Catie said.

"The problem is going to be that the wealthy countries are not going to like it, much less the wealthy people who are in control of all the industries that will undergo radical change or become obsolete."

"Yeah, the rich boys won't like you cutting into their action," Blake said. "They're likely to steal it from you."

"Yes, and with the surveillance we're under, I'm worried they're going to get help from the government," Marc said.

"Why would the government help them?" Catie asked.

"Well, people in power have rich friends, and they tend to help each other, especially those who are elected," Marc said. "Those elected officials need money to finance their campaigns, so when they get elected, they owe a lot to the people who donated millions to their campaigns. Those people expect them to return the favor via guiding the government in ways that help them out."

"That's not fair," Catie exclaimed.

"Fair doesn't generally have anything to do with life," Marc replied.

Catie crossed her arms and pouted.

"ADI and I did an economic and technology survey and have identified two promising products we should start with. A new battery and a new fuel cell that between them will dramatically lower transportation costs while reducing carbon emissions," Marc said. "The fuel cell would operate at one hundred C, instead of the several hundred that current ones operate at. The battery has three to five times the power density and doesn't wear out like lithium batteries do."

"Wow, that is so cool. You won't have to charge your phone and computer so often," Catie said.

"That's right. And although you can analyze what they're made of, it looks impossible to reverse engineer how they are made. ADI says even she can't do it based on the information someone would have available and the current technology on Earth," Marc explained. "The problem is, how do we keep them from stealing our manufacturing secrets."

"You have to totally lock down the manufacturing facilities," Blake said. "And how are you going to build machines to manufacture stuff without other people knowing how to make the machines?"

"We'll have machines to make the molds for the batteries and fuel cell elements. Based on what ADI tells me, the secret is how the materials are combined and how a specific electric field is applied during manufacturing. That will be in the programming that we control, so nobody will have access to that. It's how to stop someone from coming in and stealing the machines that has me worried."

"You need an island," Catie said. "Then you would know exactly who is supposed to be there and who's not. And if they stole something, you could stop them from getting it off the island."

"That's a good idea," Marc mused. "ADI, search for islands with low or no populations that are isolated from any major countries. Okay, we'll table that for now and come back to it later. Setting up production requires money. At first, I was planning to use the money from Hyperion to start a corporation and raise capital that way. Now I'm worried that will just expose us to compromises. So, I think we keep the core technologies private and just go public with the derivative technologies."

"What does that mean?" Catie asked.

"Yeah, you lost me there, too," Blake said.

"Sorry. By core, I mean the batteries and the fuel cells for now. But we design the cars and trucks and take those designs to existing companies or start a new one. We use our control over the core technology to control where the new cars and trucks can be built. That way we can force the wealth to be spread around more equitably, without having to have total control of each company."

"That sounds good, but it also sounds like it will take a lot of time," Blake said.

"Yes, just to build the manufacturing capacity for the batteries will take hundreds of millions of dollars. If we go too slow, we expose ourselves to industrial espionage for a longer period of time, and could lose control of the technology before we have the impact we want."

"So, you need something that will generate a bunch of cash right away," Blake said.

"That would be nice, but there just aren't that many billion-dollar opportunities lying around. And they take years to generate cash,"

Marc said with despair. "Look at Google and Facebook and how long it was before they were really worth much."

"You need to find a treasure ship," Catie said.

"What?" Marc asked. He was shocked at the suggestion. Catie was usually more practical than that.

"Sure, you have those fighters that can act like submarines," Catie said. "And you have Hyperion, even if the Navy won't let you sell it."

"That sounds good, but it's not like there are a bunch of treasure ships lying around just waiting to be discovered," Marc countered.

"But they are," Catie replied. "Just look at the San Jose they found off of Colombia. It's worth like seventeen-billion dollars, and they just found it; we talked about it in my history class. I checked, and there are dozens of Spanish and Portuguese treasure galleons that were lost between the fifteen hundreds and the late 1850s."

"I don't know," Marc said, skeptically.

"ADI, how many sunken treasure galleons are there that haven't been discovered?" Catie asked, determined to prove her point.

"The records show many ships that were lost at sea. It is not possible to determine how many actually sank versus were captured by pirates or had their crews mutiny," ADI said.

"Pooh," Catie said.

"So, you can't tell us how many ships are sitting on the bottom of the sea waiting to be discovered?" Marc asked.

"I can do that. There are eight ships sitting on the bottom of the sea in relatively intact states. There are twenty-four others that are in a close debris field that can be identified as one ship," ADI said.

"What?" Catie squeaked.

"How do you know that?" Blake asked.

"When we arrived here, the captain of the Sakira had the crew do a complete survey of your planet. That survey included a detailed mapping of the ocean floor," ADI said.

"Where are these ships located?" Marc asked. "Are any in international waters?"

"Which ships?" ADI asked.

"The ones that are intact," Marc replied.

"The eight ships are in international waters," ADI responded. "Four are Spanish galleons, one is Portuguese, two you would identify as Viking, and one is a U.S. warship and the other a British warship."

"Tell us about the Spanish and Portuguese," Marc said.

"There are two Spanish galleons about two hundred miles southeast of Bermuda. They are in very deep water, so there has been no continued damage from storms or marine life. There is another one that is one hundred miles east of Cancun, Mexico, in the Gulf of Mexico. Las Cinque Chagas is three hundred twenty miles northeast of the Azores; it is also in deep water. And one Spanish galleon east of the Philippines. I have the coordinates if you require them."

"Whoa, Manna from heaven," Blake exclaimed.

"Well it looks like we're going to become treasure hunters," Marc said. He looked at his daughter, who was just beaming. "Blake, we'll need to extend the lease on Willie. Do you think your guy would be up to doing some treasure hunting?"

"You bet he will. This is even more exciting."

"We'll probably need two guys, divers."

"I'm not sure my guy's a diver," Blake said. "He lost both legs in Iraq."

Marc grimaced. "Get him anyway. Maybe we'll come up with a third that dives. Just trying to keep the circle small."

All this time, Catie had been squirming, wanting to interject. She jumped into the pause between Marc and Blake. "But we're not going to be hunting. ADI knows where the ships are."

"But we have to look like we're hunting," Marc said. "We can't just march in and say we found some treasure ships when we've never even been looking for them."

"Oh!"

"And we'll need to recover them," Marc added.

"I see," Catie said.

"Where do you want me to ship the Mea Huli and when?" Blake asked.

"Let's go with Antigua, we don't want to tip our hand. When is the last cruise you have booked?"

"Grrr, I'll have to check. I know I have one over the fourth, but after that, I'll have to check with Macie. We don't usually get booked too far in advance. In fact, why don't I try out my new phone."

Blake called Macie while Catie and Marc sat waiting impatiently. When he hung up the phone, they both asked, "Well?"

"She confirmed the booking for the fourth, and said they had a tentative one for August eighth," Blake said. "I asked her to cancel it without costing too much and explained that we were going to move the Mea Huli to the Caribbean."

"And?" Marc asked.

"Well, she's not too happy about us moving to the Caribbean," Blake said. "She hates the idea of losing the commission."

"Oh well," Marc said. "Now, are we going to do some diving?"

They spent the rest of the day diving around Molokini. When they were tired, they cruised to Molokai and had dinner at Paddlers. The next day they cruised by the North Shore Sea Cliffs as they made their way back to Honolulu. Blake needed to get the boat ready for what he hoped was his last charter. Catie agreed to crew for him.

Once Catie was off on the cruise with Blake, Marc made the call he had been dreading.

"Dr. McCormack, please; tell her it's Marc calling."

It was only one-minute before his ex-wife came on the line. Marc had been expecting to be on hold for at least five minutes.

"Marc, is there a problem with Catie?" Dr. McCormack gasped.

"Sorry, Linda, I didn't think. Catie's fine."

"Oh good, you scared me. What do you need?"

"I need to talk about Catie. I have a change in business plans and need to move to the Caribbean in a few weeks."

"What? Are you sending Catie home?"

"You tell me. I can hang out in Hawaii for another three or four weeks, but I'd rather head out sooner. I'm not sure how you feel about me taking Catie out of the country."

"Oh!" She sounded relieved to Marc.

"What do you think? We would be in Florida, Antigua, maybe a trip to Bermuda."

"We need to talk," Linda said. "Where is Catie?"

"She's out with Blake on a charter," Marc replied.

"Okay. I can clear my calendar at three, can you call me back then?"

"Sure."

Marc called back at three, twelve o'clock Hawaiian time. Linda came on the line right away. "Hey, sorry about having to make you call back," she said.

"No worry, I know what a doctor's schedule is like," Marc replied.

"Thanks for being understanding. How is Catie doing?"

"She's only been here two-and-a-half weeks, but she seems to be loving it. We taught her how to scuba dive; she's a natural."

"That's good. How are the two of you getting along?"

"Fine. Has she complained?"

"No, not that. She seems genuinely happy," Linda said.

"Oh good. You had me worried."

"Sorry. The point is, I was wondering if you would consider keeping her full time," Linda said with a little sob.

"What, what's wrong?"

"Nothing."

"You wouldn't be talking about giving up your daughter if nothing was wrong."

"I'm not giving her up. She would still come visit; we'd just switch roles."

"Why?"

"You know my problem."

"The depression."

"Yes. It's not getting better, and I don't think Catie is happy here. She sounds so much happier when I talk to her on the telephone now. I think it would be better for her."

"You do realize she's on vacation, it would only be natural for her to be happier."

"I know. But if you don't want to keep her, I'll understand."

"That's not it. I'd love to have her. I just want to make sure you're sure."

"I am. We can revisit it every year. When I get better, she may want to stay with me."

Marc could tell Linda was crying. "This is a big sacrifice for you."

"It's for Catie."

"Would you be okay if I homeschooled her?" Marc asked. "It would make things easier and keep her busier. She has never done well with long breaks."

"What about other kids?" Linda asked.

"I could get her involved in some sports and activities, so she socializes. She never seems to have friends from school anyway."

"That's right," Linda said. "So, you'll keep her?"

"Of course, for as long as you need me to."

"Thanks. I'll have my lawyer draw up the necessary paperwork. But do what you need to. I don't have a problem with her traveling outside the U.S. It'll be a good experience for her."

"Do you want to tell her, or should I?" Marc asked.

"Would you tell her?" Linda said. "Make sure she knows how much I love her."

"I will, but why don't we wait for a bit. I think it would be better if Catie were asking to stay."

"Do you think she will?"

"She's pretty excited about the things we're doing. So, it's a good possibility," Marc said. "And then you wouldn't have to be the one giving her up."

"I'd like that. Bye," Linda sobbed as she hung up the phone.

"What else can make my life more interesting?" Marc thought.

On Sunday at 10:00, Blake made his way to the Kealoha bar. It was quite a ways inland and mainly catered to locals. Blake liked it because you rarely saw a tourist in the area. It made for a nice break from the harbor where all the bars and restaurants close by mainly catered to tourists. Besides, he liked the bartender Kal. He'd met him in the waiting room at the VA.

"Hey, Jarhead!" Blake called out as he entered the bar.

"Hey, we don't serve swabbies in here, they can't hold their liquor," the bartender hollered back.

"Bring me a drink, and I'll show you who can hold their liquor," Blake shot back. "Make it a double."

"Kind of early for you to be hitting the booze already?"

"I just finished a four-day cruise with a bunch of self-entitled rich people. I really need that drink."

"Give me a break. You spend most of your time on the bridge, and you can't convince me that sailing around on the pleasure palace you call a yacht is hardship duty."

"Maybe not hardship, but it can drive a man to drink," Blake said, as he shook Kal's hand. "Haven't seen you for a few weeks, how's it going?"

"I'm doing okay for a Hawaiian who can't surf," Kal said. "My friends take me out kayaking once in a while."

"Sounds nice," Blake said. "What would you think about signing on with Marc and me?"

"Doing what?"

"Driving the boat, providing security, some other stuff we can't talk about yet."

"Nothing illegal?"

"We might stray into the gray area a bit, but nothing illegal, no smuggling, no drugs or anything like that. We just feel we need a few more people we can trust."

"I don't know, not sure I could handle being around a bunch of self-entitled rich people, much less waiting on them."

"I've done my last charter. We're moving onto bigger things. You interested?"

"Sure, what would it pay?"

"You'll live on board mostly, that's free. If we need you to be ashore, we'll cover cost. Pay is one thousand dollars per week. If we hit something really good, a small share of the profits."

"Are there likely to be profits?"

"I'm definitely counting on it."

"How much might I wind up with?"

"I can't promise you anything. We could come up bust, but if things work out, you could own this bar."

"I don't want to own a bar," Kal said.

"Well, spend the money on something else. Upside, you'll be set for life, downside, you'll have fun sailing around the Caribbean."

"You're heading to the Caribbean?"

"Yeah, and probably some time off of Portugal, maybe the Mediterranean."

"That would be nice. I'd sure like to be able to spend more of my time on the water."

"Think about it."

"I've thought about it, I'm in," Kal said. "I'm tired of serving drunks like you."

"Hey, you would be working for me, so you'll still have to get me a beer now and again," Blake laughed. "But of course, you'd be able to get one for yourself, too."

"Sounds good. When do I start?"

"We're shipping the boat to the Caribbean on Thursday. It takes three weeks to get to Antigua ..."

"Antigua, now you're talking!"

"Yeah. We'll definitely need you in three weeks, with travel and prep. So, give your notice and start any time after two weeks from tomorrow."

"Great."

"We need at least one other guy. Someone who can dive and can handle security like you. Someone you'd trust with your life."

"Does it need to be a guy?"

"As long as she's good with a gun, I guess it doesn't matter."

"I have someone in mind. She comes here once in a while. I knew her back in Iraq. But she has a little baggage you need to know about."

"PTSD?"

"I don't think so. She was a chopper pilot; she's doing island tours now. But she was raped back in Iraq."

"That really sucks, but if there's not PTSD, why would that matter?"

"Well, the three guys who raped her turned up dead."

"Good for her. She didn't trust the brass to take care of it?"

"No, she started out that way. She reported it, they held an article thirty-two hearing, but found there wasn't enough evidence."

"How's that? Did she wait too long to report it?"

"No, she went to the hospital and got the rape kit done right away, reported it to her CO."

"So why did he let the guys off?"

"She and a friend were out drinking. The bartender brought over a couple of drinks; said they were from the guys at the end of the bar. The two of them were already feeling pretty good, but hey, free drinks. Liz, my friend, says she thinks the drinks were roofied. Her friend drank her drink, and most of Liz's too. Later, she went to the head but never came back. Apparently, she passed out. They found her later, and some nice lieutenant walked her back to her room. So, Liz wasn't all that much out of it when the guys offered to walk her home. They led her to a secluded area and well …"

"Didn't they find the roofie in her system?"

"Just a trace. Anyway, the CO said she was drunk, and he couldn't rely on her testimony. Threw the case out."

"So, the guys show up dead sometime later. Did she do it?"

"I'm pretty sure she did, she's like a fourth-level black belt in Krav Maga, but everything pointed to ISIS. They were cut up pretty bad."

"She didn't shoot them?"

"No, just used a knife, all three at the same time. There wasn't anything that pointed to her, so they didn't pursue it. But it tanked her career. She missed the next two promotion boards and had to leave."

"How did she wind up in Hawaii?"

"She's staying with her parents while she gets established. Her dad's Navy and he's stationed here. He just left on deployment last month."

"She sounds like my kind of girl," Blake said, "but Marc has his daughter with him, so I'd better check with him. I think he'll be okay with it, but better safe than sorry. I'll check with him tonight and let you know."

"Good."

"Here are a couple of our cards. If you know or hear of someone else, we might be willing to swing a third."

"Got it. She's usually in here on Tuesday with a girlfriend. Give me the word by tomorrow, and I'll talk to her and let you know."

That night Blake checked with Marc. Marc was fine with Liz, so Blake texted Kal later that night to let him know that it was okay to speak to her about the job.

That night Marc listened to the next message.

Message-4:

"Captain, I hope things are going well for you now. I wanted to make sure you had a chance to internalize everything. The most important thing to realize is that although the DI is not malicious or particularly self-aware, it does have protocols that it must follow. You need to be careful in how you interact with it to avoid triggering a protocol that requires it to contact my homeworld, or worse yet, issue a self-destruct for the ship. You can ask it about the protocols and even what will trigger them, but it is complex, so there are no perfect answers.

"The captain was poisoned by the first officer; only he had access to the captain's private stores where I found the poison. It was in one of the captain's special treats. Based on the rotation, the first officer was in stasis when the captain died. The poison had obviously been selected so that it would appear that the captain had had an allergic reaction to some of the food we had harvested from your world. I happened to be familiar with the poison from a previous experience, otherwise the first officer would have succeeded. Instead, I used the symptoms to declare a contamination by an unknown contagion and placed the crew in stasis and quarantined the ship. That puts several protocols into place, one of which restricts any other ship from our world from coming here until the issue is resolved. The first officer has powerful friends and family in the government, so I didn't risk notifying Paraxea; instead, I hoped that using the quarantine protocol and time we could find you and together we could come up with a solution.

"Now, my other concern.

"I have always believed that our government was benevolent, but I cannot understand how the first officer and his friends got on this mission. The first officer must have used his influence to make it happen, and if he did so, then he must have a bigger plan. Because of that, I think it is imperative that you get your world ready to encounter my world. If you are not capable of interstellar travel when my world comes back to check, it is possible that they would put you in a subservient position. Given what happened to our captain, it might not be a nice situation. But if you can bring your technology along over the next fifty-years so that it is on a par with ours, and if you have a means of defending yourselves, then things might be handled in a more equitable manner.

"Of course, that means you also have to find a way to keep the various governments on your world from destroying the planet. I don't have the political savvy to know how to do that. I'm just a doctor, but given

83

the altruistic nature you must have to have passed the tests, I'm hoping you do. You'll also need lots of technical help to guide the integration of our technology into yours. You must be some kind of explorer or technologist to have discovered the Sakira, but if not, you need to find someone you can trust. I recommend a small circle of people since it's difficult to find very many truly loyal people.

"After this message, all the protocols will be released to you. Until now, the DI was restricted from contacting the home planet and constrained from aborting the mission. But now you will be the unrestrained captain of this ship and its mission. Please be careful, and good luck."

"Oh, this keeps getting better and better," Marc muttered to himself as he headed off to bed.

On Monday, they took the Mea Huli out for the final cruise before having to prepare it for shipping on Friday. It was also their last chance for true privacy to go over plans for the next four weeks before they'd be able to meet the Mea Huli in Antigua.

"Captain, you are clear of all audio surveillance," ADI said.

"Thank you, ADI," Marc replied. "So, guys, let's talk about plans," he said to Blake and Catie.

"Yes, what are we going to do for two weeks without a ship?" Blake asked.

"I have to settle with the Navy. Hopefully this week," Marc said. "Then Catie and I are going to do vacation-y type things for a couple of weeks."

"Huh?" Catie said, somewhat startled. "Can't we do something to prepare for Antigua?"

"You're out here for a vacation, or have you forgotten? Your mother is expecting reports of vacation activities; besides, it'll help calm the Navy, and maybe they'll pull their surveillance."

"Okay, I'm good with that," Blake said. "I'll do some team building with Kal and Liz."

"Who are Kal and Liz?" Catie asked.

"They're two new members of our crew," Marc said. "We'll need help, and we want some more ex-military types to beef up our security."

"Oh," Catie said, wondering why she hadn't been consulted.

"And Blake, how about adding some team-building activities besides drinking together," Marc said.

"Damn, what a wet blanket," Blake laughed. "I plan on working out with them, and we'll spend some time at the firing range. Might even do some paintball."

"Ooh, can I do the paintball with you?" Catie pleaded.

Blake looked at Marc. "Why not. She's played before."

"Yes!" Catie squealed.

"We can do the paintball on Friday, and try to fit another in next week," Blake said.

"Why don't we try to get two in next week," Marc said. "I'm planning to fly to Miami the end of next week."

Catie pumped her fist.

"Why Miami?"

"We need to do some research on sunken treasure ships," Marc said. "I figure a week in Miami will look good, and we can do some additional research in Antigua while we wait for the Mea Huli."

"Okay, I'll plan to be in Antigua the week before the Mea Huli arrives on the twenty-third," Blake said. "That'll give Kal, Liz, and me a chance to scope out the local scene. What about ADI?"

"What do you mean? We'll have access via our comms."

"But it's real nice having that little spy-bot hanging around. She does a great job detecting surveillance."

"How will that help in a hotel? We can't put one in the hallway."

"Good point," Blake said. "ADI, do you have other options for detecting surveillance and providing security?"

"There are surveillance pucks in the ship's stores," ADI replied.

"What are surveillance pucks?"

"They provide EM surveillance and video stream of the surrounding area. They are eighty millimeters in diameter and fifteen millimeters thick. They can be attached to any surface."

"Oh, we need some of those," Blake said.

"We'll get some. ADI, how can we get one of your relay drones to Antigua?" Marc asked.

"Captain, it would not be able to make that long a flight. It only has enough power to stay aloft for two hours. I could deliver it using one of the FX4s."

"I don't think we want to send an FX4 flying around on its own. I'd like to have one on each of us at all times," Blake said.

"What good are they going to be in a hotel room?" Marc asked.

"They connect with the pucks and our comms," Blake said. "ADI, is there a reason we wouldn't be able to carry it in our luggage?"

"They x-ray luggage," Marc said.

"An x-ray would just show the drone as a solid mass," ADI said.

"But it's kind of a weird shape. Like a bowling ball with a flat side."

"Can't we make a shell, so it looks like a bowling ball?" Catie suggested.

"ADI, could you make a shell like Catie suggests?" Marc asked.

"Yes, Captain. A bowling ball is 21.5 centimeters in diameter. The drone is twenty centimeters; I can manufacture a shell that snaps together with the finger holes on the bottom where the drone is flat."

"Will it appear solid on the x-ray?"

"Yes, Captain," ADI said. "I can add material in the base to ensure it looks solid. It will weigh three-kilograms."

"Perfect. How soon can you have them made?"

"Thirty minutes, Captain."

"Please make them now. We need to pick them up today along with ten surveillance pucks."

Blake got up and changed their course to pass by Lehua. "It will take two hours to get there."

"I'm still worried about an inspection," Marc said.

"Hey, you're rich," Blake said. "Just charter a flight; no baggage check on a private flight."

"Yes!" Catie clenched both fists and did a little dance with her feet.

"I guess that's decided," Marc said.

"She's so excited, maybe you can talk her into paying," Blake teased.

"No way, I'm a kid. You can't use my money," Catie retorted.

"What gives you that idea?" Marc asked.

"Hey, you're my dad, you have to pay for me."

"That doesn't sound fair."

"You already told me life's not fair. You're the parent, I'm the kid. You have to take care of me."

"Good morning, Dr. McCormack," Admiral Michaels said, extending his hand to Marc.

Marc shook hands with the admiral, but he really didn't like the man. Even though the admiral was doing what Marc had expected and had even hoped for, Marc couldn't help but feel distaste at being coerced into selling his sonar invention to the Navy, even if that was his plan all along.

"Let's get down to business," Admiral Michaels said. "As you know, the U.S. Government has declared the Hyperion technology classified and would like to have exclusive access to the technology."

"Would like?" Marc retorted. "And if I don't agree?"

"We've already been down this path. We would like to make things amicable, but we will have control over Hyperion."

"Good luck reverse engineering it."

"As I reminded you, we've already been here. If you refuse, we'll seize all your assets and charge you with espionage. It is in your interest as well as the national interest to cooperate."

"What are you offering?"

"We're offering you eight million dollars for the design and all prototype materials."

"My calculations show that Hyperion would generate over thirty million dollars in the next ten years, which gives it a Net Present Value of over thirty-five million," Marc spat out angrily. "Your offer is an insult."

"I know you're angry," the admiral replied quietly, "but I have limited scope in this negotiation. And you do not want to have to negotiate with the next team. I'll lay my cards on the table. I've been authorized to go to twenty million. But that's my limit. If that is not acceptable, I will have to turn this thing over to the big boys."

"This is crap," Marc spat out.

"Best I can do."

Marc gritted his teeth. "I'll agree if you buy the company."

"What are the company debts and assets?"

"As if you don't know. There are no assets besides the Hyperion design, the debts are around fifty thousand."

"Deal," the admiral said as he extended his hand again.

Marc shook hands with him, "I'll transfer the design documents and associated data once we have a signed contract, and the funds are in my account."

"You don't trust us?"

"Haven't seen any reason I should."

The admiral shook his head and shrugged his shoulders. "You'll have the documents delivered to you by tomorrow. Funds will transfer once you sign. Where would you like us to reach you?"

"At my condo," Marc replied.

After the door closed behind Marc, the lieutenant who had been sitting next to the admiral finally spoke up. "Well, he was certainly pissed off."

"I think Dr. McCormack got exactly what he wanted," the admiral said.

"Really?"

"Yes, he saved over ten million by getting us to buy the company."

"How?"

"No corporate tax on the twenty million followed by personal tax when he took profits out of the company. This way, he only has to pay capital gains on the twenty million."

"Then, why did you give him such a good deal?"

"We are taking away his design and his company; besides, I don't work for the IRS."

"How'd it go with the Navy boys?" Blake asked when Marc joined him and Catie at the restaurant.

Marc blinked on the surveillance icon.

"Captain, I detect no surveillance."

"Good," Marc said. "We got twenty million, and they're buying the company."

"They're buying the company, that means we're set."

"For now."

"Why is buying the company good?" Catie asked.

"Taxes," Marc replied. "They're buying our shares, so we only have to pay capital gains tax."

"Oh!"

"We'll have the papers and money tomorrow. Catie and I'll pack up next week and be ready to head out on to the east coast next Friday. I've sublet the condo for the rest of my lease."

"Great, we have dinner with our team on Thursday, paintball Friday, then again on Monday and Wednesday next week," Blake said.

Chapter 6   MacKenzie Discoveries

Blake set their first team meeting at Orchids, a Japanese restaurant down the street from Marc's condo. He made a point to arrive well before everyone else. He wanted to make sure that everything was set in the private dining room he'd reserved. He had ADI use his comm to scan and make sure there were no listening devices. He confirmed all the arrangements with the staff, a raised table so Kal would be able to sit, complete privacy during the dinner.

Kal was the first to arrive. "Hey, Kal, you're early."

"Only a bit, thought I'd see how things were shaping up."

"You're not getting cold feet, are you?"

"Nah, I'm ready," Kal said. "By the way, I can't get cold feet."

"Ah, give me a break."

"I'm just messing with you. And thanks for having a raised table."

"No problem."

Kal took a seat and relaxed while he waited for the rest of the team to show up. Marc and Catie came in about five minutes later.

"Hello, you must be Kal," Marc said as he walked over to Kal. He waved Kal back to his seat before he could start to get up. "I'm Marc, and this is my daughter, Catie."

"Hi," Catie waved as she took a seat next to Kal, where Blake had indicated.

"And this must be Liz," Blake said as a tall blond woman entered. She was obviously athletic. She wore nice slacks and a simple blazer over a white blouse, but she looked like she could just take off running if she needed to.

"Yes," Liz replied. "Commander McCormack?"

"Just call me Blake, or Captain if we're aboard," Blake replied. "You know Kal." Liz gave Kal a nod. "And this is my brother Marc, our fearless leader. And the young lady is his daughter, Catie."

Liz looked at Catie, shocked. "This is the fifth team member?"

"Yes, didn't Kal tell you Marc's daughter would be our fifth?"

"Yes, but I was thinking seventeen or eighteen, what is she, like ten?"

"Twelve," Catie snapped as she gave Liz a cold, dead stare. Marc was shocked at the look. He'd never seen Catie look so much like her mother. She was showing the same steel her mother used to have before. It made him proud.

Liz stared back at Catie for a minute before she broke eye contact. "Well, youth is good," she smiled. She shook hands with everyone and took the empty seat on the other side of Kal. Marc and Blake sat down.

"Let me first welcome everyone to MacKenzie Discoveries," Marc said. "The name was selected by Catie to honor our Scottish roots. Alexander MacKenzie was one of the first explorers to reach the Arctic Ocean. He was also the first European to cross from the Atlantic to the Pacific Ocean north of the Rio Grande; his crossing was in Canada."

"That's interesting," Liz said. "And I think a good choice for the company name."

"The waitresses will be here in a moment to take our orders, so check out the menu," Marc said. "Once they serve dinner, the staff will leave us alone so we can discuss our plans and answer any questions."

With that, Blake pressed the call button, and three Japanese women entered the room. Two of them served each diner a glass of water while the third simply stood at the back of the room and observed. After serving the water, the other two joined her and quietly waited while everyone perused the menu.

When everyone had set their menu down, indicating that they had made their selection, one of the women made the quick round to take drink orders then hurried off. The second explained the menu options, answered a couple of questions, and then took the orders. By the time she was finished, the first woman had returned with the drinks.

Blake stood and raised his glass in a toast. "To MacKenzie Discoveries."

Everyone raised their glass in reply and drank.

"So, Liz, Kal tells me that you fly helicopters," Blake said, trying to fill the time until their dinners arrived.

"Yes, I'm flying between the islands, quick hops for those who don't want to hassle with regular airports."

"That must be fun," Catie said. "You get to see every island and catch all the beautiful scenery."

"It is kind of fun, but a little tame for me," Liz replied.

"Yes, I guess everything is tame after flying a Viper," Blake said.

"Kal, what did you do in Iraq?" Marc asked, bringing Kal into the conversation.

"I was a grunt," Kal said. "Incursions, house to house, that sort of thing."

"That must have been scary," Catie said.

"It definitely got your motor running," Kal replied.

"He had quite the reputation," Liz said. "His men thought he was some kind of war god."

"Why?" Catie asked.

"I think it was some Hawaiian war cry he'd let out," Liz said. "That and the fact that they always made it back safe."

"Except that last time," Kal said.

"You all made it back," Liz said. "That's safe in my books."

"What happened the last time?"

"They knew we were coming and had a trap set."

Catie looked at him expectantly.

"The house was booby-trapped with explosives."

"Was anyone hurt?" Catie asked.

"Just me, I was too slow."

"He wasn't slow. He grabbed the last guy and pushed him out in front of himself," Liz said.

"What happened to you?"

"Lost my legs," Kal said.

Catie looked aghast. "Your legs?"

"Yeah. But the Marines gave me these new titanium legs. So, except for the fact that I can't surf, I'm doing okay."

Thankfully, by this time, their dinner arrived. Once everyone was served, Blake indicated to the staff that they should leave them.

"Okay, let's eat," Blake said. "The room is secure, so you're free to ask any questions."

"Why all the security?" Liz asked.

"We're talking about an opportunity to make a few hundred million," Marc said. "We're worried someone might want to take an unauthorized share or even beat us out of it entirely."

"That's a lot of money," Kal said. "How are you dividing it up?"

"Kal is a cut-to-the-chase kind of guy," Blake said with a laugh.

"I respect that," Marc said. "We're guaranteeing one million for each crew member. We might have to hire another one or two, but we'll see. Crew shares are two percent of the gross return for each."

"Two percent doesn't sound very generous," Liz said.

"You have to decide that," Marc said. "We're taking all the financial risk, providing the intel, and covering all expenses. Not to be blunt, but ignoring the percentages, what would you expect to make in six months? We're talking about one million to over twenty if we find what we expect."

"Hey, that sounds good to me," Kal said. "Six months of adventure, then we're set for life, or worse case, we have one million to start our own business."

"I can roll with that," Liz said.

"Everyone, please eat, don't let the food get cold," Marc said as he took a bite of his sushi.

"Sushi doesn't get cold," Catie said.

"Not everyone is having sushi," Marc replied.

"Okay, so what's the big secret?" Liz asked. "Treasure ships?"

"Exactly, how'd you guess?"

"You wanted divers," Liz replied.

"Smart woman," Blake said. "You sure know how to pick them, Kal."

"Hunting for treasure ships is risky business. What makes you so confident you're going to find something," Liz asked.

"We have excellent intel," Marc said. "In fact, our intel is so good, we aren't going to be searching, but pretending to search."

Liz and Kal both looked dumbfounded. "Pretending to look!"

Catie giggled. "We already know where they are."

"On screen," Marc said. The 64-inch TV on the wall in front of their table lit up. It displayed the image of a huge ship sitting on the bottom of the ocean.

"We have two options," Marc said. "The first is the <u>Las Cinque Chagas</u>. It is a Portuguese ship that was returning with plunder from the conquest of Goa in India. It was riding the trade winds back toward Portugal when the British started chasing it. They caught it by the Azores and attacked. After a pitched battle, it was sunk. It is reputed to have been carrying over four billion dollars in treasure at today's prices."

"But what about all the competing claims for salvage?"

"Our plan is to negotiate directly with Portugal," Marc said. "We'll promise to deliver the ship whole to them in the Azores. They can deal with the competing claims. Possession is nine-tenths after all."

"You think you can move that ship in one piece?!"

"Blake."

"As you can see," Blake said as the image panned around the ship, "the ship is surprisingly whole. It is in deep water, so there hasn't been the usual rot and decay. We're just starting to do the engineering on how to raise her, but the thought is to put a big rubber sheet under her, attach baffles and raise her. Once she's on the surface, all the excess water will pour out, and we'll tow her to an agreed-upon location to meet a Portuguese escort."

"You guys certainly don't think small," Liz said.

"Small is for chipmunks," Catie said.

"Says the smallest member of our crew," Blake laughed.

Starship Sakira

"Our second option is in the Caribbean," Marc continued. The display changed to the image of a Spanish galleon sitting on the bottom much as Las Cinque Chagas had been.

"Looks like the same play," Liz said.

"Not quite," Marc said. "This one isn't as isolated as Las Cinque Chagas. And if we decide to go for both, then everyone will know about the recovery of the Chagas, so we'll have lots of scrutiny."

"Do you need a wheelbarrow for those balls?" Liz asked Marc.

Marc laughed. "Audacity is part of our Scottish heritage. We're distant relatives of Robert The Bruce."

"Hey, so am I," Liz said. "So big shoes to fill."

"I prefer, a great example to follow," Marc said.

"I like that. So how are you going to pull this off?"

"We're still planning that," Marc said. "Catie and I are off to Miami and the Caribbean in a few days. We'll see you in Antigua. You guys and Blake are going to do team training to make sure we're ready with security. Liz and Blake should tune up their dive skills. We're all dive qualified. Catie will probably be manning the underwater rover most of the time, but she'll be able to pitch in with diving. We'll work on her deep dive skills in Antigua."

"I can dive," Kal said.

"You can?" Marc asked. He didn't want to comment about Kal's legs, but the question was obvious.

"Yeah, it ain't pretty," Kal said, "but I can maneuver around pretty good. Just put a wetsuit over these and lock the knees, and I can get a bit of thrust. Of course, I'd rather use a sea scooter."

"So would I," Blake said.

"It looks like most of the work will be done standing up, and I can walk underwater as well as I do above water."

"Okay, then get what you need, and maybe we'll have enough divers," Marc said.

"How deep are we talking about for the dives?" Liz asked

"Four to five hundred meters," Marc said.

"That's deep, Hydrox?"

"Something a little better," Marc said.

"What's better?"

"We start out with standard CO_2 scrubber and pure O_2, switch to Hydrox at thirty meters to get rid of the nitrogen, then switch back to the CO_2 scrubber and O_2. So, you're carrying mostly pure oxygen. It gives you five times the air supply."

"Isn't that dangerous?" Liz asked.

"It fails safe to pure O_2, but you're still carrying a small amount of standard air for the last thirty meters of the ascent," Marc said. "You can switch earlier if there's a problem. We focus on the O_2 for the working time."

"Clever," Kal said. "You invent the rebreather?"

"Yes."

"So, we have to figure out how to get the liner under the ship," Liz said.

"That's why we have Blake," Marc said. "Mechanical engineering from the academy, masters in aerospace engineering from MIT."

"I've got my ME from the academy," Liz said. "Hopefully, I can help."

"Plus, we have our secret weapon," Blake said.

Kal and Liz both gave him the 'And' look.

"Catie. She doesn't know what can't be done, so she comes up with some killer ideas."

"Really."

"Yes, she was the one who figured out the treasure ships."

Catie grinned at everyone. "It was obvious."

"Something only the young and brilliant can say," Marc added.

"How did she figure it out?" Liz asked.

"That touches on our intel source," Marc said. "That's something we are not willing to share at this time. Maybe on our next mission if you're still with us."

—

"I cannot stress how critical it is to maintain operational secrecy," Blake said. "We've already detected some surveillance. We cannot afford for any of this to get out. I trust Kal with my life, and he says we can trust you, Liz."

"This sounds like an adventure," Liz said. "You won't have any issues with me."

"Other questions?" Marc asked.

"What is the Spanish galleon worth?" Kal asked.

"Right to the chase again," Blake laughed.

"We believe it's worth about two billion," Marc said. "Again, we'll negotiate with the Spanish government for delivery. We're hoping in both cases to get between forty and sixty percent."

"And you avoid the months cataloging and such by bringing them up all in one piece."

"There's not any debris?" Kal asked.

"As you can see," Marc said, panning the view on the display, "there are a few cannons and some minor debris around each ship, but they are mostly intact. They apparently broached and capsized in a hurricane and sank. Again, deep water so very little rot."

"Whose territorial waters are we going to be working in, and how will you deal with that government?"

"All the ships are in international waters. In fact, they are outside the economic zone of the closest land. So, our problem will be pirates, not governments."

"Arg!" Blake bellowed.

He got a laugh from everyone as he was sitting there with his eye patch and scarred face.

"We Scots like to toast the beginning of a new venture," he added, as the waitress came back in. They made the rounds giving everyone a highball glass and then poured a small dose of Glenlivet 15-year-old scotch in each glass. Marc gave the waitress a nod when she got to Catie using his fingers to indicate how much she should give her.

"To success and adventure," Marc toasted.

———

Catie took a sip. Maybe a bit more than she should have, but she managed not to spew any of her whiskey out as she coughed. She took a much smaller sip and managed to take the third sip, finishing off the glass.

"There we go," Blake said, patting her on the back as she coughed some more. "We'll make a proper pirate out of you yet."

"Oh, she's a pretty good pirate already," Marc said. "Just ask my wallet."

Chapter 7   Paintball

The next day they all met at a paintball arena. Blake had signed them up for a thirty-minute run through, then a 5-on-5 competition against another paintball team. He'd rated them intermediate given the military training that three of them had.

Kal ran them through the basics of the equipment. Catie thought the helmet looked like a motorcycle helmet, and she decided to wear her wraparound glasses under it.

After their team completed the basic safety training and had practiced aiming and firing the paintball rifles, Kal started with tactics.

"Anyone left-handed?" Kal asked.

Catie and Marc raised their hands. "Marc, you'll take the right side of any doorway or hallway. That way your rifle is away from the wall or jamb. Liz, you take the left side, Blake, you'll play frog. When they call clear, you leap into the hallway and cover the way we're going. Once we're in, you play point."

"What if the door is locked?" Blake asked.

"Then you should lie on your back and punch it out with your feet; roll to the left and come up behind Liz. Everything is the same after that. I'll follow and cover behind us. Catie, you're our backstop. You make sure to cover our rear when we're going through a doorway, so you'll be the last one through. Don't let them shoot us in the ass."

"Right," Catie said. "No shots in the ass."

Marc rolled his eyes and laughed at his daughter. She just couldn't resist the chance to say ass in front of her father.

"Good. Then you get to the middle once we're through and cover wherever Blake isn't looking. Got it?"

"Got it," everyone replied.

"And Catie. If I fall or get knocked down, you cover me until I can get back up, okay?"

"I'll cover your … back," Catie said. Marc had coughed before she could say ass. He figured once was enough for now.

"Now hand signals," Kal continued. "Point the way you want us to move with four fingers. Use two fingers when you want someone to look that way. Hand up means halt, fist up means take cover. It's okay to yell, but then they'll hear you."

He decided they were as ready as they were going to be, so he called the operator, who met them at the entrance to a second set of rooms.

"Guys, the other team is already in there. Your job is to go in and root them out. Because they get to pre-position, you guys get three extra lives. That's total, not each. If you get hit, you have to come back here. If your team still has lives left, you can go back in. Got it?"

"Got it," Kal replied.

"One minute then you go in," The operator told them.

The first hallway was easy. Nobody was home, and they cleared the three rooms in no time. At the corner to the second hallway, Liz saw movement and let off a burst of three paintballs. She waved Blake in, and he jumped to the center of the hallway in a crouch and let off a burst of three. Then he waved the rest of the team in. Blake pointed at his eyes and shook his head; he hadn't seen anyone.

The first room was clear. When they got to the second room, the door was locked or jammed. Blake lay down, scooched close to the door, and waited until Marc and Liz both gave him a thumbs up. He reared back and kicked his feet forward with all his strength. The door burst open, and several paintball shots flew over him. He rolled to the left and came up behind Liz as he was firing back into the room. Marc took down the guy who was shooting and then scanned right. Liz was already firing to the right and took down a second person. Just after Blake jumped into the room and Marc was getting ready to follow, he heard Catie on the comm. "Dad, left, left, left," she called out in a harsh whisper.

She was already on her stomach, firing down the hall. Marc dropped and rolled up beside her and fired blindly. Then he got his bearings and took one guy out. Catie had already taken care of one.

"That's five," Kal called out after he turned around and surveyed the scene.

The opposition team got up and walked over to Kal. "No way you guys are intermediate," the lead guy said as he took his helmet off.

"It's our first time," Kal said. "I bumped us to intermediate because three of us have military training."

"I'd have gotten at least one of you if weren't't' for the kid. How did she signal you?" he asked, looking at Marc.

"Tapped me," Marc said.

"Well, good show. I wish I could say we'll get you next time, but I'm going to tell the guy up front he has to push you up a level."

"Not a problem," Kal said. "Like I said, we were guessing at levels."

"Cool, at least we learned some things."

The five MacKenzies did high-fives all around. "Good job everyone," Kal said. "I didn't even get to shoot."

By then, the operator came back to show them out. "You guys are getting pushed up to upper-intermediate," he said. "That team wanted me to push you to advanced."

"Well, we thought we had a couple of weak links," Kal said, looking at Catie. "Apparently, that was a bad call on my part."

"I'd say so," the operator said. "It's not often I get five sets of equipment back without any paint on them."

"And one gun that was never fired in the competition," Kal said as he handed his rifle to him.

"Well, that team has been doing pretty good, ripping up the intermediates, so you should think about advanced. But your call. You only used up twenty minutes of a forty-five-minute slot, so you might want some stiffer competition."

"I'll think about it," Kal said as he handed the rest of his gear over.

"Iraq?" the operator asked.

"Yeah."

"Good team skills, had to be from real combat," the operator said as he gathered up the rest of their equipment.

"Pizza?" Marc asked.

"Perfect, we'll debrief then," Kal said.

After they ordered pizza and the drinks arrived, Kal asked, "Okay, how did you alert Marc?" He was looking at Catie hard.

"It's our phones," Catie said. "They act like comms, and we all wear an earwig."

Marc started to stop her from answering but realized she was doing just fine, providing only the information necessary without hinting at anything proprietary.

"That would have been nice to know," Kal said. "That kind of communication is critical in those types of situations. But I don't see a mic."

"They're really cool," Catie said. "They pick up the sound from your bone, so you don't have to yell, and they're almost invisible."

"I'd like to get one like that," Liz said, looking into Catie's ear. "How can they be so small, where's the battery?"

"It's super small," Catie said. "Daddy, we should upgrade their phones. Set up a team comm." She coughed into the crook of her arm and whispered, "they don't need to know about ADI."

"Again, my daughter points out the obvious," Marc said. "After pizza, we'll go back to the condo and set you guys up. Once we have the comms up, we can talk about some of the other options." Marc gave Catie a pointed look to make sure she wouldn't add anything else until they had a chance to secure their communication from any eavesdropping.

"Pizza," Blake called out.

"Great, let's eat."

They had a good time talking about the paintball exercise and eating pizza. They especially gave Kal a hard time about not getting off a shot. He just claimed it was superior leadership on his part. After pizza, they walked back to the condo.

"Come on in, guys," Marc said as he let everyone go in before he entered and closed the door.

Marc focused on the surveillance icon in his HUD and blinked to activate it.

"Captain, there is no active surveillance at this time," ADI reported.

"Okay, guys," Marc said as he went to the safe and opened it. "We've got some nice goodies here to hand out. This stuff is brand new high-tech gear, so keep it confidential."

"Not a problem," Liz said.

"First, you have to decide if you want to keep your existing phone or replace it with the new comm. It will mimic whatever UI you have on your phone, and Catie can transfer all your apps."

"No reason to carry two phones," Kal said.

"I agree."

"Good, unlock your phones and give them to Catie. She'll get them cloned."

Kal and Liz both handed their phones to Catie.

Catie turned away and focused on the phones. "ADI, clone Kal's phone first," she whispered. She accepted the new Bluetooth device prompt, then let ADI do all the work. "Now take care of Liz's phone."

After ADI was finished, she turned back to the group. "Here you go. Your old phones are unregistered, you can do whatever you want with them." She handed Kal and Liz each a new comm unit.

"That was fast," Liz said.

"We have it automated," Catie explained. "Now it will register your fingerprint. You can use any finger, so give it all ten," Catie said, "anywhere on the glass, and you only need to do it once."

"How do you turn it off?"

"You don't," Catie said. "You can put it in airplane mode, or quiet, so it doesn't ring and bother you, but it's always on."

"What about a charger?"

"The battery will last over a week. We have a wireless charger; you should get one of those," Marc explained. "The computer is super-fast, and the voice recognition is almost perfect. There's an app on the home screen for you to train it. You should do that right away."

"Looks just like my old phone," Kal said, "except it's just a bit bigger."

"It's smaller than my old phone," Liz said, "but the UI is the same."

"We have cases for them," Marc said. "They're kind of non-slip, and I just leave mine in my pocket unless we're going to be active, like today. They're also pretty unbreakable, you can't even scratch the glass."

"That is definitely nice," Liz said. "I'll take a case so that I have a choice to go without my purse."

"I'll take one, too," Kal added.

Marc handed Liz and Kal each a case and an earwig. "Here you go. Now you put the earwigs into whichever ear you wish. If you press it for three seconds, it will seal to your ear and turn on. Three seconds toggles on or off, and an eight-second hold will make it release from your ear. Like Catie said, it's all waterproof, so I just take mine out when I want to clean my ear."

Liz and Kal pushed the earwigs into their ears and looked at Marc expectantly.

"Can you hear me?" Marc whispered.

"Loud and clear," Liz said. "That is definitely better than anything I've used before."

"It must do some kind of sound leveling," Kal said, "otherwise Liz would have blasted my eardrum."

"I hadn't noticed, but I guess it does," Marc said.

"Now for the pièce de résistance," Blake said as he handed each a set of wraparound glasses. "These babies are like a combat pilot's head-up display. You use your eyes like a mouse to change the display, answer your phone, etc. Catie will give you a rundown later. They are set to automatically adjust to the ambient light. You can also set them to be reflective or not depending on your mood."

"Wow, this is some serious tech," Kal said.

"Nothing but the best," Blake said. "They even have cameras pointing forward and to the rear, so the comm unit can analyze a three-hundred-sixty-degree view. They will sort of bond to your head and hair if you press on them here above the nose. Three seconds to attach, three to let go. So, you don't need to worry about a lanyard."

"Wow, that's way better than we had in Iraq," Kal said. "Where do you get this stuff?"

"Another one of those things we're not ready to share right now. Suffice it to say it's experimental but very rugged, but it does take some getting used to."

"You'll pick it up right away," Blake said. "Especially you, Liz, since you're already used to a HUD. Also, I had mine set to camera-only during our exercise. That means they're opaque, and all I can see is the video projected on the lenses. That way, it compensates for my missing eye, eliminating the blind spot I would normally have."

"Oh baby, come to papa," Kal said as he put his on. "Cool, so how do I activate the menu?"

"You focus on the choice you want, then blink," Catie said. "If you double blink, they'll bring up options, just like a mouse."

"Oh man, and you say you can make them show video?" Kal asked.

"Yeah, you can watch a movie on them," Blake said.

"Even in three-D," Catie added.

"I definitely could have used these in Iraq," Kal said. "I'd probably still have my legs and be some kind of general even."

"They are super cool. We can do some practice and games to get better," Catie said. "Dad really needs to practice more."

"Some of us actually have work to do," Marc said as he gave Catie a light tap on the back of the head.

"Okay, so for next week, we focus on using the comm. I'm not sure we can handle much more."

"Well, you can set it to highlight in red where it hears a noise or detects movement," Catie added. "I had that on during paintball."

"Is that how you caught those guys?" Kal asked.

"I saw them at the same time," Catie said. "Maybe a second later. But being able to tell Dad to help made the difference."

"It sure did. Okay, when can we meet to practice before the next paintball exercise?"

"How about tomorrow afternoon? That way you two can get comfortable with them before we meet here."

"You can meet early with me," Catie said. "Then Dad and Uncle Blake can work on getting things ready for Antigua."

"Okay, we'll see you here at one o'clock," Liz said. "We do an hour with Catie, then we can do team practice after."

"It's a plan."

On Saturday morning, Catie convinced her father to introduce the surveillance pucks to the team. She pointed out they could slide them into the room and get a full three-hundred-sixty-degree view without having to expose anyone to fire. Since it was consistent with the capabilities of the wraparound specs, Marc didn't see how it would compromise anything they weren't already sharing, so he agreed.

Sunday, Liz came over and spent the day with Catie while Marc and Blake got the Mea Huli on her way to Antigua. Liz spent some time teaching Catie a few Krav Maga moves while Catie helped Liz get more comfortable with the comm gear.

On Monday, they all met up again at the paintball arena. With their new tech, Kal had upgraded them to Advanced. Expert was the only higher level, but they were still a new team, so he didn't want to push their luck too much.

The operator led them to the arena entrance. "Okay, these guys are the A-team of the advanced group. They specifically asked for you after hearing from the team you guys took out Friday. Like before, they're already dug in, you get three extra lives. Let's see if you can come back clean this time," he added with a smirk.

"We'll try our best," Kal said.

"Okay, a quick review. Call signs are just our first names, except for Catie, you okay with Cat?" Kal said. "We like to keep it to one syllable."

"Fine by me," Catie replied. She had her game face on; Marc had never seen her look so grown up.

"Okay, and I guess Marc will answer to Dad as well," Kal added.

That gave everybody a chuckle. "As long as she doesn't call me Pops," Marc said, getting another laugh from the group.

"Okay, same as before," Kal continued, "except Blake will slide a puck in when we get to a room or new corridor. Catie, you recover the puck once everything is clear."

Blake, Liz, and Marc had each programmed their HUDs to give them a view of the room for ten seconds after the puck went in. Then it would fade the view out so they could see normally, but still be able to pull it back up. Catie and Kal were back-cover, so they didn't want to be distracted by what was going on in the room. They had added a menu item to their HUDs so they could bring up the puck's view with a flick of their eyes.

They entered the first hallway after the puck showed it clear. Like yesterday, there were three rooms, but unlike yesterday, there weren't any doors on the rooms. They quickly cleared the three rooms, the puck showing each of them was completely empty. No furniture or doors.

"I don't like no doors," Kal said over the comm.

"Me either. You figure they have a barricade set up?"

"Exactly, probably one on each end of the corridor when we get to the T."

"What should we do?"

"We'll go check it out and then make a plan," Kal said.

The team followed Blake down to the T. He slid a puck out into the hallway. It was exactly what Kal had expected. About ten feet down each branch, there was a door propped up as a barricade with the opponents crouched down behind it.

"Damn, that's going to be hard to crack," Kal said.

"What are our options?"

"We can try lobbing paintballs over the barricade or bouncing them off the ceiling. They've made one mistake. The doors are completely horizontal, so it doesn't do much to cover something coming at a high angle or arc."

"Okay, so we start lobbing paintballs, then what?" Marc asked.

"We charge them and hope we take them out before they recover," Kal said.

Catie was holding her hand up, almost doing a dance as she tried to get Kal's attention.

"Okay, Cat, what are you thinking?"

"Let me show you," Catie said. "Dad, give me your rifle."

Marc handed Catie his rifle. She held it in her right hand, with her rifle in her left hand. Then she walked up to Marc's left side. "UP!"

Marc looked at her a little shocked then shrugged his shoulders. When she was little, he used to raise her up by putting his hand under her butt and lifting her. It was a favorite thing for her to demand at parades, and anywhere a little kid had trouble getting a view. But this time she was asking him to pick her up backward. He bent down and put his hand out. Catie sat on his palm and texted, *"UP."*

As Marc started to lift, Catie hopped up. He continued lifting her, thankful for the bounce. She was a lot heavier than the seven-year-old he'd last lifted. Catie wrapped her legs around Marc's arm and she leaned back, and extended both rifles. "On full auto, I should be able to get a few. They're looking at the floor or just above it. They'll never see me."

"Looks like a plan," Liz said, "but set her down first."

"How good are you going to be with your right hand?" Kal asked.

"She's ambidextrous," Marc said.

Liz had pulled off her four-X1 paintball harness and removed two Velcro straps. "Let's stabilize these rifles." She wrapped a Velcro strap around the stock and Catie's forearm for each rifle. "Now, Cat, you go paint 'em blue."

"Okay, Marc, raise her up again. Slide her into the hall slowly, we'll watch the puck sensor and tell you if you need to hurry. Cat, you have the hall up on your HUD?"

"Yes," Catie replied.

"Let's do this. Blake and Liz cover left and right; poke your rifle in to create a bit of a distraction, but be ready to charge in and cover Cat."

"Roger."

Marc raised Catie up, and she leaned back. She kept the rifles crossed over her chest so she could immediately deploy them once her shoulders were into the hallway.

"Easy, easy. You're still good," Kal called out as he watched the surveillance feed from the puck. "You're weapons free."

Catie extended the rifles and pulled both triggers at the same time. The rifles were on full auto and started dropping paintballs on the guys behind the barricade.

"Go, Go, Go," Kal called out. Blake and Liz jumped into the hall, each turning to their assigned barricade. They ran along the edge of the hallway. When they came to the barricade, they each found two paint-covered opponents glaring at them.

"I've got two," Blake whispered.

"Same here," Liz said.

"So that leaves one bad guy," Kal said as he entered the hallway looking each way. "Any thoughts?"

Marc let Catie down, and she walked over and picked the puck up. "We're still missing one door," she added.

"They've got one guy as a backstop in case we got by the first group. Okay, we'll go left first. Really watch our backs, this guy could be waiting for us to move so he can sneak up on us."

"Should we take the doors with us?" Marc asked.

"I don't think so. We can always come back for them, but they'd be awkward to carry, so let's just keep them in mind. Lay them flat, so we'll have plenty of time if we see someone trying to sneak up and use them."

"Gotcha."

The team worked their way down the left hallway. There were two rooms they had to clear first, but both were empty. When they got to the turn in the hallway, Blake signaled a stop.

"I'm thinking he's going to be behind this corner," Blake said.

"I agree, slide the puck out," Kal said.

Blake slid the puck into the hallway.

"Oh, that's clever," Kal said with a whistle.

"What?" Catie asked. She wasn't looking at the puck feed since she was covering their backs.

"He's got that third door sitting on top of two partially open doors. They make a Vee, which gives him stability, and he's lying on top so he can catch us coming around the corner."

"Should I go up again?" Catie asked.

"No, I don't think that would work this time. Besides, I think all we have to do is start lobbing paintballs at him. He seems to think we would be coming around the corner without looking too much. Even with just a mirror, we'd have him. The puck makes him a sitting duck."

"Okay, Marc and Liz, you're up. Liz, you go high, Marc, you go low, keep your heads back."

"Kal, do you want to take my place? You were complaining about not getting to shoot anyone. Besides, I'm sure you're a better shot."

"Sure, you help Catie cover our rear."

"Why, there's only the one guy?"

"First rule of combat is never trust anything, not even your own intel."

"Roger that," Liz said.

"Here, this will help," Blake said as he stuck a surveillance puck on the wall so that it was sticking about two inches into the hallway. "Use that with your HUD, it'll help you line up the shots."

Marc lay down, but let Kal take the first few shots. It only took him three tries before he managed to catch the guy with a paintball right on his helmet.

"That makes five," Kal called out. "Anyone else still up?"

"No, we were only five," the guy on the door called out. "Good shot."

"Thanks. Nice traps you guys set up."

"How did you guys get by the first barricades?"

"We've got someone light enough to lift," Kal said, pointing at Catie. "So same principle as your door there. Shoot from above where nobody's looking."

The operator walked up to the group while they were talking. "Hey, I've got some ticked off customers who say you're cheating," he said.

"How are we cheating?" Kal asked.

"They said you have some device you're using to get an edge. Apparently, you slid it into the hall before you took them out."

"I'm amazed that a crack team would be distracted by a hockey puck," Kal said as he held out a surveillance puck. "What they should really think about is mirrors," he added, as he pulled a mirror from a pocket in his combat vest. "I would think anyone playing at the advanced level would be carrying one."

The fifth guy laughed. "Don't worry, it's probably Bill complaining. He hates to lose, especially when it was his plan. You're right, we carry mirrors," he said. "By the way, my name is Aaron." He extended his hand and shook with Kal.

"I'm Kal, and this is Blake, Liz, Marc, and our gymnast is Catie. Call sign Cat."

"Like Cat Woman," Aaron said. "I like that. Ron, they played well. Don't let Bill confuse you. Doesn't matter what tech is, you have to plan for everything, and Bill's plan didn't cover Cat here."

"She's our secret weapon," Kal said.

Catie smiled at the praise.

"Anyway, see ya around," Aaron said as he headed off.

"Hey, you guys have to put the doors back on," Ron yelled.

"I'll take care of it," Aaron hollered over his shoulder.

Ron looked at the MacKenzie team. "No paint this time either."

"You did tell us not to mess them up," Blake laughed. "We try to do our best."

"You guys are going to have a price on your heads now."

"What's that mean?" Marc asked, not looking happy at the comment.

"They'll form up an A-team picking the best of the best to take you on, then they'll bet on everything from the number of survivors, to how many paintballs they use."

"Tell them to bring it on," Kal said.

The third match happened on Thursday. They had been asked to come and meet with the opposition before the competition. They arrived thirty minutes early.

"Hey guys," Aaron said. "Surprised to see me?"

"I guess not," Kal said. "So, what do you want to talk about?"

"Just wanted to review the rules and see if you agree."

"Sure, what's the deal?"

"We get six people, and you guys don't get any extra lives."

"You guys nervous?"

"Maybe, but it works out better this way. Now the deal is we've all chipped in five hundred apiece to be on this team. Each one of you is worth a five-hundred-dollar bounty."

"What's the other five hundred for?" Kal asked.

"Party for the winning team. Losing team cleans up."

"What if you don't get any of us?"

"Then you guys are having a really big party."

"Anything else?"

"Not really. Each of us has a unique paint color, so we know who gets the bounty. You guys are blue like last time. We're still setting up," Aaron said. "Match starts in fifteen minutes."

"Good by us," Liz said as she gave Aaron a cold stare. "We like to eat at expensive restaurants."

With that, Aaron turned and headed into the arena.

"What do you think they're up to?" Liz asked Kal.

"I don't think they're setting up," Kal said. "I think he wants us to be thinking barricade."

"Makes sense, so what do you think?"

"What would you do?"

"Not sure."

"I would stay mobile," Blake said. "I think they'll try to get us from both sides."

"That's my thinking. They'll do something to engage us on one side, and have half the team attack us from the rear. Like when we're busting into a room or clearing a new hallway."

"So, what do we do?"

"Watch our backs," Kal said as he pulled a surveillance puck from his pocket. "We can stick these on the ceilings. If we center them in the junction, they can cover both hallways."

"It's time, you guys ready?" Kal asked.

"Born ready," Liz said. "Oorah!"

Everyone else gave an Oorah, and they entered the arena.

"Okay. Blake, go right; let's get the right intersection covered."

Blake leap-frogged into the hall after Marc and Liz declared it clear. He slid the puck they'd tossed in, to the left, past the doorway. Then he headed right toward the end of the hallway.

"Rear guard, stay alert," Kal called out as he took up his rear-guard position. He and Catie walked backward down the hallway until they caught up with the team. Blake was waiting to start clearing the hall. When they arrived, he slid a puck into the hall. His head-up display showed everything was clear.

"Clear."

"Okay, Cat, you and Marc are up."

Catie pulled a puck from her vest and held it over her head. Marc grabbed her around the waist, and with a little hop from Catie, lifted her up so she could attach the puck to the ceiling.

"Okay, now back to the left, we'll proceed as usual. Cat, you watch with your HUD, I'll use my eyes."

"Roger."

Once the team had backtracked to the entry and then to the next junction, Kal called for a stop.

"I think the action is going to happen in this hallway. It's going to have to be something that makes noise so it will alert the enemy. So, watch for tripwires and anything else. If the hallway is clear, we go to the end and put a puck at the junction, then come back and clear the rooms."

"What if someone is hiding in the room waiting for us to do that?" Liz asked.

Kal pulled something from his vest. It was L-shaped with an elliptical metal shape on the end. "Door jammer," Kal said. "Won't stop them, but it'll slow them down and cause a lot of noise."

"Good."

"Let's go."

Blake slid the puck into the hallway. It was clear, so Marc and Liz entered and took up left and right positions. Blake assumed point as Catie and Kal backed into the hall.

"Okay, Cat, you're up again."

Catie and Marc repeated their puck-planting process, and everyone moved on down the hall. They stopped at each doorway as Kal used one of his jammers to lock the door. To use the jammer, he slipped it under the door then used his foot to force the handle around. The edges of the ellipse were rough, so it grabbed on the floor and the door, jamming it tight. They repeated the process on the other two doors in the hallway, and then checked the next junction. It was clear so they planted another puck and went back to the first door.

Blake stopped in front of the door and reached for the handle. Kal touched his arm to hold him up.

"What do you want to bet there's nobody in there?" Kal said.

"That makes sense, so not taking that bet," Blake said.

"Right," Kal said. "So, let's make a little noise like we're' going to breach this room. Try the handle nice and hard, then give it thirty, then put your shoulder into it. Cat, we still clear?"

Catie had the display from all three pucks up on her HUD, showing four separate views of the hallways. "We're still clear."

"Go."

Blake twisted the handle to the door; it moved a little then jammed. "Locked."

"Still not taking the bet," Kal said.

Blake continued counting down from thirty. He'd just reached fifteen when Catie called out "incoming, from behind. Three. They're in the side hall, just reaching the main hall now."

"Good. Marc, Liz, you take them. Marc, on the right, Liz, on the left, Blake, you get down and cover the middle. Cat, you and I have to cover the rear. Lean up against the wall to minimize your exposure. Yell out if someone comes into that hallway."

"Got it."

Thirty seconds later, the enemy made the corner. Catie counted down until they hit the turn. Liz took out the first one to uncover, then Marc got the next guy. Liz shot the third just as he realized he was going the wrong way.

"Three down."

"They're behind the second door," Catie said. "I heard them try to open it."

"What do you want to do now?" Blake asked.

"Let's clear the other two rooms. No sense taking any chances that they split up more."

"Okay, same process as usual?"

"Of course."

The team went back to the first room. Marc and Liz took up positions on each side of the door, and Catie and Kal each covered one direction. Kal took the direction back toward the second room.

"Cat, we clear?"

"Clear."

"Blake, go."

Blake kicked the door in, and Marc slid a puck into the room. Looks clear, Blake called out as he checked the room out on his HUD. Marc and Liz covered the sides, and Blake, who'd rolled over behind Marc, jumped into the room. "Nobody home."

"Okay, the third room now," Kal said.

It only took them another minute to clear the third room, then they gathered in front of the second door.

"Okay, so we're pretty sure our last three bogies are hiding in there," Kal said. "By now they're going to be pissed off, and they probably know we already took out half their team."

"So how about we go get some doors," Blake said.

"What are you thinking?"

"We build a kill box around the door. Force it open and jam it so it can't close. Then we shoot 'em. Got any tape?"

"You know it."

Marc, Blake, and Kal went around the corner and removed one door, after making sure the room was clear. Then they removed the other two doors in their hallway and brought them back. During this time, Catie and Liz stood guard at the door, listening for any activity inside.

"Okay, we've got the doors, now what do we do with them?" Kal asked.

"When I kick the door in, someone is going to push this one in so the door can't close. Use your door jammer to lock it into place. Put it at about a twenty-degree angle away from the opening; same thing on the other side, except we can lock it in right away. Then Marc yanks me back beyond the doors, and we drop the third one between them,"

Blake explained. "Then we control the access, and we start picking them off."

"What stops them from nailing you after you kick the door?" Liz asked.

"Marc needs to pull me out fast."

"I don't like that," Marc said.

"Other options?"

"Why don't we lay the third door on top of him?" Catie suggested.

"How do I kick the door out, then?"

"We need to have it set on a fulcrum," Marc said. "What can we make one out of?"

Catie pulled out one of her paintball guppies and handed it to her father. "These?"

"We have plenty of them," Marc said. Each team member had a 6X harness of guppies for paintball refills. "I can make a three-by-two stack, so they're kind of stable. But it will still be a little unstable."

"The pucks will stick on either side," Catie said as she pulled one out. She stuck it onto a guppy and then stuck it on the floor. She pushed it, and it held the guppy straight. Squeezing the side, she got it to release and handed it to her father.

"Perfect. How did you know they did that?"

"Too much time on my hands," Catie said with a shrug.

Marc quickly assembled four stacks of guppies. Each was about 22 inches tall. He placed two of them about two feet from the door on each side, then the other two about six feet back. Then he and Blake laid the door on top of them like a table

Blake lay down underneath the door and brought his knees up. They bumped the door before he got them all the way up. He pushed the door up with his hands and brought his knees all the way up. "I can just let it rest on my knees. When I kick, it'll drop down and stop on the guppies so it won't nail me in the shins."

"Good, then I'll pull you back," Marc said. "Cat, tell me when his feet are clear of the end of the door, so we can drop it down."

"There," Catie called out when Blake's feet passed the end of the door. His head was just below the top of the door. "Okay, Blake, when you see the top of the door, you push it up. I'll let you go so you can sit up, and then I'll keep it going until it's against the other two doors."

"Easy peasy," Liz said.

"Then we toss a puck in and figure out where everyone is," Kal said. "I expect them to be along the front wall, so there isn't a line of fire to them from the hallway. But that means they won't have a line of fire on Blake, either."

"Alright, let's get this thing done," Marc said.

They locked the left door into position. Catie put a puck on it right at the end at the top of the doorway. Then they placed the right-hand door into position with the door jammer under it to lock it in place once they kicked the door in, and Liz slid it into the room some. Blake lay down under the door table and got his knees into position.

"Okay, this needs to go like clockwork," Kal said. "After Blake kicks the door in, Liz, you push this door into position, I'll lock it into place since I've got the weight. Cat, you're on the left side looking over the top of the table door, you'll need to shoot right-handed."

"No problem."

"As soon as the door gets kicked, you start laying in cover fire. Pull back when you feel the table door raising up, so you don't lose your weapon," Kal said. "Anyone not ready, give us a heads-up now … Okay, Blake, you're on."

"On three; one, two, three."

Blake kicked the door. As soon as Marc heard Blake's feet impact the door, he yanked him by his harness, falling down as he pulled Blake back into the hallway. It was only a second, and Blake was pushing the door up.

"Got one," Catie called out.

Marc was lying on his back when Blake sat up into a crunch position. He used his feet to push Blake up. Blake pushed the door up with him, and their box was closed. Liz and Kal had the right-hand door jammed into place.

"Good job, everyone," Kal called out.

"I'm out," the woman in the room called out.

"Told you I got one," Catie said.

"Hey guys, let me through," the woman said again.

"Not going to happen unless your friends want to surrender."

"Hey, I need to pee."

"Sorry about that, you'll need to hold it for about ten or fifteen more minutes while we finish up here."

Aaron laughed at that and hollered, "You haven't gotten into the room yet."

"We'll be there, just relax," Kal hollered back.

"Don't count on it."

Kal signaled everyone to listen up. "Okay, he's on the left side against the wall. I assume the other guy is on the right side up against the wall so we can't get a line on him. Liz, we'll boost you up so you can sit on my shoulders. That'll put you above the door. Cat, you're on Marc's shoulders. Blake, make sure they don't push our door down."

"I should slide the puck in farther so we can see the room," Catie said.

"Okay, do that. Now you'll want to reach down with your gun and fire around the corner blind, or I guess using your HUD. You need to line up the shot before you let them see your gun, then just let loose with it. Recoil's not too bad, but plan on your shots going wild. Pull back after a few rounds and try again if we need to."

Catie slid the puck in about 1½-inches. The view of the room came up on her HUD. She focused on the left-hand view and saw Aaron standing against the wall about three feet from the door. He had his rifle zeroed in on the doorway at about chest height. Looking at the right-side view, she saw another guy standing right after the door. It was giving him some cover.

Liz indicated that she was ready, so they both laid their rifles horizontal and eased them into the room.

"I'm good," Catie said when she had Aaron lined up.

"Go for it," Liz said, and they both started firing. After five shots each, they pulled back.

"I'm out," they heard Aaron yell.

"I couldn't get the other guy," Liz whispered. "He's got the door protecting him."

"I see that," Kal said. "Okay, last round. We'll open this center door. Liz, grab a handful of paintballs. Blake and Marc get ready to roll into the room. When I open the door, Liz, run in and throw your paintballs at the ceiling, so they bounce off it and the wall behind the door. Blake, you hit the floor just past the door and unload on him. Marc, you follow Blake."

"I'll gently shove the door against the wall after I unload," Liz said. "That'll either force him into the room or pin him."

"Good idea. Everyone ready, on three; one, two, three."

Kal yanked the door sideways using the handle. Liz immediately ran in and tossed two handfuls of paintballs over the door, then she leaned against it. Blake was already rolling past the end of the door, firing.

"Oomph," the last man gasped as the door smacked him. "Alright already, I'm down."

Aaron walked over to Kal, "No hits again?"

"I think we're all clean," Kal replied.

"Well, if that doesn't beat all. I can't believe we didn't get at least one of you," Aaron said. "And the kid got two of us."

"She's a pretty tough cookie," Kal said. "Might want to be careful calling her a kid, she might take a few more shots at you."

Aaron laughed. "I guess we have some cleaning up to do. Looks like you're having a big party tonight."

"Why don't you guys join us?" Marc said. "We had fun and learned a lot going against you. We'll be at the Orchid at five o'clock; you guys can cover the check. Whatever's left over, you can use to drown your sorrows over the weekend."

"Hey, how about my sorrows?" Blake whined.

"Okay, you can make them invite the three of you over for drinks. Catie and I are off to Miami tomorrow."

"Sound like a plan?" Blake asked Aaron.

"It's your money; we lost. But we'll be happy to help you spend it."

"See you guys at the Orchid," Marc called over his shoulder, as team MacKenzie headed out.

"Wow, are we hot or what!" Catie gushed.

"Don't get overconfident," Kal said. "I'd give us a C+ as a team. Maybe with the tech, a B. But against a real A team, we'd have been toast. Much less if it had been real combat."

"How so?" Marc asked.

"They weren't using real guns," Kal said.

"What's the difference?" Catie asked.

"Real bullets go through walls."

"Oh!"

"Real pros would have had the halls covered. When we tried to put the pucks up, they'd have taken us out. Probably would have gotten two or three of us. Then down to three, we would have had a hard time."

"But we could have put the puck on the corner like I did on the door. Then we wouldn't have been exposed."

"Why didn't you suggest that?"

"I didn't realize we're were exposing ourselves that much. And the pucks are less noticeable if they're on the ceiling."

"See, B performance," Kal said. "That would have helped, but still nothing like real life."

"Again, how so?" Marc asked.

"A five-hundred-dollar bounty is nice, but real bad guys get paid a couple hundred grand, and they've got good tech and a lot more practice than these guys," Kal said. "And when they play, losing means you're dead."

"Yikes!" Catie squeaked.

"Yeah, real life can suck," Kal said.

They were lucky and got a separate room at the Orchid. As everyone filed in, Aaron and Kal made the introductions.

Sheri, Jake, Paul, Charlie, Mae, and Aaron had been their opponents.

"Aaron, you said they had a kid on their team. But she's like what, twelve? We'll never live this down," Charlie groaned.

"Charlie, you'd better dial it back, or you're going to have to go mano-a-mano with Catie," Liz said.

Catie was giving Charlie a mean stare. "Sorry, no offense," Charlie said. "I'm just hurting from all the paintballs I had to eat."

Everyone talked back and forth about tactics, then somehow the discussion turned to poker.

"Yeah, same skill applies to poker," Kal said. "You have to be able to read your opponents, do the math in your head on the odds, then make the right play."

"You want to put your money where your mouth is?" Aaron said.

"Sure, bring it on," Kal replied.

"Where can we play?"

"The Mea Huli," Blake suggested.

"The what?" Aaron asked.

"Our yacht," Blake replied.

"How will that work?" Charlie asked. "We could get what, five players?"

"Oh no, we have room for everybody," Blake said. "It's a big boat."

"Who's in?"

Sheri, Charlie, Paul, and Aaron raised their hands, along with Blake, Liz, Kal, and Catie.

"The kid wants to play?" Charlie said.

"Keep digging that hole, Charlie," Liz said.

"Does she even know how to play?" Sheri asked.

"I learn fast," Catie said.

Blake looked at Marc, "Well, Bro?"

"Don't look at me. If all of you want to give her your money, I'm not going to argue."

"We're not going to give her our money," Charlie said. "We just want to make sure you're okay with us taking hers."

"You can try," Marc said. "But Catie doesn't lose at cards. Ever."

"Hah!" Aaron shot back. "Where's this Mea Huli? We'll grab a case of beer and meet you there."

"What about cards and chips?" Sheri asked.

"We've got them on the boat," Blake said.

"I'd prefer new cards," Charlie said.

"We have brand new decks," Blake said. "But feel free to bring your own new deck."

"As long as they're wrapped, I'm cool."

"See you guys there."

Thirty minutes later, everyone was aboard the Mea Huli, setting up the card tables. Blake brought out the poker chips and two new decks of cards.

"Which game are we playing?" Catie asked.

"Texas hold 'em," Charlie suggested.

Blake could see Catie accessing her HUD to look up the game. After she finished, he motioned her to remove her specs and her earwig.

"What!" Catie gave him an indignant look. "Okay."

"You sure you don't want to play?" Blake asked Marc.

"I have to give her enough money already without letting her just take it from me," Marc said with a laugh. "But please go ahead, the more money she gets from you guys, the less she'll be asking me for."

"Bawk, Bawk, Bawk," Blake squawked.

"Don't say I didn't warn you," Marc said as he headed up to the sundeck to relax.

"When is the kid's curfew?" Charlie jested.

"We won't need to worry about that," Marc called over his shoulder. "I give you two hours before she has all your money."

"Psych-ops," Kal laughed.

"What's the buy-in?" Aaron asked.

Catie was already handing Blake a $100 bill.

"One hundred, it is," Aaron said. "Who's in?"

Blake gathered up the eight hundred dollars and put it into the card box that he'd just unwrapped and removed the cards from.

"High card deals," Charlie said as he shuffled the cards. Liz cut the cards, and then Charlie dealt out a card to each player. "Aaron's deal."

Blake handed out the chips. "Whites are one-dollar, reds are five, and blues are ten. You can buy more chips before each deal, but you have to have the chips to bet. No borrowing, no side bets."

"No limit?" Kal asked.

"Pot limit," Sheri suggested.

Blake looked at everyone. "Pot limit it is. Catie, you get all that?"

"I think," Catie replied. She was grinning ear-to-ear. "Pot limit means you can only raise what's in the pot, right?"

"Got it in one," Charlie said, winning him a glare from Catie.

An hour later, Marc wandered back down to check on the game. "How's it going?"

"We're doing fine," Charlie said. "Your daughter is up twenty dollars, but nothing exciting."

"How many hands have you played?"

"This will be our twelfth," Charlie said.

"Okay, I'll watch for a while, then."

Catie won the next hand, filling out a flush on the river card. She folded the hand after that on the ante. The next hand, she ran the pot up to $300 before winning it on a full house, aces over fours getting the third ace on the river card. On the next hand, she bluffed her way through, and everyone was getting a little gun shy.

"Anybody need to buy chips?" Blake asked. "I'm buying another one hundred from Catie." Blake handed Catie a $100 bill, and she counted out the chips for him.

"I'll buy mine from the bank," Charlie said, handing Blake a $100 bill.

Sheri bought another $100 from Catie; Aaron and Liz said they had enough to play, and Paul bought $50 from Catie.

Catie folded on the next hand, lost the next after feeding $100 into the pot. The next hand she ran the pot up to $300 and caught another full house on the river card. It only took another hour before Catie had everybody's money.

"Gawd," Charlie cried. "It's like she knows every card."

"She does," Marc said.

"What, you mean, she marks them?" Charlie snapped.

"No, you do," Marc said.

"What does that mean?" Charlie asked.

"By the tenth hand, most of the cards are slightly different, a crease, a smudge, folded curve," Marc said. "She just memorizes them all."

"That's impossible," Aaron said.

"Catie, show them."

"Ah, Dad!"

"You're not going to be playing them again. And I think Blake, Kal, and Liz have learned their lesson," Marc said.

"Shuffle the cards," Marc told Blake.

Blake shuffled, then dealt out five cards face down.

"That's the ace of hearts, the four of clubs, the jack of clubs, don't know, the seven of hearts," Catie said.

Blake turned the cards over.

"She got four out of four," Aaron whined. "Do the next five."

Blake dealt the next five cards.

"The six of diamonds, the queen of spades, don't know, the eight of hearts, don't know."

Blake turned them over, "Three out of three."

"She does better when you're holding your cards," Marc said. "With Texas hold 'em, they don't get handled as much, so it takes her longer. Try playing gin with her."

"Jeez, not fair," Charlie whined again.

"I warned you," Marc said.

"And you had to go and make her mad," Sheri smacked Charlie on the shoulder.

"We should play again, with a new deck," Charlie said. "This time, we won't handle the cards."

"It'll just take her longer," Marc said. "You can't shuffle them without marking them. And besides, she'd beat you just playing the odds and your tells."

"I'm glad to hear you're leaving Hawaii," Aaron said. "I'd prefer word didn't get around that a twelve-year-old cleaned my clock."

"In poker and paintball," Liz said, giving Catie a high-five.

Chapter 8   Treasure Ships

"You guys ready?" Blake asked Catie and Marc as they walked to the taxi. He'd stayed up after the poker game drinking expensive scotch whiskey from the Mea Huli's bar.

"We're ready. Not so much to worry about with a private flight."

"It's definitely going to spoil you," Blake said.

"I like being spoiled," Catie added.

"We've noticed," Marc teased.

Catie stuck her tongue out at her father.

"I'll see you guys in Antigua on Wednesday, Dude," Blake said.

"We'll be there."

The crew from the plane met Catie and Marc when they arrived at the private terminal. They immediately took their luggage, and the flight steward escorted them onto the plane.

"It's just the two of you, so take any seat you wish," she said. "My name is Fatima, and I'll be taking care of you today."

"Thank you," Marc and Catie said together.

"Would you like anything before we take off? It should only be about ten minutes."

"Orange juice for both of us," Marc said.

"Only ten minutes," Catie gushed. "Uncle Blake was right; this will definitely spoil us."

Just as Fatima indicated, they were wheels-up ten minutes later. After the flight leveled off, Marc turned to Catie and said, "You know summer is almost over. We have to talk about when you head back to school."

"No way!" Catie squeaked. "You can't send me back."

"You have to go to school," Marc persisted.

"I can homeschool," Catie shot back. "With ADI, it'll be easy."

"What about socializing with other kids?"

"I don't socialize much anyway."

"That's a problem. You have to learn how to get along with others."

"I get along with you and Uncle Blake. And then there's Liz and Kal."

"But you didn't do too well with Sally."

"We did alright when we were diving," Catie defended herself. "But she was just silly."

"You have to learn to get along with silly people. Sometimes you have to make nice, so you can accomplish your goals. What if you need Sally's help one day? Do you think you bonded with her enough that you could count on her?"

"I wouldn't want to have to count on her."

"But if you had to. One day she could be the only person who could help you."

"But, isn't that using people?"

"No, it's making contacts that you can count on. Even though she was silly, she seemed like a nice girl."

"Yeah, she was."

"Then you should have sucked it up and made friends with her. You don't have to become best friends with everyone, but you need to create bonds with people. That takes practice."

"Can't I practice on adults?"

"Yes, but one day you're going to find that the people in a position to help you are all around your age. You have to start learning how to make that work."

"Okay, but that doesn't mean I have to go to school," Catie complained.

"Maybe not. But your mother is expecting you back in San Diego."

"But she's always at work. At least I can be with you when you work."

"Maybe she needs you."

"I think she was happy when I left for Hawaii."

"Sure, she was glad to see you get a vacation, to get to see Uncle Blake and me."

"I don't know. She was pretty stressed. I think she was happy not to have to worry about me."

"You'll have to work things out with her when we get to Miami."

"Why can't I just call her now?"

"We're on a plane."

"We have our comms and ADI; besides, they have Wi-Fi."

"Oh, then go for it. I'm going to go sit in the back."

"ADI, call Mom," Catie instructed.

"Hi, Catie," Dr. Linda McCormack said as she answered the phone.

"Hi, Mommy, guess where I am."

"In Hawaii."

"No, I'm on a private jet on the way to Miami."

"Oh, your father said you were going to Miami. But a private jet?"

"Pretty cool, huh? We're the only two passengers."

"It sounds like your father is spoiling you."

"I kind of like it."

"Hmm, I'm not so sure about that."

"He's making me read and work on my studies. With the bucks he got from the Navy for selling Hyperion, we're splurging on this flight."

"Okay. What are you going to do in Miami?"

"Daddy needs to do some research, so I'll tag along with him and help. It'll teach me how to dig up information and stuff. And we'll do some fun stuff. I think we'll go to Disney World, too."

"Sounds like fun."

"It will be. Later we're going to the Bahamas and Antigua."

"The Caribbean, nice. What about hurricanes?"

"We definitely plan to avoid those. We'll watch the weather and move Mea Huli out of the path if we have to. She's really fast."

"That's good."

"We might even go to Europe."

"Sounds like a lot to accomplish before you have to come back for school."

"Uh, that's why I'm calling. Can I stay with Daddy for a while? I'll do homeschooling on the internet. I promise to study hard and everything. But this way, I get to spend a lot more time with Daddy, and do some cool stuff."

"I'm not sure."

"Please, please. You're always at work, and either Daddy or Uncle Blake is always around, so I get lots of *supervision*." Catie said 'supervision' like it tasted bad.

"And we all know how much you like supervision."

"But they're fun to be around, and I am learning lots."

"Well, I need to think about it. I'll discuss it with your father, and we will decide."

"Do you want to talk to him now? He's right here."

"No, let me think about it first. Then I'll call him. You'll just have to be patient."

"Okay. I love you, Mommy."

"I love you too, Baby. Have fun in Miami."

"I will, bye."

"So, how did it go?" Marc asked when Catie came back and sat next to him.

"She said she'd think about it."

"That sounds promising."

"You think so?"

"Sure. If she didn't push back right away, then she's open to it. She just has to come to terms about being apart from you for a long time. That's hard on a parent."

"I guess. Anyway, I told her we'd go to Disney World."

"You did? Funny, I never heard that," Marc said as he poked Catie in the ribs. "How come I let you con me into things like that?"

"Because I'm your daughter and you're supposed to spoil me," Catie said. "I'll even pay."

Marc laughed. "I think I can cover Disney World. I wasn't sure you'd want to go."

"We can't go to Florida and not go to Disney World. I am still a kid. And what would other kids think about me if they found out I passed up a chance to go to Disney World?"

"You definitely have a future in negotiations," Marc laughed. "Do you want to see if the pilot can redirect to Orlando, and then we can go tomorrow?"

"Sure."

It only took the pilot ten minutes to reroute to Orlando. Marc made reservations for a suite at the Four Seasons.

"Admiral Michaels, I have that report for you."

"What does it say?"

"The guys at the NSA are really impressed with the math, but they say it's way above his previous work."

"So?"

"They think he had help."

"Interesting. Tell our friends to keep watching him."

"Yes sir."

The flight to Orlando was eleven hours. The time went by pretty fast, given that they were traveling in the lap of luxury. Marc dove into the work he was doing to research the ships and their histories. Catie went back to her study of geometry and practicing with the flight simulator. She also kept up her querying of ADI about the technology on the ship, at least what she was allowed to know without getting the *Captain's permission*.

Fatima served them breakfast right after Catie finished talking to her mother. Lunch was served at the halfway point, after which both Catie and Marc took a nap. It had been a long day with the paintball and the late celebration. Fatima was just serving them dinner now.

"Wow, this is pretty nice," Catie told Fatima.

"Only the best," Fatima answered. "The charter company always uses a gourmet chef to prepare the meals. This pasta primavera is one of my favorites."

"I can see why. Thanks for being so nice to us."

"It's my job; besides, you guys are pretty easy to be nice to."

"I'll be back in twenty minutes to pick everything up," Fatima said. "Press your call button if you need me sooner. We'll be landing in about one hour."

"Great, what time will it be?"

"It's nine o'clock now, we'll land at about ten."

Catie and Marc spent Saturday at Disney World. Catie made Marc go on all the rollercoasters: Space Mountain, Expedition Everest, Splash Mountain, Rock 'n Rollercoaster, and finally Slinky Dog Dash. Then she had them finish up with Mission Space, the simulated journey to Mars. Catie insisted it was the prep for when they got to fly one of the spaceships.

On Sunday, they flew to Miami. Marc had the private jet under contract for the next few months. It was a comfortable flight with Fatima taking excellent care of them. They arrived at Miami-Opa Locka Executive airport right after 10:00 in the morning. Catie thought it was perfect timing since they could get to Surfside, check into the Four Seasons, and be on the beach before noon.

Once they checked in, Catie spent five minutes checking out their two-bedroom, ocean-view suite, three minutes changing into her swimsuit, another minute urging her father to get changed, and then they were heading to the beach. Beach robes and beach sandals were provided by the hotel. Both wore their wraparound specs; they left their comms in the hotel since they had unpacked the comm-drone so ADI could take over that function. Once they found the lounge chairs that the hotel had reserved for them, Catie dumped her robe, kicked off her sandals, and ran into the water. Marc marveled at her tan. When they had lived in Boston, she had been pretty pasty, but after a couple of years in San Diego and five weeks in Hawaii, she now sported a soft cocoa tan that would easily handle the Florida sun.

Marc lay back under the umbrella and continued his prep work for their day at the University of Miami library tomorrow. He would be researching the history of various Spanish treasure fleets that had been lost in the Caribbean and off of Florida. Although they knew right where the ships were, he needed to establish a credible trail of how they had found them. He needed to minimize any suspicions that would lead to the wrong kind of surveillance and questions.

Marc was having ADI look up the various books and documents that he would have the librarian pull for him tomorrow when Catie came running up.

"Daddy. You have to come in the water. It's so warm; it's nothing like San Diego or Hawaii."

"That's because of the Gulf Stream," Marc said. "Warm water from the equator flows through the Gulf of Mexico and gets warmer, then it flows by Florida before it heads north to New England and over to Europe."

"Yeah, Yeah, Yeah. I'll ask ADI to go over it with me if you'll just come in and swim with me."

"You're about to 'yeah, yeah, yeah' yourself back into the room," Marc said right before he chased Catie into the water. She got him to let her stand on his shoulders so she could dive into the waves. They did that a few times before Catie was hungry enough to want to go back to their beach chairs to order lunch.

They each ordered a chicken sandwich with chips. "I believe you promised to study up on the Gulf Stream," Marc said.

"Oh, come on, can't I do it later?"

"Well, you're not going in the water for at least an hour, so why not take care of it now. Maybe you'll be able to use it for a school paper."

"Okay," Catie acquiesced. "Have you talked to Mommy yet?"

"Not yet," Marc replied. "I'm sure she's still processing."

Catie rolled her eyes. Marc could barely tell since they both had their specs tinted for the sun. But the umbrella they were sitting under provided enough shade that the specs were partially see-through.

Catie got a lesson on the Gulf Stream from ADI and continued her study of geometry; she'd started studying it so she would be able to navigate. All she really cared about was getting to fly one of the fighters sitting in the flight bay on the spaceship.

Finally, enough time passed, so she was allowed back in the water.

Catie ran down and jumped into the water. She swam out and floated while she waited on a wave. She caught one and rode it toward the shore, using her hands to keep her up on top of the wave. When the wave broke over her, she rolled out of it and popped to the surface. Another girl was standing on the beach, cheering her. "That was so cool."

"Thanks," Catie said. "I learned to body surf in Hawaii."

"Oh, I hear they have the best waves there."

"I think so," Catie said. "My name's Catie."

"I'm Julia," the girl said, pronouncing the J as an H, Spanish style.

"Do you ride the waves with a wave board?" Catie asked.

"No, I like to run down the beach and jump on it," Julia said. "I can slide for a long way."

"If we had a rope, I could pull you along. I wonder how far we could go."

The girls looked along the shore and finally found a piece of ski rope. "This will be perfect."

Catie pulled Julia down the beach. They got going very fast before the wave board slide out from under Julia's feet. She landed on her butt. "Ouch," she squealed. "That was fun. Your turn."

Julia pulled Catie down the beach, but she had a hard time getting her up to the same speed that Catie had gotten her to; finally, she ran out of gas. "Sorry."

"Hey, that was good," Catie said. "Watch out, incoming," Catie added as she pointed toward a couple of boys coming toward them.

"Why don't you let us pull you?" the tall blond asked. "We can make you go faster."

"Sure," Catie said. "It's Julia's board, so she should go first."

"I'm Bill," the tall blond said. "This is Hank."

"Hi, guys, I'm Catie, and like I said, that's Julia."

Julia grabbed the board, "Great, let's see how fast we can go."

The guys grabbed the ski line and started pulling Julia. She squealed, "Faster, faster," just before she caught a wave wrong and went spilling into the water and sand.

"That was so cool," Julia shouted. "Catie, you're going to love it."

"My turn," Catie hollered back.

"Want me to hold your glasses?" Bill asked.

"No," Catie answered. "I can't stand the sun in my eyes. They're attached pretty well."

"Are you sure? Julia took a pretty gnarly spill there."

"I'm sure."

Bill handed Catie the end of the line, then the boys took off, pulling Catie. They were going even faster than they had pulled Julia. When Catie finally lost control and crashed, Bill was right there to help her up. He grabbed her hand and pulled on her; just as she was getting up, he reached for her specs. As he grabbed at them, Catie pushed his hand away.

"They're fine," she said angrily.

"Come on, I want to see how they stay on."

ADI warned Catie that Hank was coming up behind her, highlighting him in the HUD display. Catie tried to push by Bill, but he grabbed her. She immediately brought her knee up into his crotch and pushed his face with the flat of her hand.

"I said, no! Now get lost!"

Bill bent over in pain after the knee to the groin. "Get her," he yelled at Hank.

Catie put her right fist into her left palm, extended her elbows horizontally to the side, and whipped around to face Hank. She caught his left shoulder with her elbow, then she did a palm strike to his face, aiming for his nose. She got a good hit on it, making it bleed.

"Run," Catie yelled at Julia, who was standing behind Hank, trying to figure out if she should run or attack. The two girls ran up the beach toward Marc, who, having been alerted by ADI, was already running toward the girls.

"Are you girls okay?" Marc shouted when he got close to them.

"Yeah, we're alright," Catie gasped. "I've got some snot on my hand," she added as she went to the water to wash it off.

"What happened?" Marc asked as he and Julia followed her.

"A couple of jerks wanted my specs," Catie said. "I used some of the moves that Liz taught me, then we ran." Catie then gave her father a big hug as she let out a little sob.

"I was so scared," Julia said. "I didn't know what to do."

"I'll call the police," Marc said.

"Don't, Daddy," Catie said. "They've run off by now, and I don't want to have to answer a bunch of questions."

"Are you sure?"

"Yes. Boy, those moves Liz taught me really work," Catie laughed. "But it's not really the same as hitting someone."

"You really laid into Hank," Julia said. "He was crying when we ran. And Bill is going to be sore for a month."

"Serves him right," Catie said.

"Okay," Marc said. "Why don't we go to the hotel and get some ice cream. I think you two girls need a break."

After ice cream, Catie and Julia decided to watch a movie on the suite's big-screen TV. While the girls were watching the movie, Marc hid out in his room and prepared for his research trip to the library.

"Do you want to tour the campus before we go to the library?" Marc asked Catie the following morning.

"Why?"

"You might want to go to college here; and if not, it'll give you a sense of what college life would be like."

"I plan on going to the University of ADI," Catie replied.

"That might get you a great education, but I don't think it'll be a very marketable degree."

"I think that by the time I'm twenty, that won't be very important," Catie replied.

"Why not?"

"You're going to change the world," Catie declared with confidence.

"Oh, there is that," Marc replied. *"Just what I need, more expectations."*

"Come on, my dear Oracle, the library is this way," Marc said, "but of course you already knew that."

"Yeah, sure."

"While we're there, you should write your paper on the Gulf Stream. If you homeschool, you'll need to start submitting papers and doing homework."

"Killjoy!"

"Just being a good father."

Marc spent the afternoon having the librarian pull the documents and books he and ADI had identified as pertaining to the Spanish galleons they were looking for. They documented the time that they were sailing through the area when the hurricane hit. There were some papers written by a couple of college professors that tried to predict where they would have sunk. Fortunately, they were a few hundred miles off, which left the galleons for MacKenzie Discoveries to find. The work was interesting, but given that it was just for show, it was hard for Marc to really dig in. He kept up the motions, thinking about how they were going to negotiate with the government of Spain more than the research he was doing. He really wanted to work with ADI on developing additional scenarios for introducing Paraxean technology to Earth, but was unwilling to do it where he couldn't guarantee privacy.

After six hours of pseudo-research, Marc decided they had done enough and went to look for Catie. He found her alone in a side room. She looked like she was playing, definitely not writing.

"That doesn't look like you're writing a paper."

"I'm finished," Catie shot back.

"Did you write it or did ADI write it?"

"I wrote it," Catie said, giving Marc a hurt look.

"Okay, I'll read it on our way to Antigua. What are you doing now?"

"I'm practicing on the flight simulator," Catie said.

"Flight simulator?"

"Yes, the one for the FX4. ADI is running me through the qualification training."

"Very ambitious of you," Marc said. "I hope you're just as ambitious with your studies."

"I am. I have to learn geometry and trigonometry to qualify to fly the FX4. So, I'm studying geometry now."

"Very impressive. Are you ready to go? We're flying to Antigua in one hour, and we'll have dinner on the plane."

"Sure."

As they made their way out of the library, ADI alerted Marc. "Captain. I've highlighted a person on your HUD. I observed him at two other locations that you have been to since arriving in Miami. I predict that he is with the group that was observing you in Hawaii."

"Has he been close enough to observe anything important?"

"He has not been able to observe Catie and her flight simulation work, but he has been checking with the librarian. I predict it has been about what you've been taking out."

"I hope he enjoys the reading," Marc said.

"What's up?" Catie asked.

"Someone's following us, like in Hawaii," Marc replied. "It's not a problem. We just need to be careful that they don't see us using the new tech. So good thinking doing your flight simulator thing in a private room."

"Duh, I'm not stupid," Catie said. "These specs are cool, but way ahead of anything that exists on Earth. So, I'm careful."

"I didn't say you were stupid; in fact, I was saying you were smart."

"You should expect me to be smart."

"Praise doesn't mean you did something unexpected, just that you did something good," Marc said. "Now, don't be sensitive. I've always thought you were too smart for your own good."

Catie laughed, "Good one, Daddy."

Blake met Catie and Marc at the airport when they arrived in Antigua. "How was your flight?"

"It was great," Catie said. "Nothing beats flying on a private jet."

"I agree. We loved our flight from Hawaii," Blake said. "The Mea Huli just arrived by the way. Should be unloaded in about four hours; Kal is sitting on it."

"Good," Marc said. "Are you checked in?"

"Yes, we're all in the same building at the Admiral hotel. Gunpowder suites, here are your keys."

Marc laughed. "Yeah, they're really working the Admiral Lord Nelson thing. Let's go, the flight steward will bring our bags to the hotel."

"Nice service," Blake said. "We had to carry ours. Anyway, our taxi is just over here." Blake led the way to the exit and to the waiting taxi. "Isn't that the same jet you guys flew from Hawaii?"

"Yeah, I contracted to keep it for a few months," Marc said. "I figure we'll be doing a lot of flying, and having our own G6 and a dedicated crew will make it easier. Besides, we really like the crew. I hope you don't mind me jumping on it without talking to you."

"Yeah," Catie said. "They've been really nice and responsive."

"Sounds good to me," Blake said. "You are the senior partner, old man."

"Funny, junior," Marc said. "I want to be able to be decisive and move fast, but we're still partners."

"Good by me."

"I'm going right to the National Archive," Marc said. "Catie, I assume you would rather hang out with the rest of the crew."

"Oh, Yeah!"

"Alright, since you did such a good job on your paper on the Gulf Stream, you can have the day off."

"Cool."

"Captain," ADI interrupted Marc's preparation for bed.

"Yes, ADI?"

"I have a fifth message for you."

"Thank you, please put it on my comm," Marc said. He had kicked himself when he realized he should have put all the other messages on his comm also. That would have avoided all the extra complications that came with Catie discovering them on his computer.

"The message is available now," ADI said. "I am cutting off my audio from you. Ping the interface when you want to re-engage me."

"I will," Marc said as he used his eyes to click 'play' on the message. The voice of Dr. Metra came through clearly on his comm.

"Captain, this is my fifth and final message for you. By now you should be well into understanding how you want to proceed. I don't know what year it is; I had planned that ADI would actively seek out a new captain after we were dormant for forty-nine years. The protocol for a medical quarantine requires that every twenty-five years, the doctor will be awakened to check that the stasis pods are still functional and that the crew is still safe. At that time, I will be required to check whether advances have been developed that can handle the reason for the quarantine. I have already been awakened once.

"Of course, I maintained the quarantine since the quarantine is a ruse to lock up the people who killed the captain. There is no choice. The same will be true when I awaken next, but I hope that you will have been found, and we can find a way to end the quarantine without waking the crew. My hope is that the timing is such that I will be awakened shortly after you find the Sakira or ADI finds you. If for some reason, you have discovered the ship earlier than the year two thousand thirty-five, I will not be able to provide any assistance to you because the protocol will not allow for me to be brought out of stasis earlier than the scheduled date. Unfortunately, the protocol doesn't allow for the captain to override it and to bring me out earlier. An oversight in the design. Again, I wish you good luck and look forward to seeing you. Hopefully, that will be soon."

"Great," Marc sighed. "I'm always early, this time by eighteen years." He went to bed, knowing he would be thrashing about trying to digest all the ramifications of the message.

The next day the team moved to the Mea Huli. Marc had had everyone gather in the main lounge after they had stowed their gear in their berths. Blake took that time to get them underway, and they were now out of English Harbor and on autopilot in the open water.

"Okay everyone," he said once they were all gathered, "we're going to the Bahamas to pick up some extra dive gear that I have waiting for us. Then we'll be doing survey sweeps as we move to Bermuda. We'll take a couple of days of rest there and then do a few more survey sweeps on the way back to the Bahamas."

"While we're sailing to the Bahamas, we'll be doing some dive training," Blake added. "We want everyone familiar with the gear, and comfortable with deep dives before we actually have to do any real work down there."

"Questions?"

"Do we know how we're going to raise the ships?" Liz asked.

"An excellent question," Marc replied. "I'm hoping Blake has a good answer," he laughed.

"I have an answer," Blake said. "You guys will have to tell me whether it's a good one or not."

"Well, that's why we're here," Marc said.

"Las Cinque Chagas is going to be the most difficult," Blake said. "It's the biggest by far, and I mean big. It's one hundred fifty feet long with a forty-five-foot beam and displaces over twelve thousand tons."

"That's a lot of ship."

"So?"

"So, the concept is that we wrap it in PVC-coated canvas sheet like they use when they termite a house. The material is readily available and comes in nice large sizes. That will stabilize it. Then we attach lift bags to it until it floats."

"That's going to be a lot of lift bags," Kal said.

"Yeah, but I don't know of another way to get her to float," Blake replied.

"Didn't the ship used to float?" Catie asked.

"Of course, but now it's full of water."

"Can we just empty the water out?"

"If it was on the surface, and didn't have any holes in it, we could. But it's under more than four hundred meters of water," Blake said.

"Couldn't we fix the holes?"

"Probably."

"Then, couldn't we replace the water with something else?"

Blake mulled this over, "Hmm, like what?"

"Foam," Catie replied.

"How would we get the foam inside the ship?"

"Spray foam. I used some last year at school to build my diorama."

"But this needs to be foam that can expand under the huge pressure the ship is at, not interact with the water and be very light," Blake said.

"I'm sure ADI can find some for us," Catie said.

Blake looked shocked at the mention of ADI in front of Liz and Kal, but Marc jumped right in. "I bet she could. Why don't you go contact her and see?" Catie got up and went to the bridge so she could talk with ADI. "ADI is the fourth founding member of MacKenzie Discoveries," Marc continued. "She's our computer geek slash general technologist. She's pretty much an agoraphobe, so we just tie her in via our comms. But she's a dynamo when it comes to searching the Web and has a lot of techie contacts."

"Sounds like a good person to have," Kal said.

Catie came back into the lounge with a big smile on her face. Blake thought it was more of a smirk. "I assume by your pleased look that ADI found some foam," he said.

"Yes and no," Catie said. "Nobody sells it, but she has the formula for it and says almost anyone can make it. It uses nitrogen to expand, sticks to just about anything has a density of 0.016 grams-per-cubic-centimeter."

"Wow, that's pretty amazing," Blake said. "Did she say it could expand under pressure?"

"Oh yeah, she said you have to add 0.013 grams of nitrogen per-cubic-centimeter for each atmosphere of pressure."

"So, at our depths of around four hundred meters, that's about 0.1. Definitely will make it buoyant," Blake said.

"Won't the foam cause problems with the artifacts?" Liz asked. "How will anyone get it off of everything."

"ADI and I thought of that. The foam melts at forty-five C, and when it's liquid, it just washes off, something about its surface tension," Catie replied.

"Cool. Sounds like it will make the job a lot easier," Marc said.

"Wait, wait," Blake said. "I see two fatal flaws."

"What?"

"When we raise the ship, the nitrogen will expand, and so will the foam. We'd be talking about five times as big."

"Hah, thought of that too," Catie said. "The foam will outgas as the pressure around it decreases. ADI says it won't let water in, but it will outgas to equalize the pressure so it won't expand."

"Okay, second flaw," Blake said. "With all that lift from the foam, the ship won't be able to hold it. It's designed to be held up by its hull, not the decks. They'll just tear out of the ship."

"Rats," Catie said. "Can't we reinforce the ship?"

"Wait, wait," Blake said. "Foam displaces the water, makes the ship lighter. Thus, being more buoyant, the lift comes from the water pushing on the lighter ship, so... Sorry, my bad. It's a great idea, Catie. What would we do without you?"

"So how come it's okay now?" Kal asked.

"I was thinking about the foam wrong," Blake said. "It's not floating, it's just pushing the water out of the ship, so the total weight enclosed by the hull and decks is lighter. Then the pressure from the water outside the ship forces the whole ship up. No extra pressure on the deck."

"Good, so what does that do to your plan?" Marc asked.

"It means we don't need so many big lift bags," Blake said. "That will make everything easier. But now we have to wrestle the foam containers. We'll have to come up with some tubing to use when we disperse it. I have to calculate how many containers we will need."

"You're going to need like five hundred or six hundred containers," Marc said. "Sounds unwieldy."

"Probably not as unwieldy as so many lift bags would be. And we'd have to have almost as many containers to inflate the bags," Blake replied. "We should get the material and put it and the gas in the cylinders on the Mea Huli like I planned to do for the lift bags. The cylinders are going to be a big part of the weight and volume. I might get a compressor and refill the cylinders. I'll work with ADI on the process.

"Okay, so these cylinders are going to be heavy," Blake continued. "We'll get a lift bag for each; we can drop them down a line with the lift bag, and we'll adjust the setting based on the depth, so they stop at the right depth. That way, the divers can stay at depth while they work."

"Sounds like a complex set of logistics," Kal said.

"Nobody said it was going to be easy," Blake said. "That's why we're getting the big bucks."

"Alright, I'll arrange for a few cylinders to be added to our package, so we can practice," Marc said. "I already have some for some lift bags and a few big sheets of the canvas. We'll pick them up in the Bahamas."

When they got to the Bahamas, they docked at the port in Hamilton Harbor. The pier was stacked with their supplies.

"What are these?" Catie asked as she pulled a Seabob out of the stack.

"Trust the kid to go right to the toys," Blake said.

"You should know," Marc said, giving his brother a tweak about his propensity to act like a kid. "Those are Seabobs. They're underwater craft that you can ride when you dive, so you don't have to swim everywhere. We'll use them to maneuver around the ship and to get down to it."

"Cool, and we're going to do lots of practice with them, right?" Catie insisted.

"Of course," Marc said. "Now load up the canisters, canvas, and, of course, the Seabobs."

The crew was heading back to the Bahamas to have the Mea Huli shipped to Portugal. They had made numerous practice dives with and without wrestling the cylinders.

"Okay, that was a good dive practice," Blake said. "We managed to deploy a cylinder every ten minutes. That's our best time yet."

"Yes, but that still means we're going to be working at Las Cinque Chagas for three days," Kal said, "and that's if we can set up around the clock shifts."

"I know, I know," Blake replied, "It's a big ship."

"If what we're doing leaks out, we're going to be vulnerable," Kal added.

"Maybe we should use a ship that's a little less conspicuous than a yacht," Liz suggested.

"We could," Marc said, "but we'll still have the problem of a ship hanging around in one place for three to four days. Since the general area where the Las Cinque Chagas went down is common knowledge, that's going to be a dead giveaway."

"We'll need to be prepared for problems," Kal said.

"That's why you're here," Blake replied.

"Catie, do you have something to add?" Marc asked.

"Nooo," Catie replied. "Just thinking."

"Okay everyone, we're three hours from the Bahamas," Blake said. "We're making port in Hamilton, and we have to have the Mea Huli ready to ship by tomorrow. We get two days of downtime, and then we fly to the Azores. The Mea Huli should arrive the day after we get there."

"We're staying at the Hamilton Princess," Marc said. "It's right on the harbor, so it'll be convenient."

"Is convenient code for a Motel Eight?" Liz made air quotes around the word convenient.

"No, it is not. It's a luxury hotel; so, you'll have a nice two days after Blake works your ass off get the Mea Huli ready. I hear it has a nice spa."

"Good thing," Liz said as she headed out.

As everyone left the lounge, Blake nodded to Marc to hold back. "I'm worried about sitting in one place for that long," he said.

"So am I," Marc replied. "I think Catie may have a solution for you."

"Really? What makes you think so?"

"I know that look," Marc said. "She been working on something since we left Antigua, but I can't get anything out of her."

"Hey, you're her father, can't you get her to talk?"

"Hey, twelve-year-old geniuses aren't easy to parent," Marc said. "Besides, I think she has another agenda she's trying to weave in. I think the meeting today gave her a way to advance it."

"What do you think it is?" Blake asked.

"Not sure. She'll let us know when she's ready."

"I hope it's good."

"She's been working with ADI on it, so I'm sure it will be good."

"How's your plan going?" Marc asked Catie over breakfast the next morning. They were alone since the rest of the crew had partied late into the night after sending the Mea Huli off.

"What plan?" Catie asked, looking all innocent.

"Be that way," Marc said. "I know you've got something cooking, just don't wait too long before you bring it up. We don't want to waste a bunch of time working on one thing, then have to make a big change."

"Don't worry," Catie said.

"So, there is a plan?"

"I didn't say that."

"Then why shouldn't I worry?"

"Ahhh," Catie growled as she realized the trap she'd fallen into. "Hey, have you talked to Mommy yet?" she asked, quickly changing the subject.

"I'm talking to her in two hours when she gets up," Marc replied.

"Do you think she'll let me stay?"

"I don't know," Marc said. "How's your schoolwork going?"

"I've just finished my report on To Kill A Mockingbird for my English class," Catie said. "And for biology, I finished the section on amino acids and proteins. ADI says I'm picking it up pretty fast."

"Are you learning it or just memorizing it?"

"You know ADI is smarter than that," Catie scoffed. "She doesn't just have me do the homeschool test, she creates her own tests, and those are hard."

"Good," Marc said. "Are you going with Liz when she goes shopping today?"

"Does that mean you want me out of the way when you talk to Mommy?"

"Yes."

"Then shopping it is."

◆ ◆ ◆

"Hey Linda," Marc said as his ex-wife answered the phone.

"How's Catie doing?" Linda asked.

"She's fine. She really wants to stay," Marc said. "But we have to do what's best for her."

"How's her schoolwork?"

"She's working at it. Much more diligently than I remember, but it's been a couple of years since I had to monitor her schoolwork."

"If she's working at it, that's good. She's been just doing what it takes to get an A, and with her talent, that's not too hard," Linda said. "That damn memory of hers makes it too easy for her, she gets away with just memorizing things too much."

"Well, that's not cutting it here. I've got an assistant that reviews her work and works up challenging tests for her. She complains some, but I think she's enjoying the challenge."

"Then, I think we have our answer," Linda said. "I'm in group therapy, and I think it's helping, but I still think she's better off with you for now."

"If you're sure."

"Please tell her I love her, and we're doing this for her," Linda said.

"Hey, she thinks I'm here begging for her," Marc said. "She's going to really think you love her when we let her stay. She really wants to and is afraid you'll say no. So, this will make you the good guy for once."

"I hope so. Thank you for being so understanding after everything."

"You're welcome. I know you've gotten a raw deal, and I wasn't much help. But things will get better. She'll probably want to call and thank you over a video chat tonight, so be prepared."

"I will be. Thanks for the heads up."

That evening Catie called her mother.

"Hi, Mommy!"

"Hey, Sweetie, how are you doing?"

"Great, thank you so much for letting me stay with Daddy. I promise to be good and study hard."

"I'm sure you will," Linda sniffed. "You have to call me all the time. I don't want to miss my little girl growing up."

"I promise. And I'll be home for holidays and vacations. I'll see you at Thanksgiving and Christmas. Since I'm homeschooling, we can just pick the time I come to visit," Catie gushed on.

"Oh, that will be nice," Linda said. "We'll do vacations together."

"Yeah, that will be fun."

Catie spent another hour telling her mother about all the exciting things she was learning and doing.

The flight to the Azores was uneventful. After two weeks of hanging around the beach, eating and drinking, the Mea Huli finally arrived. Everybody was tired of vacation and wanted to get to the real mission. They got the Mea Huli back in the water as quickly as they could.

They continued working on their diving skills while they wandered around the general area of Las Cinque Chagas. They carefully avoided actually coming closer than 100 miles to the actual ship, in case they were being monitored somehow.

"It's been three days, I'm ready to push a pencil through my forehead," Kal whined.

"Yeah, when do we get to start the real mission?" Liz added to the whining

"Okay, okay," Marc said. "We'll do a fast loop to the northeast and then continue on to Lisbon."

"It's almost two days to Lisbon," Kal whined some more.

"We have to pick up the foam and canvas we ordered," Marc snapped. "We'll suspend dive practice for the trip."

"Thank God," Liz said. "I'm starting to turn into a porpoise."

"Get your rest now, you have to load up the supplies and head back here right away," Marc said. "Catie and I will fly back after we finish negotiations."

"Are you sure you two should be alone?" Kal asked. "We still seem to have our friends checking up on us."

"Yeah," Blake said. "We spotted them in the Bahamas and here on the Azores. What did you do to that admiral that makes him so interested in you?"

"Nothing I know of," Marc replied. "I suspect they're just curious about Hyperion's creation. Maybe they think I have something else."

"Well, I think one of us should hang with you," Kal said.

"Okay, why don't I keep Liz with me."

Liz did a little fist pump as she realized she would get some shoretime.

"It's a plan," Kal said, deciding that Liz could do a better job keeping an eye on Catie than he could.

"Blake, go ahead and crank her up to full speed," Marc said.

"Yeah," Catie shouted.

"What's this baby's top speed," Kal asked.

"Thirty-two knots," Blake replied.

"How is that possible? I thought these things topped out around twenty-five knots."

"We made some mods," Marc said. "She's fitted with a new prop design that increases her efficiency and speed. Blake and Catie are speed demons, so I thought I could improve my life by helping them get their fix."

"Yep, we'll make Lisbon by this time tomorrow," Blake bragged.

Chapter 9   She's Gone

Marc, Catie, and Liz waited in the reception area of the Portuguese Minister for Antiquities. It had taken two days to get an appointment, and although their appointment was for 10:00, it was already 11:30.

"Are they ever going to let us in?" Catie whispered.

"Important people like to make others wait," Marc whispered back. "It lets you know how much more important they are than you."

"How childish," Catie whispered.

"Yes, it is."

"The minister will see you now," the secretary announced in heavily accented English.

"Thank you," Marc replied as the three stood up and made their way into the minister's office.

"I'm sorry to have kept you waiting," the minister said. "It's been a busy day."

"Minister Sampalo, I thank you for seeing us," Marc replied. "This is my daughter, Catie, and my associate, Elizabeth Farmer."

"Pleased to meet you," Minister Sampalo replied, gesturing for them to be seated at the table in his office.

There was a knock at the door, "Dotour Verissimo," the secretary announced.

"Ah yes, please join us, Dotour. Dotour Verissimo is our expert on lost galleons."

"Pleased to meet you," Marc extended his hand. The dotour shook hands and sat down.

"Minister Sampalo tells me that you think you've found one of our lost ships," Dotour Verissimo said.

"We are quite confident that we have found one," Marc replied as he laid his briefcase on the table and opened it. "As you can see, it is definitely a galleon." Marc laid a picture of Las Cinque Chagas on the table.

"Meu Deus," the dotour exclaimed under his breath. "This looks like Las Cinque Chagas."

"We're confident that it is," Marc said.

"But how can it be," Minister Sampalo said. "Las Cinque Chagas caught fire and sank; this ship is whole."

"It mostly is," Marc replied. "Based on our survey, we surmise that the fire destroyed its sails and masts. Also, either the fire or the enemy cannon destroyed its steering. She then was caught abeam by the waves and capsized."

"Meu Deus," the minister said. "And you say she is mostly whole?"

"Yes," Marc replied. "We are confident that we can effect repairs and raise her in one piece."

"That would be a miracle," the minister said. "And for this, you would want?"

"Four billion U.S. dollars," Marc replied.

"Isso é insano!"

"I don't think so," Marc said. "The estimates of the cargo's value are well over four billion. Imagine how much having all that and the ship in one piece would be worth. The publicity would be enormous."

"What is to stop us from finding it ourselves now that you've let us know she's just sitting there waiting to be discovered?" Dotour Verissimo asked.

"We've been very cautious in how we surveyed the area," Marc replied. "We're very confident that you will not find her on your own. If you don't want it, we'll approach the Indian government; we understand they also have a claim."

"Ridiculous," the minister said. "It is our ship."

"For four billion dollars, you can have her delivered to one of your military vessels by the Azores. We'll be happy to tow it into port, but we think an escort would be prudent."

"I will need to consult with our Presidente," Minister Sampalo finally said after several more minutes of posturing and declarations of Portugal's sovereign right of possession over Las Cinque Chagas. "I will contact you within two days. Please allow my secretary to show you out." The minister buzzed his secretary from the phone on the table. "Please show our guests out."

The secretary opened the door and motioned for them to follow him out. Catie and Liz followed Marc out of the office.

"Might I ask where you are staying in case the Minister needs to contact you later," the secretary asked.

"You have my number," Marc replied.

"Of course. Would you like a recommendation of where to dine?" he asked. "We have some excellent establishments here in Lisboa. You would not want to miss the opportunity to dine at one of our better restaurants."

"Where would you recommend we dine?" Marc asked.

"Tavares is one of the oldest and most prestigious restaurants in the world," the secretary replied. "It's in the heart of our historical Chiado district, our theater district, as you say."

"What do you think?" Marc asked.

"Sounds nice," Liz said.

"I can get you reservations," the secretary said. "A call from the minister's office will ensure you a nice table. What time would you like?"

Marc looked at Catie, "I think eight o'clock would be good; we don't want to be too late."

"Of course," the secretary said. He made the call while they waited. After a brief exchange on the phone in Portuguese, he hung up. "You are confirmed for eight o'clock p.m. at one of the finest tables in the restaurant. Please enjoy your time here in Lisboa."

"This place is cool," Catie said as she spun around to look at the chandelier hanging above them in Tavares Restaurante.

"It certainly is," Liz added. She was especially impressed with the wall paneling and the mirrors that surrounded the dining room. "It's like stepping into the Seventeenth Century."

"Definitely nice," Marc agreed.

"Senhor e senhoras, please follow me," the Maître d' gestured toward the dining room. He led them to a lovely corner table where they could observe the whole room.

"Well, he certainly delivered as promised," Marc said.

"Hey, what was his name?" Catie asked. "We were never introduced."

"I think it is Muzah Harrak," Liz said. "At least that is what was on the nameplate on his desk."

"We'll have to remember to thank him," Marc said.

The waiter came by and took their drink orders, and then Liz and Catie excused themselves to go to the lady's room.

"I'll bet the bathroom is really cool too," Catie said as they made their way down the hallway.

"I'm sure it is."

When they got to the bathroom, a woman was exiting it fiddling with her purse. At the same time, a man was exiting the men's room. Liz's warning bells went off, and she turned to check him out. Just then the lady with the purse pushed a Taser to her neck. Liz collapsed, and the woman grabbed Catie. As Catie was trying to put her elbow into the woman's face, the man put a bag over Catie's head and then wrapped his arms around her. She felt a needle in her neck, and then she went limp.

"Captain, someone has grabbed Catie," ADI's voice echoed in Marc's head. He was dashing toward the restrooms before he even internalized what ADI had said. As he got to the hallway, two men were coming out of the men's room. They bumped into Marc as he was rushing down the hall knocking him into the wall. He gathered himself up and kept pushing toward the back door at the end of the hall.

"Captain, they've put her into a car and have driven away. I have called the surveillance drone from the hotel. I can track them via satellite until it gets close enough. She still has her earwig and specs, but her comm is on the ground next to the back door."

"Can you talk to her?"

"No, she appears to be unconscious."

"Where is Liz?"

"She is inside the lady's room," ADI said. "She is just regaining consciousness. I believe they tasered her."

At that time, Liz came out of the restroom. "I'm so sorry, Marc. They were waiting for us."

"I can tell," Marc said as he looked around for the two men who had delayed him. "This was a complete setup."

"But who?"

"The secretary, Muzah," Marc guessed. "ADI, can you find him?"

"Captain, he has an apartment about two miles from here. I haven't determined if he is home or not. I'm trying to access his cellphone now."

"Should we call the police?" Liz asked.

"I'm not sure. I think they'll just get in the way. ADI, does the drone have the car yet?"

"Not yet, it is still two minutes out, Captain."

"Okay, let's move. ADI, I need Blake ... Blake, I need you guys back here in Lisbon."

"What's up?" Blake asked.

"Somebody has grabbed Catie," Marc said. "We're going to need help getting her back. We think we know one of the instigators; we're heading over to his place to see if we can grab him."

"We're three hours out," Blake said.

"Okay, just get here. Liz, let's go. We'll grab a cab and head to his apartment while ADI tries to determine if he's there."

"Right behind you," Liz said. "By the way, what's this surveillance drone you mentioned?"

"Arrg," Marc cried. "Long story, I'll fill you in later. Think of it as an aerial drone."

"Okay, so it's going to be able to find the car Catie's in?"

"Yes, ADI is tracking the car via satellite until the drone gets close enough."

"Okay," Liz said as she signaled for a cab to wait for them. A couple of men who were also waiting for a cab stepped up to argue who's cab it was. One look at Liz and they decided that they could wait.

ADI gave Liz the address, which Liz relayed to the cab driver. Marc was just coming out of the door after giving the Maître d' money to cover their hasty departure.

"Let's move," Marc said. "Bônus para rápido," he shouted at the cab driver. The cab squealed its tires as it pulled away from the curb.

"Captain, the drone is now tracking the car, and I have a connection to Cer Catie's comm," ADI said. "She is breathing calmly, but still unconscious. Based on what I have recovered from her comm, they are headed for Faro, where they plan to transition to a ship. We don't have the name of the ship yet."

"Blake, change of plans. I need you to head for Faro. Liz and I will take the plane and meet you somewhere close to there. ADI keep Blake updated with any intel changes."

"Yes, Captain."

"We're on our way," Blake said. "We're actually a little closer to Faro than Lisbon, so two and a half hours."

The cab squealed to a stop in front of an apartment building. Marc just threw money at the cab driver as he and Liz bailed out of the cab. The cab driver was obviously pleased with the money. So pleased, in fact, that he pulled to the curb and waited to see if they might want to engage his service when they came out.

"Is he in there?" Marc asked.

"Captain, his phone is in the apartment. It is either in his pocket or some other dark place, so I cannot be sure he is there."

"Which apartment?"

"Captain, it is twenty-two B."

Marc and Liz rushed up the first flight of steps. They were trying hard not to make too much noise, but speed was critical. As they approached 22B, they slowed down and continued their approach quietly. The door was very solid with a keyed lock.

"Can you open it?" Marc asked Liz.

"I can, but he might hear."

"I'll take care of that," Marc said. "ADI, can you call Muzah and speak to him in Arabic as a distraction?"

"What should I say?"

"Hmm. Say you are from the ministry and that there has been a problem at the office. Act like you cannot hear him. We only need a minute," Marc said while looking at Liz for confirmation. Liz gave him a nod.

"Yes, Captain."

Momentarily they heard the phone ring inside the apartment. "Go ahead and pick the lock."

"On it," Liz said as they could hear Muzah talking loudly on the phone.

It only took Liz a minute to pick the lock. When they opened the door, Muzah was sitting on the couch, yelling into the phone.

Liz ran over and grabbed him by the wrist. She twisted it and wrenched his arm up behind his back, forcing him to his feet.

"Unhand me," Muzah yelled, then he squealed in pain.

"Quiet, one more yell, and I'll break it," Liz said.

"What have I done to you? Why are you accosting me in my apartment?" Muzah protested more quietly.

"Where is my daughter?" Marc hissed.

"I don't kno…" Muzah winced as Liz twisted his wrist more.

"Now if you lie to me, try to escape, or do anything to piss me off, I'm going to let Liz take you apart," Marc said.

"I haven't done anything to you!" Muzah hissed.

"I'll give you that one for free," Marc said. "Now I know you're involved with the people who snatched my daughter. Now you'd better start cooperating, or I won't have any use for you, and we'll just leave your body here."

Liz applied a little more pressure to Muzah's wrist. "I suggest you start talking," she said. "Or I'm going to see how many bones I can break before you pass out."

"I'm sorry, I'm was just doing what I was tol…. Aack" he cried out in pain as Liz dislocated his thumb.

"You just had to start by being uncooperative," Liz said.

"If you harm me, it would be bad for your daughter," Muzah said.

"I'm confident that whoever has my daughter will be happy to negotiate with me whether you are alive or not," Marc hissed. "So, what did you do?"

"I just called my uncle when I realized what you had found. He told me to get your hotel room number or find out what restaurant you were going to tonight. That's all I did."

"Who's your uncle, and where is he?" Marc demanded.

"He is Omar Harrak; he is a big chefe in Casablanca."

"Is that where they're taking my daughter?"

"I don't know, but it would make sense. He has many friends in the police there. And he has an estate outside the city."

"ADI, we need a flight plan to an airport close to Faro, that will let us meet up with the Mea Huli and get ahead of the kidnappers."

"I have alerted the flight crew to file a flight plan to Lagos. It is close to Faro but closer for the Mea Huli. They will be ready to depart when you reach the airport."

"Call us another cab," Marc requested.

"No need, Captain, your last cab is waiting outside."

"Great! One word or problem from you," Marc hissed at Muzah, "and she will break your neck!"

Marc headed toward the cab with Liz still holding onto Muzah's wrist. "The Humberto Delgado Airport," Marc shouted at the cabbie.

"Muito rápido?" the cabbie asked.

"Sim," Marc replied, using the Portuguese for yes.

It only took them ten minutes to make it to the airport as the cabbie dodged traffic and cut down side streets. Marc tossed him another handful of money as he piled out of the cab, followed closely by Liz and the whining Muzah.

"Get this plane in the air," Marc demanded as they climbed aboard their jet.

"We start taxiing in one minute. Everyone, please get strapped in," Fatima said as she closed the hatch.

"Wheels up in two minutes," the pilot announced over the PA.

"ADI, we will need a speed boat to take us out to the Mea Huli."

"Yes, Captain. I am arranging that now. It will be ready when you arrive."

"You're sure good at this for an academic," Liz said.

"Necessity," Marc replied tersely.

They were halfway to Lagos when Marc finally got the answer he wanted from ADI. He'd been asking her if Catie was awake yet every few minutes. The answer came when his HUD pinged an incoming text. "*DADDY,*" it said.

"Catie, can you hear me," Marc replied over the audio channel.

"*Yes, I'm gagged,*" Catie texted back. Marc could hear her sobbing through the gag.

"Are you hurt?"

"*No, I think I'm OK. I'm in the trunk.*"

"We know where you are. The surveillance drone is tracking you. We're putting together a plan to rescue you."

"*Good. How long?*"

"It will probably be a few hours," Marc said. "They are going to move you onto a boat. ADI says it's a fishing boat. We'll try to get you once they're out to sea. Uncle Blake is on his way."

"*Okay,*" Catie texted back.

"Anything I can do for you?"

"*AMOF have ADI bring the LX9 to the Azores.*"

159

"What, you're tied up in the trunk of a car, and you want to talk about bringing that jet here?"

"*4my Plan, you said no WOMBAT*" (Waste of money, brains, and time), "*I was going to tell you tomorrow.*"

"Can't we talk about this tomorrow?"

"*No WOMBAT.*"

"Okay, ADI, can you bring the LX9 to the Azores without it being detected?"

"Yes, Captain. It has stealth technology far superior to your technology's detection capabilities," ADI replied.

"Then do so," Marc said. "How long will it take?"

"It will be there in approximately twelve hours," ADI replied. "Where should I put it?"

"Put it on the ocean floor next to the Las Cinque Chagas."

"Yes, Captain."

"We'll be landing in ten minutes," the pilot announced over the PA.

"Please buckle your seatbelts," Fatima said.

After they landed, the pilot came back into the cabin, leaving the co-pilot to taxi them in.

"Sir, would you like a couple of additional men?" he asked. "Walter and I have military experience, and we would be happy to join this fight, I like kicking a little ass now and then." He gave them a feral grin.

"We're going to infiltrate via scuba," Marc said. "We've all trained together, so I don't want to upset the team dynamic. But we could use someone to drive the boat, how are you at that?"

"I haven't sailed anything as big as the Mea Huli, but I've sailed a few yachts in my time. I think I could handle it."

"Well then, Fred, welcome to the strike team. We'll leave Walter with the jet in case we need it. We'll fit you with our comm gear when we get to the Mea Huli."

"Glad to be on the team," Fred said.

It took twenty minutes from the time they landed until they were on the speedboat heading for the Mea Huli. "You are thirty minutes from the Mea Huli, Captain," ADI said. "Once you are aboard the Mea Huli, it will arrive outside of Faro approximately ten minutes after the car with Cer Catie arrives at the port."

"Blake, Kal, I'm thinking we should let them set sail and take them on in the open sea."

"I agree," Kal said. "We should let them get well into their trip to Casablanca before we make our move."

"Catie, can you hold out that long?" Marc asked.

"*I'm good,*" Catie texted back. "*Just wake me up first.*"

"Is she serious?" Liz said. "*Just wake me up first.* Any other twelve-year-old would be screaming her head off."

"She's not just any twelve-year-old," Marc said.

"She takes after her father, neither of them is very excitable," Blake said over the comm.

"Kal, are we good?" Marc asked.

"It's a plan," Kal said. "There's nothing like the drone of a ship's engines to put you to sleep or off your game."

"We've got five Seabob F55s on board. So, we should be able to have the whole team get to the boat," Blake said. "We just need to slow them down."

"I think we can accomplish that," Kal said. "We just need Liz to drive the boat. The way she drives would make anyone slow down and try to get some maneuvering room."

"Har, har," Liz said. "Good thing you're not on this speed boat, or we would only need three Seabobs." Liz was thinking she'd just toss the joker overboard if he was at hand.

"I think our man Fred will be able to handle the lousy driving," Marc said as he gave Fred a quick smile. He was listening in on the conversation over Marc's comm unit.

"I'm sure I can make like a drunk playboy," Fred said.

"Good, we just need ADI to find us the optimal location with the right weather and sea conditions," Kal said.

"ADI?"

"Working, Captain."

"Am I wrong, or is ADI getting smarter?" Blake asked.

"*ADI is getting smarter,*" Catie texted.

Chapter 10   The Rescue

"Okay, guys, we've got about two hours to plan this thing, and we have to get it right." Marc collapsed onto the sofa on the sundeck behind the pilot's chair. Blake was giving Fred a crash course in how to drive the Mea Huli.

"We'll put her on autopilot, so we can pay attention," Blake told Fred. "I'll alert us if the radar picks up anything close."

Everyone picked a seat around Marc, and after a few more words of support, Marc started the meeting.

"We've already decided we're going to take them on the fishing boat. ADI says it's really a smuggling vessel dressed up to look like a fishing boat. She estimates that there are twenty or so crew aboard. The ship's designed for twelve crew, so they're going to be crowded."

"That's a lot of men to neutralize," Liz said.

"Yes. Now's the time to change the plan, so anyone with a better idea, feel free to speak up," Marc said.

"I think taking them on the boat is still the best play," Kal said. "They won't be expecting anything, and there's no chance for additional support. If we wait until it reaches Casablanca, there's no telling what will be waiting on us."

"I agree," Marc said. "So, what we have so far is:

1: We wait until they're nice and comfortable.
2: We have Fred cut across their bow like some distracted playboy to slow them down.
3: The four of us use the Seabobs to approach the ship underwater.
4: We board and take out anyone in our way.
5: We grab Catie and get out.

Sounds easy. What are we missing?"

"We need to secure the Seabobs to the hull underwater," Kal said.

"I've got magnetic clamps that should work for that," Blake said. "What about your legs, Kal?"

"They'll be fine, I can use my arms to climb up and position myself at the rear of the ship; I'll just cover everyone from there," Kal said. "I shouldn't need to move around much."

"Is the ship metal-hulled?" Marc asked.

"Yes, Captain, it is."

"Thanks, ADI. Blake, can we use your magnetic clamps to climb the side?"

"Sure."

"You guys might want some kind of night vision," Fred suggested.

"Got that covered," Marc said as he pointed his specs. Fred just nodded.

"Weapons?" Liz asked.

"Silenced nine millimeters and Tasers," Marc said.

"I've got a couple of the mini FX air rifles. I'll keep one, and I suggest one of you carry the other," Kal said. "We approach underwater, I'll go up first and set up cover next to the skiff they have tied down at the stern. The rest of you come up midship right behind the cabin area, port side, so you're away from the crew access."

Everyone nodded their head.

"We do all that without alerting the pilot. Once you're on board, make your way to the starboard side and enter the cabin areas," Kal continued. "There are six cabins, so we move forward, clearing them one at a time."

"I'm in the forward cabin port side," Catie texted.

"Scratch that, we go forward and cover that cabin first," Kal corrected. "Catie, are you alone?"

"Most of the time."

"Are you still tied up and gagged?" Kal asked.

"Yes, but working on it."

"Be careful, Catie," Marc said. "We don't want them to start sitting on you."

"I am."

"This is good," Kal continued. "So, whoever has the rifle stays at the back of the hall; take out anyone who sticks their head out of a cabin. If you miss, they'll at least duck back in. The rest of you secure Catie's cabin then clear the rest prow to stern. Keep one person on her cabin, and they can cover the hallway from the forward position."

"That's a lot of carnage," Fred said.

"These guys are smugglers, not exactly innocent," Marc said. "Besides, anyone who wants to stay alive just has to stay in their cabin."

"Don't get me wrong, I'm fine with taking them out. We just need to consider how we clean up," Fred said. "I guess we could just sink the boat."

"We'll deal with that once we have Catie," Blake said. "Then we'll know the exact situation."

"Alright everyone, it's a plan," Marc said. "Prep your weapons and get some rest. ADI, do we have a time and location yet?"

"Yes, Captain, in two hours, your target will enter an area of relatively calm seas. You should attack there."

"Catie, you good?"

"*Yes!*"

Marc didn't get any rest during the two hours. Now he was bobbing off the stern of the Mea Huli in a shorty wetsuit while getting his rebreather attached. The Mea Huli had stayed ahead of the smuggler boat, they were fifteen minutes ahead as the four of them were getting into the water. They would take off at full speed, aiming for the port side of the target. They had to leave enough room for whatever maneuver the boat's captain made after Fred brought the Mea Huli across his bow. The other three members of the infiltration team gave him a thumbs up, signaling that they were ready. He launched and headed for the rendezvous spot. They would proceed on the surface so ADI could navigate for them. Then they would submerge before they closed on the target.

Ten minutes later, Marc signaled for everyone to stop. They gathered around resting high on top of the Seabobs. The water temp was only

20 degrees C, or 68 F. A bit cool for just wearing a shorty, but they couldn't afford the loss of mobility that a full wetsuit would cost them.

"Here she comes," Marc said. "Where's Fred?"

"I don't see him, but I can hear him," Liz said. "He should be here momentarily."

"Ah there he is, no lights," Blake said. "Now he's turned them on. And now they're off."

"Pretend fight," Liz said.

"They're on…. They're off," Blake continued calling off the state of the lights.

"I think our friends see him; they're slowing down," Kal announced.

"ADI, what's happening on the target?" Marc asked.

"Captain, the ship is slowing down, but the men in the pilothouse don't seem too excited. Two of them are with him keeping track of the Mea Huli."

"Fred, you're a genius," Marc said. "Keep it up. Let's go guys."

The team submerged and jetted to where the smugglers' boat was coasting along. It only took them three minutes to reach it, and they easily kept pace. They had decided to release the Seabobs with the depth set for three meters. That would avoid the risk of them getting caught in turbulence and bumping against the hull. The Mea Huli's sonar wouldn't have any trouble finding them later. They each clamped onto the hull, took their rebreather off and attached it to their Seabob, then pushed it away.

Kal made quick time climbing up the hull. His above-average upper-body strength made short work of the one-two climbing rhythm required by the two clamps. He dragged himself across the back of the skiff and up to the edge of the ramp. He pulled his rifle from his back, took it out of its watertight package, and set up.

"I'm good back here," Kal said. "Time for the party."

Blake climbed up about half a meter then stopped. Liz used him as a stepladder and crawled up his back then stood on his shoulders so she could climb onto the deck. She pulled her nine-millimeter out of the plastic bag and signaled Marc to come up. Marc used the same procedure that Liz had used.

"Ugh, brother, you need to lose some weight," Blake complained as Marc was standing on his shoulders.

"Yeah, I'll keep it in mind." Marc swung onto the deck, letting Liz provide cover. He reached down and helped Blake make the final climb. "Speaking of needing to lose weight."

"I know, it's all the gear," Blake said as he pulled the rifle off his back and removed it from its case. "I'm ready."

"Catie, what's your situation?"

"I'm alone and ready," Catie replied.

"And not gagged or tied up, I'm guessing," Kal said.

"Of course not," Catie whispered back.

"Jam the lock to your cabin," Marc told Catie.

"Already done."

"Let's go."

The three made their way along the bulkhead to the hatch that opened on the hallway for the cabins. "You're good," Kal said.

"Ready?" Marc asked Blake.

Blake shouldered his rifle and gave Marc a nod.

Marc opened the door quickly. A guard was sitting in a chair at the end of the passageway. He reached for his gun and started to stand up. Blake shot him in the left eye, and he collapsed back into the chair.

"Go," Blake hissed.

Marc rushed to the front of the hallway with Liz coming behind him. When he passed the galley, there was a gasp. Liz shot the surprised crewmember in the head and moved on, meeting up with Marc at the front.

"Just one in the galley," Liz said. She tried the door to the cabin next to Catie's. "It's open."

"Wait," Kal said. "We have one coming down."

"Should I take him out?" Blake asked as he turned back to the door.

"No, I'll get him," Kal replied. "I just want to wait until he's on the deck, so it doesn't alert the other two up top."

Kal watched the man make his way down the ladder. When he turned toward the starboard side entry, Kal shot him. He fell with a thud, but the engine noise was loud enough to mask the sound, so nobody was alerted.

"You're clear," Kal said.

"Good," Marc said, nodding to Liz, "On three, one … two … three."

Liz opened the door, and Marc rushed into the room, dropping low. Liz came behind him high. Four crewmen were lying in the bunks. Two were awake and reaching for their guns. Liz shot the one in the top bunk, and Marc took care of the one in the lower. They quickly dispatched the other two sleepers before they even realized what was going on.

"Seven down," Liz said, "Thirteen left, an unlucky number."

Another member of the crew came out of the back cabin yelling toward the galley. Apparently, the man Liz had shot was supposed to bring something back. Blake shot him. "Unlucky for him. Eight down now, I need you to clear this back cabin, they're apparently wanting snacks from the galley."

Liz made her way back to Blake while Marc stayed at the front. Marc undid the cleats that were locking the door to Catie's cabin and waited for Liz and Blake to clear the rear cabin.

"I'm guessing two more in there," Blake said. He pulled his nine-millimeter out and strapped the rifle on his back. "On three."

They entered the room, acting like the missing crewmen coming back. Three men were sitting at what was obviously some kind of card game. "Alhudu' 'aw tamut, quiet or you die," Blake called out.

The three men raised their hands. "Now, what do we do?" Blake asked.

Liz gave an exasperated sigh and walked over to the men. She used her gun to knock the first one out, a blow square in the center of his head. He fell over unconscious instantly. The other two pulled away and started to yell. Liz pointed her gun at them, she pointed to the barrel and then to the handgrip, essentially telling them to choose. They both quieted down and waited until Liz had knocked them unconscious.

"Eleven down, two up top, so we have seven left," Liz said. "A lucky number."

"These guys are really slow," Blake said.

"Can't you smell the hashish?" Liz asked.

"Oh, counting their money early, aren't they?"

"Good for us, bad for them," Liz said. She made her way forward to Marc, and they prepared to enter the fourth room. When they entered, there were four bunks, each occupied by sleeping crewmen. Liz dispatched each of them with a blow to the top of the head. "Fifteen."

The fourth room they entered had four bunks, but only one of them was occupied. Liz was able to knock him out quickly, and they made their way to the 5th room.

"Okay, here goes," Marc said as they rushed in. The room only had two bunks, and neither was occupied. "They're up top," Marc said.

"But that's only eighteen," Liz said.

"Cer Liz, twenty was only an estimate," ADI said.

"Yeah, unless they were hot bunking, this should be it," Marc said. "ADI, any activity up top?"

"Captain, the ship's captain is bringing the boat back up to speed; the second man is keeping an eye on the Mea Huli. Fred has stopped turning the light on and off, so they seem to be relaxing."

"Can you let me out?" Catie asked.

"Are you locked in?" Marc replied. "We need to secure the two up top before they realize we're here and alert someone."

Catie pulled out the piece of wood that she'd used to jamb the door and opened the door. "I'm free. Can I go to the bathroom?"

"Go ahead," Marc said. "Kal has you covered. We're going up to the pilothouse and finish this."

Blake grabbed one of the caps that the crew wore and put it on, Marc did the same. "Keep behind us," Blake instructed Liz. They slowly made their way up the ladder to the top deck. The pilothouse was huge, with consoles to manage the various winches around the sides of the boat when they were pulling in a net full of fish. The man piloting the ship was staring toward the front while the second man was looking forward out the port window to keep an eye on Fred.

Once they were well inside and had both men covered, Marc coughed.

"Ahem, gentlemen. If you remain calm, we won't have to shoot anyone," Marc said.

The second man spun around quickly, so Liz put a bullet in his head.

"Like I said, remain calm," Marc repeated.

The other man raised his hands and slowly turned around. "What do you want?"

"We have what we wanted," Marc said. "The question is, what can you give us. Now please stop the boat."

"The girl," the pilot said with recognition as he turned and pulled the throttle back to idle.

"Yes, my daughter," Marc said. "Now that I have her, why shouldn't I just sink this tub?"

"I can tell you who ordered her taken."

"I already know that," Marc said. "We have his nephew tied up on our boat."

"Ahh, I can tell you how to get to him."

"Now that might interest me," Marc said.

"He is expecting us to make port in Casablanca. There is a warehouse there that will have a van. Four of the men below are supposed to take her in the van to his estate."

"No welcoming committee?" Marc asked.

"Just a driver. He doesn't know anyone. He is just expecting the girl and four men."

"Do we go to him, or will he come to the boat?"

"I go to him, then he will bring the van to the boat."

"Okay, what about the compound?" Marc asked.

Starship Sakira

"I have only been there twice," the pilot said. "It is walled, there are guards."

"How many?"

"Eight, ten."

"ADI," Marc said.

"Captain, I have dispatched the drone to surveil the compound. It will be there in six hours."

"How long for us to arrive at Casablanca?" Marc asked the pilot.

"We are supposed to arrive in nine hours, I can make up the lost time," the pilot replied.

"Fred, come and get Blake, Catie, and Kal. Then you three can pick up the Seabobs and follow us. We'll work on a plan on the way," Marc said. "We can always decide to sink her later."

"Hey, I want to stay with you," Catie begged over the comm.

"Not a chance," Marc replied.

Chapter 11   Retribution

Nobody wanted to sleep in any of the bunks on the smugglers' ship, so they planned that Blake and Kal would get four hours of sleep, and then the Mea Huli would rendezvous with the smuggler. Blake and Kal would trade places with Liz and Marc so they could get some sleep. Marc decided they would have to make do with three hours so that they would have two hours to plan once ADI had the surveillance data. Catie would take over piloting the Mea Huli for four hours so that Fred could get some sleep.

Once they were underway again, the pilot turned to Marc, "Sayid, we should get rid of any bodies," he said, motioning to the body on the bridge.

"Liz, can you go see if you can wake up any of the crew?"

"Sure." Liz made her way to the crew area. She decided on the three guys who had been playing cards. They had seemed very eager to cooperate and appeared to just be sailors, not directly involved in the smuggling or the kidnapping. She woke them up and motioned for them to drag the bodies out onto the deck.

"I should attend to this," the pilot said when all the bodies were on the deck. "Hasad can pilot the boat."

"Liz, Hasad, up here," Marc hollered. One of the men moved toward the ladder, and Liz motioned him to continue to climb. Marc covered the men on the deck while keeping a watchful eye on the pilot. Once Liz was up, he motioned to the pilot, "After you."

When they got to the deck, the pilot shouted at the other two men, and they went to one of the side lockers and brought out some tools. They then stripped the men, going through their pockets and taking any valuables while they did.

"You, of course, may have anything you wish," the pilot said.

"Just get on with it," Marc said.

After they had stripped the men, the crew put their clothes in a bag. They mixed up what looked like concrete and poured it into the bag on top of the clothes. Marc looked at the pilot.

"We wouldn't want any of it to float to shore; some enterprising police officer might decide to investigate."

Marc nodded as he watched the two men toss the bag over the side. Then they pulled a couple of large knives out of a toolbox. Marc made a show of bringing his Beretta up to discourage any foolishness.

"Not to worry, Sayid. They just need to make sure that the sharks do their part," The pilot said. He motioned to the men to hurry up.

Marc watched with disgust as they slit each body from pelvis to the solar plexus so that the intestines and internal organs were exposed. Then they simply pushed the bodies over the side.

"The sharks will be attracted by the smell of blood and organs," the pilot said. "Soon, there will be no trace of what happened. Those men were simply too drunk to make the ship before we sailed."

Two hours out and everyone except Catie, much to her chagrin, was gathered on the smuggler. They were all seated in the large pilothouse. The boat was idling, and the pilot was locked below in his cabin, as were the rest of the crew.

"ADI, please provide us the intel you've gathered. First, who is this Omar Harrak?" Marc asked as he started the planning session.

"Omar Harrak is a mid-level crime lord in Casablanca. He has powerful friends in the government, especially the military and the police force. He is primarily involved in smuggling drugs and other goods into Portugal and Spain and luxury goods back into Morocco" ADI went on to list various other crimes and connections.

"Okay, how about enemies?" Marc asked.

"There are factions within the government that have been trying to eliminate him, but his friends have been able to protect him. He is also enemies with other crime lords in Morocco. I have traced another enemy, a Berber Chief. His name is Ayyour Dahmani, and he is from a city in the Atlas Mountains."

"That one is interesting," Blake said. "Why are they enemies?"

"Omar also participates in the trade of sex slaves," ADI said. "Two years ago, his men kidnapped a small group of girls who were shopping in Rabat. The girls had wandered into a secluded area, and the men saw them as a target of opportunity. The chief's daughter was one of them; the other girls were from the same village. The men killed the girls' bodyguards and brought the girls to Casablanca for Omar."

"I guess that would piss you off," Blake said.

"Go on, ADI. What happened to the girls?" Marc asked.

"When Omar realized who they were, he had them all killed. He worked hard to eliminate any trace to himself. However, the locals in Rabat recognized one of the men who took them, and Dahmani's investigators discovered this. They captured him, and after interrogation, he divulged the fate of the girls."

"Okay, try to contact Dahmani, let's see if he wants to join the party," Marc said.

"Yes, Captain."

"That gives us a potential ally," Marc continued. "Now, some of you might wonder why we don't just sink the tub and sail away. Well, Omar knows who we are and has plenty of resources. If we don't take care of him now, I'm sure we'll be seeing him in the Azores later."

"I agree," Kal said. "Let's look at the compound layout."

They spent the next hour reviewing the layout of the compound and discussing how they would secure it. The main thrust of the plan was to take advantage of the fortress-like structure. The main house was well fortified, so if they could secure it, they should be able to hold off the rest of the security force, the majority of which was along the wall and in the outbuildings.

"What are we going to do about the Arabic thing," Fred asked.

"We'll all be wearing a keffiyeh to hide our faces. Each of us will have a comm under it. They'll let ADI, our tech wizard, speak for us. She'll feed a translation to yours and then speak for you if necessary," Marc explained.

"What about Liz?" Kal asked. "I'm not sure she's going to pass as a twelve-year-old girl."

"You ass," Liz said. "I'll be wearing a hijab, so my face won't show. Very proper, other than that Catie and I are almost the same size."

"Sorry," Kal said, but he was smiling at the jab he'd got in.

"What are we going to do about the crew once we're off?" Fred asked.

"We're rigging the ship with explosives. Catie will have the trigger. Once we're off, the captain will need to take her back to sea," Marc said. "I've shown the captain the surveillance pucks we have on the bridge and in the main deck area. He knows that if we don't get an accurate headcount after they make sail, or if anyone alerts Omar, Catie will trigger the explosives and send this thing to the bottom. He seems very eager to be cooperative."

"I'd guess so," Blake said.

"Okay, let's get this tub moving again," Marc said. "We dock in thirty minutes."

Once they had docked, Marc and the pilot made their way to the warehouse to collect the van. Marc allowed the pilot to do all the talking. He hadn't shown him that he was able to understand Arabic, so this was a good test of the man's commitment to keeping himself and his crew alive.

They entered the warehouse and found the driver standing next to the van. The pilot walked over and yelled at the man. "Why is the van not ready?" he demanded.

"It is ready, Sayid," the driver replied.

"It is not running, you should be in the driver seat ready for me to open the door," the pilot yelled.

"Yes, Sayid."

The driver ran to the van while the pilot opened the door. When the driver exited the warehouse, the pilot closed the door, and he and Marc got into the back of the van.

"Who is he?" the driver asked.

"That is none of your business. Too many questions and Omar will need a new driver," the pilot yelled.

"Yes, Sayid," the driver drove the van up to the gangway to the smuggler's boat.

Three men came down the ramp leading Liz. Liz had her hands tied in front of her. They crawled into the van while the pilot got out and hurried up the gangway. He motioned for the dock crew to remove the ramp, then rushed to the bridge to get the boat moving.

"Let's go," came from Marc's keffiyeh as he slapped the driver with his Beretta.

When they arrived at the compound, the security guard at the gate let them in with only minor questions; they were obviously expected. The driver drove to the front steps of the house and exited the van. He opened the side panel, and the four men led Liz out of the van and up the stairs to the house.

A security guard met them at the door. "The Effendi is waiting for you. Follow me."

As they walked toward the office, Blake and Marc held back, and once the guard turned down the hallway, they split up, Marc rushing to the roof while Blake ran back to the van to get their equipment. He yelled at the driver to help him carry things into the house. His manner confused the other security guard enough that he simply allowed them to take their bags from the van to the house.

Marc had strapped the parts of a small rifle to his legs. When he reached the roof, he had to use his Beretta, which still had a silencer on it, to dispatch one security guard. Then he assembled the rifle and took position on the edge of the roof to provide cover.

Kal and Liz entered the office behind the security guard. Omar was behind his desk when they came in. He was smiling until he realized that Kal was not who he was expecting.

"Who are you," Omar demanded of Kal as he came out from behind his desk.

"I'm Tarik. Muammer fell overboard, a disagreement about a gambling debt," Kal said. "Zaud sent me in his place."

"You lie, Muammer was a good Muslim, he would never gamble," Omar yelled. "Tell me, who are you?"

Kal stood there stoically holding onto Liz's arm. Omar pulled out a pistol, "I said, who are you?"

"I told you, I'm Tarik," Kal replied.

Omar pointed his pistol at Kal's foot and looked at him. "This is what I do for the first lie," he said as he pulled the trigger.

Kal just stood there looking at Omar as the bullet smashed through his foot. Omar was stunned at the lack of reaction. Liz took the opportunity to drop the ties on her hands, kick the gun out of Omar's hand, and pull her own weapon from beneath her skirt, all while she dove to the ground. She rolled over, coming up to one knee and then put a bullet into each of the two guards, who had also been stunned at Kal's lack of response.

"You let him shoot my foot," Kal yelped.

"Hey, you can patch it up," Liz said. "It made a good distraction."

"Yeah, right."

"You need to head up to the roof," Liz said. "Here, use the elevator."

"I need my rifle," Kal shouted.

"Coming," Blake called back. He ran into the room and threw Kal his rifle case. "I think the shots have the locals a bit concerned. They're heading for the house now. Marc is already on the roof, holding them off."

"Yeah, and I could use some help," Marc hollered in the comm.

"On my way!" Kal called out as he entered the elevator and pressed the button for the roof.

Now that Liz had Omar pinned down, she used some zipties to secure his hands and feet.

"You're all dead," Omar yelled. "My men will stop at nothing until they free me and kill you."

"Oh, put a sock in it," Liz snapped as she shoved a gag into Omar's mouth.

"Fred's covering the front," Blake yelled. "I'm going to cover the back. You'll need to stay here and watch him. Of course, you're free to use that window to discourage any guests."

177

"Just get out of here," Liz shouted as she made her way to the window.

Marc's cover fire from the roof had the security detail pinned down behind the van and in the outbuilding. Liz could see that there were several men on the wall, making their way to positions that would let them get an angle on Marc's position. "Come on, Kal," she urged.

Kal arrived on the roof and immediately assembled his sniper rifle. He moved to Marc's position and lay down. "I can scoot along if I have to," he said. "But I need you to move back behind the chimney there and take care of any fast-moving targets."

"Got it," Marc shouted as he moved back to the chimney.

Kal lined his sights up on the van, "ADI, give me the angle for one of these guys; let's work through them."

ADI, using the drone overhead, outlined the various security men on Kal's HUD. Kal aimed the rifle at the target and fired, shooting through the van. He shot the two men behind the van in quick succession. Then he concentrated on the men on the wall. The top of the wall was a channel giving the men an adobe shield between them and anyone on the inside or outside of the compound. Unfortunately for them, it was no match for the M40 Kal was using. He quickly dispatched four more security men before the rest ducked into the outbuilding for cover.

"Okay, anybody got a hot target?" Kal shouted.

"Nope, everyone has ducked into the security shed," Blake called out. "Can you cover me while I open the gate?"

"We've got you covered," Marc called out as he took up position beside Kal. "Go for it."

Blake rushed out using the van for cover. He made sure that the bodies behind it were dead before he made a mad dash to the gate. A shot rang out as Kal took out one of the security men who was trying to get a bead on Blake from the window of the shed.

Reaching the gate, Blake unlocked it and swung it open. A Moroccan security van entered the compound, followed by two military jeeps.

Four men from one of the military jeeps jumped out and ran to the security shed, demanding that the men inside surrender themselves.

After pointing out that they had grenade launchers, they were able to persuade the six men inside to surrender.

Marc and Kal took the elevator down to the main office. "How's it going, Liz?"

"I'm fine. Omar here seems to be a little upset," Liz grabbed Omar by the arm and pushed him into the desk chair. He had managed to spit the gag out and was screeching in Arabic.

"You sound like a child," Marc spat out. "I'm going to be happy to hand you over."

Omar smiled when he realized that Marc was going to hand him over to the authorities, or so he thought. "I will be back, and I will enjoy killing you," he spat out.

"I don't think so," Marc said. "I'm pretty sure this is the last time we will ever meet."

"I have friends in high places. They will get me out, then I will come for you."

Marc smiled, "Sayid Dahmani may have something to say about that." Omar's eyes went wide as Ayyour Dahmani entered the room.

"Sayid, I think you can take things from here," Marc said.

"My deepest thanks, Sayid McCormack," Dahmani said. "You may take one of my jeeps back to the port. Just leave it there, and we will collect it later."

"Thank you," Marc said.

"No, it is I who is indebted to you. If you ever need anything, please do not hesitate to call."

"We won't," Marc said. "But we don't have any immediate plans to be in Morocco after today."

"May Allāh be with you."

"Hadāk Allāh," Marc replied.

Everyone climbed into the jeep Dahmani had loaned them. "I think that was a successful mission," Blake said.

"Yes, nobody got shot," Marc said. "That's the mark of success."

"Nobody got shot," Kal squawked. "What about my foot?"

"Don't be a baby," Liz shot back. "It's not like it's a real foot."

"You owe me a new pair of shoes," Kal shouted.

"Sure, sure, I'll be happy to buy you a pair of shoes if you just quit whining."

"You think it's funny," Kal shouted back at Liz.

"It is pretty funny," Blake said. "I would have loved to have seen the look on Omar's face when he shot you."

Liz laughed, "It was priceless. I've got a shot of it saved on my comm; I'll send it to you."

"Send me one, too," Marc said.

"Me too," Fred added. "Wow, he was pretty confused," Fred started laughing after viewing the video, and soon the whole jeep was laughing, even Kal.

◆ ◆ ◆

The Mea Huli was waiting for them at the same dock that the smuggler had used. They all quickly climbed aboard, looking forward to leaving Casablanca behind.

"Let's get out of here," Marc said to Catie, who was waiting to greet her father.

"Wait, what about the nephew?" Catie said.

"Oh crap, I forgot all about him," Marc said. "Blake, will you go bring him up. Fred, get us ready to leave."

Blake pulled Muzah out of the stateroom, where he had been locked for two days. "Here he is. Can't we just chuck him over the side once we get out to sea?"

"I wish," Marc said. He gave the nephew a harsh look. Marc dragged him down the gangplank and shoved him into the back of Dahmani's jeep. He tied his legs again and left him there.

"Dahmani will take care of him for us," he explained when he reboarded the Mea Huli. "Let's get out of here."

"We might need to stop for fuel," Blake said.

180

"Nope, all fueled up," Catie said.

"Smart girl," Marc said. "After it, Captain Blake."

"Aye, aye."

Chapter 12 Selling the Chagas

Blake and Kal had dropped Marc, Catie, Liz, and Fred off at Lagos before heading on to the Azores. Fred had then flown the trio back to Lisbon to continue the negotiations, now they were waiting outside of Minister Sampalo's office. The minister had a new secretary sitting outside his office, an attractive woman named Carolina Henriques.

"The minister is just finishing up his call," Carolina said. "He should be with you momentarily."

A moment later, the minister opened his door. "Welcome back," he said. "Would everyone like some coffee?" He got nods from everyone, so he turned to Carolina. "Carolina, would you please bring us each a coffee and some of those nice pastelarias from the café downstairs, and bring one for Senhor Bosco also."

"Of course, Minister," Carolina said as she got up from her desk and headed to the elevator.

"Please come in and have a seat," the minister said. "Senhor Bosco should be here shortly."

"Senhor Bosco?" Marc asked.

"From the finance ministry," Minister Sampalo said. "If we are going to talk about money, we must have a finance lawyer to help us."

"Of course."

"Please be seated. I'm so glad you could make it," the minister said.

"We were happy to accept your invitation," Marc said. "You have a new secretary?"

"Yes, my last one didn't show up for work the day after your last visit. He didn't even bother to call, unforgivable. I never liked him anyway. He was forced upon me by someone in HR; undoubtedly someone's nephew."

"I'm sure," Marc said.

"Ah, Senhor Bosco," the minister said as an older gentleman entered the room. "Let me introduce Senhor McCormack; his daughter, Senhorita Catie; and his colleague, Senhorita Farmer."

"Pleased to meet you," Senhor Bosco said. He shook Marc's hand and gave a bow to Catie and Liz.

"Now we can get down to business," Minister Sampalo said. "Coffee will be here shortly." He motioned for Senhor Bosco to start.

"The Presidente has authorized us to negotiate the fate of Las Cinque Chagas with you," he started. "We are very interested in reaching a mutual agreement, but I must tell you that four billion dollars is far too much money."

"Well then, thank you for your time," Marc said as he started to rise.

"Please, Senhor McCormack, you must allow us to negotiate," the minister said.

"I'm happy to negotiate," Marc said. "But if we're so far apart in what is reasonable, then I feel it will be a waste of everyone's time."

"Possibly I overstated the difference in our positions," Senhor Bosco said. "What would you consider a reasonable starting point for negotiations?"

"Four billion," Marc said.

Senhor Bosco sputtered a little. "The government of Portugal would be far more comfortable with something in the one-billion-dollar-range."

"I'm sure they would be," Marc said. "I am far more comfortable with something in the four billion range."

"We could continue to dance our way toward the middle, but why don't we just go there," Senhor Bosco said. "What about 2.5 billion."

"We have incurred a lot of expense getting to this point," Marc said. "And we still need to raise the ship."

"But surely your expenses cannot be so great, possibly another ten million?"

"I think we're talking about closer to one hundred million dollars," Marc replied. "We've had to pay for extensive research, and develop new techniques and chemicals to ensure we can raise the ship in good condition."

The door opened, and Carolina entered. "Your coffee."

"Thank you, Carolina," the minister said. "Please serve us. Ah, and such nice pastelarias you have selected."

Carolina placed the tray on the table. The coffee was in an elegant silver demitasse coffee pot with beautiful antique china coffee cups. Carolina passed out the coffee cups and the matching plates, then she poured each of them a cup of coffee while offering cream and sugar to everyone. After passing the pastry plate around, she set it in the center of the table next to the coffee tray. "Will there be anything else?"

"No, Carolina, thank you for taking care of us," the minister said. "Please everyone, enjoy your coffee before we get back to business."

After everyone had eaten their pastry, and the minister had poured everyone a second cup of coffee, Senhor Bosco leaned forward.

"Senhor McCormack, I think the government could work with 2.6 billion U.S. dollars. I fear that is the most I can offer."

"I think we can accept that," Marc said.

"How would you like to proceed?"

"We want the money placed in a Swiss escrow account," Marc said. "The escrow account is to be for a term of two years. It is to have an automatic payout to MacKenzie Discoveries two days after the bank receives verification that we have delivered Las Cinque Chagas to you."

"I can arrange that. But why two years? I was led to believe you would be able to deliver her much sooner."

"We believe so also, but we don't want to be overconfident," Marc said.

"What else?" Minister Sampalo asked.

"We want an escort provided by the Portuguese Navy. We'll transmit coordinates and a time to you for the rendezvous."

"A prudent precaution."

"Also, an agreement by your government that they will not interfere with our attempts to raise the ship."

"Of course," the minister said. "May I ask that you provide some documentation of your efforts to raise the ship?"

"We will provide video documentation, but we will retain the rights to the video."

"Could we not share the rights?" Senhor Bosco asked.

"I will agree with that; however, the video is not to be released until we say or until six months after delivery."

"Agreed."

"Then all that's left is for you two to create the proper contract," Minister Sampalo said. "Please continue to use my office. I have another matter to attend to."

"Thank you, Minister," Senhor Bosco said.

Catie gave her father a look. "Catie, why don't you and Liz go back to the hotel?" Marc said. "I'm sure you have something you would rather do than sit through a bunch of contract talks."

"Definitely," Catie said.

After Catie and Liz left the room, Liz gave Catie a hug, "Thanks, girlfriend. I don't think I could have survived a few hours of legal contract talk."

"Me neither," Catie said. "Can you believe 2.6 billion dollars?"

"Pretty awesome negotiator, your dad."

"Yeah, I really liked Daddy's opening move, getting up to leave."

"That was priceless. Did you see the look on Minister Sampalo's face?"

"Yeah, he looked like he was going to have kittens. Daddy does a good job when he acts like a hard ass."

"That's acting?" Liz said. "I thought he was a hard ass."

"Not really," Catie said. "Sometimes he just forgets to have fun."

Chapter 13   How to Raise Her

Everyone was gathered on the sundeck. Marc, Liz, Catie, and Fred had arrived that morning after a quick flight from Lisbon. "So, we're ready to start the next phase of this operation," Marc said.

"How are we sure the Portuguese government will pay up once we give away the Chagas' location?" Kal asked.

"First, we're not planning to give her location away, more on that later," Marc said. "Second, they have put the money in the escrow account, so they can't back out."

"That's great," Liz said. "Now we can finally get down to some real work.

"Just remember you said that," Marc said. "It's going to be a lot of work to raise the Chagas."

Fred's eyes bulged out. "You're going to raise a shipwreck?"

"Not only a shipwreck but one of the richest ones that are out there," Blake said.

"Hey, now he's going to want a raise," Marc chided.

"No, I'm good with the hazard pay," Fred said. "But if you feel compelled to, I won't refuse."

"Smooth," Liz said.

"Ahem," Marc coughed. "We'll headquarter at Vila Franco Do Campo since that's the closest Marina to the east of the Azores."

"Will we have a ground base?"

"Yes, I've had ADI book rooms at the Vinha D'areia Beach Hotel. It's the closest to the marina, although I think we'll be on the Mea Huli most of the time."

"It's always nice to be able to take a bath, or visit a spa," Liz said.

"I agree." Marc turned to Catie. "Now young lady, it is time for you to tell us your mysterious plan. Why did you have ADI send the LX9 out here?"

"Well …." Catie paused for dramatic effect. "Since we now have pirates to worry about, it's even a better plan. We should stage the work from the LX9 instead of the Mea Huli."

"What is this LX9?" Kal asked.

"Um…" Marc hesitated.

"It's a submarine," Catie said. "Very top secret. But we can put the material for the foam base on board it, and it has the ability to extract nitrogen from the seawater. Then we just pump it all through the mixer and into the ship. We'll be right at the same depth, so we can take breaks in the LX9 and not have to worry about pressure changes."

"That's a good idea, at least I think it is," Marc said. "What made you think about using it? And how do you know it will work?"

"You know I've been spending a lot of time learning how to fly her, I mean drive her. So, I've studied up on all her capabilities. It just popped into my head when Uncle Blake was complaining about having to move all those canisters down from the Mea Huli. Then I worked it all out with ADI."

"You couldn't have mentioned this before we did all that practice with the canisters," Kal complained. "My arms still ache from wrestling with those things."

"Well," Catie hemmed, "I wasn't sure it would work then."

Catie texted ADI on her HUD. "*#3 please.*" She had created a short list of private explanations she might need and given it to ADI.

"Captain and Cer Blake, Cer Catie asked me to give you this additional information," ADI told Marc on a private channel. "The LX9 can stay submerged when you board from the Mea Huli. That will limit its exposure to others in the crew and minimize the view by Liz and Kal. As you know, it is very stealthy, Cer Catie's word."

Marc gave Catie a nod to go ahead. "What we do, is extract nitrogen from the ocean water using the LX9's systems. Then we pump it and the foam base out to the Chagas where it's mixed and, voilà, foam."

"How do we get the hose through the LX9's hull?"

"It has a couple of small ports for that. Since we're at the same pressure, there's no risk of decompression or anything," Catie said.

187

"Okay, how much foam base can she carry?"

"Lots, at least half of what we'll need. We can pump it from the Mea Huli whenever we need more. We should be able to use the same container that Uncle Blake got for the Mea Huli, we'll just use them two at a time instead of all four."

"It will help that the Mea Huli isn't hanging around the same spot all the time," Blake added encouragingly.

"Even better," Catie jumped back in. "She doesn't even need to get close to the spot. We can have her stay miles away. We just jump out, board the LX9, and the Mea Huli can sail off somewhere else while I drive the LX9 to the Chagas."

"While you drive her?" Marc asked skeptically.

"Sure, I'm the only one who's qualified, just ask ADI."

"I can see why you like this plan," Blake said.

"And we can use the pumps to pump water and clear the silt from around the Chagas."

"I see you've thought of everything," Marc said.

Catie just beamed at her father.

"Okay, so it does make sense to use this to avoid having anyone know where the Chagas is," Marc said. "We just need to hide the fact that five of us are gone for hours at a time."

"Yeah," Kal said. "If we can rest on the LX9, we could put in two shifts before we have to come back up, we could even stay out for a few days at a time. I'd say we go for two six-hour shifts with a two-hour rest period. That's a fourteen-hour day. No sweat. An hour for dinner, an hour for personal time and eight hours of sleep, we'd be golden."

"Hey, fourteen-hour days doesn't sound very golden to me," Liz objected.

"Hey, Marine, have you lost your edge?" Kal barked.

"Oh, screw you," Liz said. "I can run you into the ground."

"Well duh," Kal said as he pointed to his legs.

"Bite me!"

"Then fourteen-hour days it is."

"I'm not so sure about my daughter working fourteen-hour days," Marc said.

"Hey, she can rest all she needs in the LX9," Blake said. "Once we're in place, and the process is primed, there's not much to do on that end."

"Hey, I can help out in the water, too," Catie said, clearly miffed at being treated like a kid.

"Of course, you can," Marc said. "But someone has to be in the LX9 to keep contact with ADI. We don't have any comms underwater, remember."

"Oh yeah," Catie said. "But I can still help if someone needs extra rest, I can spell them."

"That sounds okay," Marc said. "But I think we'll be better doing one-four-one-four for shifts. It's hard to stay mentally alert for that long, and when you're over four hundred meters down, you need to stay sharp."

"And now we're not going to have to drop canisters four hundred meters," Liz said. "Easy peasy."

"We'll load up tomorrow with the material and containers," Marc said. "We'll do a short day to get a feel for things. Everyone, think about what time we should start out each day."

"Right!"

"Right!"

"Gotcha."

The other four divers followed Catie on their Seabobs. They could just see the LX9 that was sitting at ten meters of depth, waiting for them. Catie zipped toward the rear of the spacecraft and drove her Seabob right into the cargo bay. The other four cautiously followed.

They all followed Catie's example and secured their Seabobs to the opposite bulkhead. Then they followed her to the airlock. Catie cycled herself through the airlock and then helped each of the others do the same. Inside the main cabin, Catie had removed her rebreather, so everyone followed suit.

"Wow, nice sub," Kal said. "It looks more like a G6 than a sub." There were eight rows of seats, one on each side, a galley with a head across from it, then another head at the back with a small table against the bulkhead across from it.

Marc, Liz, and Kal spent some time looking around the main cabin. Catie had the door to the cockpit sealed since Marc really didn't want Liz and Kal to realize that the LX9 was actually a spacecraft.

"As we descend, the nitrogen will get replaced with hydrogen, so no risk of nitrogen narcosis as we go down. When we ascend, we'll pull out the hydrogen and replace it with nitrogen so we can get back to normal depths. We can change the pressure quickly in the cabin independent of the external pressure so we can go down faster. There's also a cargo hold below the deck here, that's where the nitrogen extractor and pumps go. We'll have to put the containers with the foam base into the rear hold. There's just enough room for them and the Seabobs."

"Do these seats recline?" Kal asked.

"Yep, all the way," Catie said.

"Great, then with that galley up front and the two heads, this will be a perfect base to work from. We even have a worktable to do planning."

"Didn't you notice the shower?" Catie said. "I told you it would be perfect."

"A shower, oh thank god," Liz said. "I was having visions of having to take a sponge bath three times a day."

Blake headed to the front. He tried to open the cockpit door but found it locked. "Hey, what's up with this?"

"I'm the captain of this boat," Catie said. "So, I'm the only one allowed up there."

"I think you're taking too much liberty there," Blake said, looking at Marc.

"Her plan, her rules," Marc said. He gave Blake a hard look to ensure there would be no further argument.

"I'm gonna owe you one," Blake gave Catie a mean look.

"Alright, now that we have the lay of the land, so to speak," Marc said, "Catie, you pilot; the rest of us will go back and get the container for the foam. We should be able to get it pumped on board in a couple of hours. We'll bring the other equipment aboard and set it up. Liz can bring in food and other comfort items. Blake, Kal, and I will set up the equipment. We'll pump the foam while we do that. Then we'll go back to the marina for our last day on shore for a while."

It took them three hours to get everything transferred to the LX9. Marc wasn't worried about anyone noticing their position since they were south of the Azores, well away from the Chagas.

Aboard the Mea Huli, they regrouped on the sundeck. Catie had some mango juice, while all the adults had grabbed a beer. "Everyone, let's talk through logistics."

"Daddy!"

"Hey, we've got three hours before we make port," Marc said. "Better now than over dinner. Besides, we need the privacy."

Catie pouted but turned in her seat to face the others.

"With the distances involved, we're going to need to stay aboard the LX9 for days at a time. I'm suggesting we do a five-day workweek, with two days ashore, to keep us sane."

"That's not too bad, the LX9 looks pretty comfortable. We can scrape together pretty decent meals in the galley," Kal said.

"We could. But let's plan on having the Mea Huli come out and give us a good meal twice. That means we get a good meal, then long drive to the Chagas. We work two days, then meet the Mea Huli somewhere close to the Azores," Marc continued. "We get five hours of travel time, so that's one hundred eighty miles."

"Nuh-uh," Catie said. "You have to subtract the time we're on board the Mea Huli unless we're just going to wave at each other."

"Oops," Marc said, glancing at a very smug-looking Catie. "Okay, so only one hundred forty-four miles. I'm worried that it won't take long before someone can map out the general area we're interested in. Are you happy now?"

"Better," Catie laughed.

"But one hundred forty-four miles, if you assume a circle, that's over sixty thousand square miles of ocean," Blake said.

"But they'll guess we're meeting on the periphery once they realize we've got a second vessel involved."

"Then take a short day on the days we have a meal," Catie said. "That lets you add to the radius."

"Alright, if we take four hours off, that gives us another two hours of travel," Marc said. "Then we've got one hundred eighty miles. It feels a little better, but we're going to be at this for three or four weeks."

"Yeah, that's a lot of meets," Kal said. "Drop off, pick up, and two meals."

"You only have to do the meals," Catie said. "The drop-offs and pick-ups can be close to the marina. Since we're traveling, we might as well do it on the LX9. It's got a good autopilot, so we'll be sleeping anyway."

"You're right," Kal said. "So that's only six data points."

"Feels right," Marc said. "Okay."

"How is Fred going to make it look like we're all aboard?" Liz asked.

"Yeah," Fred said. "I'm going to have a hard time looking like Liz or Catie. I've got great legs, but I still don't fill out a bikini very well." He got a laugh from everybody.

"I've been thinking about that," Blake said. "I think we should have Walter and Fatima on board as well. I'll sleep in one of the crew bunks so they can use my cabin. Looks like I won't be using it anyway."

"I can bunk there too," Kal said.

"Good, that gives us the two extra suites we need for them," Blake said. "Then, with three of them, they should be able to make out like they're having a good time playing as they cruise around the Azores."

"You'll generally need to stay out to sea when we're not aboard," Marc said

"Hey, not a problem," Fred said. "This baby's way better than most hotels we're used to staying in."

"Do you think Walter and Fatima will go for it?"

"I'm pretty sure they will," Fred said. "I'll definitely be happy to have some company up here. This is a great toy, but a week all by myself doesn't really float my boat."

"Okay, everyone, relax," Marc said. "We've got an hour and a half before we make port."

"Anyone up for a game of poker?" Fred asked.

"I am," Catie said as she popped up.

"Forget it," Kal said.

Blake and Liz seconded him and headed down to the main deck.

"Do you want to play gin?" Catie asked Fred.

Chapter 14   Working Deep

"Wow, she is big," Blake said as they looked at Las Cinque Chagas. It was lying on its side and covered in a deep layer of silt. It had obviously had a lot of silt deposited on top of it since the last survey.

"I wonder what caused so much extra silt to fall on her," Marc questioned.

"Captain, there were several efforts on the Azores to clear out their harbors. They dropped the debris in the ocean, and this is downstream of one of their dumpsites," ADI explained.

"That explains it," Marc said.

"We need to wash as much of the silt off of the top of her and from around her as we can," Blake said. "ADI, which way does the current flow?"

"There is a slight current that goes ten degrees off the port bow," ADI replied.

"Okay, we wash her from stern to bow," Blake said. "Then we'll start pushing foam into her to lighten her up. The foam will also add some structural support as we go and plug any holes. Of course, with her full of foam, the holes won't matter much."

"Uh, not to be indelicate," Liz said, "but will there be bodies or skeletons?"

"She was carrying almost one thousand passengers," Marc said. "But I would have expected an all-hands abandon ship announcement when she started to go down. And then just flotation would have pushed many of them out of her. We'll have to be prepared to deal with them. The minister and I agreed we would leave them in situ."

"Alright, once she starts to float a bit, we can try to straighten her up and balance her," Blake continued. "That will probably be the most dangerous part, but with the LX9, we can probably do it with acceptable risk."

"Anything else we need to see before we start?" Marc asked. "Did everyone sleep okay last night?" The Mea Huli had dropped them off south of the marina, and the LX9 had taken ten hours to get them to the Chagas.

"I'm good," Blake said.

"Let's review the plan before we head out," Marc said. "We've got limited communication when we're out there. By touching helmets, we can text each other via the comms, but otherwise, it's all hand signals."

"I'll clamp myself to the bulkhead," Kal said. "Then I'll feed the hose out to you guys. I'm not going to be much good for stretching it across. But once it's there, I can handle the nozzle just fine."

"How heavy are the hoses going to be?" Liz asked.

"We're washing the ship for now. So, we'll be using the small line. It'll be filled with water, so it's going to be just slightly heavier than neutral. Same for the big line when we run it. But once we start pumping foam, the small line will be buoyant, so you'll need to tie it to the big line. It balances out and makes the pair neutral."

"We should lay the small line first. Then, while two of us are washing the silt away, the other two can run the big line," Blake said. "Catie, you can feed it to me. That way you'll be on board, and Marc and Kal can start washing."

"Sounds good," Kal said. "Let's gear up."

Catie had set the LX9 down at the halfway point along the length of the Chagas. She'd given them another 10 meters between the LX9 and the Chagas for maneuvering and safety. They would run the line to the Chagas's stern then start washing the silt away. They needed 30 meters of hose so they could reach every part of the Chagas. It only took them one hour before Marc and Kal were washing the silt away. Blake, Catie, and Liz took another hour to get the big hose run and strapped to the smaller hose. Blake strategically located weights at each coupling in the hose.

By the time the first four-hour shift was over, everyone was tired. That is, everyone except Catie.

"Boring," Catie said after they all cycled into the main cabin.

"Hey, I'm happy to let you take some of my onsite time," Liz said. "I'm exhausted."

"Me too," Kal said. "It's a lot more work lugging that hose around than I thought it would be."

"And we've barely gotten started," Blake said. "But I don't think we need four of us on the hose at one time. Two managing the hose, one handling the nozzle seems about right. We can just cycle through the team; one hour on the nozzle, then you come back to the LX9 for a rest, and the next person cycles in. That means you get two hours of rest and three-hours on the hose."

"I don't think Liz and Catie can handle the nozzle," Marc said. "I struggled with it, and I outweigh both of them together."

"You're probably right," Blake said. "How about, they cycle every other hour in the third position. That's the one doing the most movement, not heavy work but a lot of it. Then the rest of us can do one hour of rest, one hour at second position, then one hour on the nozzle."

"You ladies okay with that?" Marc asked.

"Hey, I'm not trying to prove anything," Liz said. "I had enough trouble in the second position."

"Sure," Catie said glumly.

It took them the entire first week to get all the silt off of the Chagas-- well, at least most of it. Now, after a relaxing weekend at Vila Franco Do Campo, they were back into the grind.

"Let's review how we're going to spray the foam," Blake said after everybody had awakened following their trip back to the Chagas. "Tyrant," Catie groaned as she sat up and turned around on her couch.

"Better that than we have an accident because we're not prepared," Blake countered.

"Just give us the lecture," Liz said. "You can squabble with Catie later."

"Alright," Blake said as he gave Liz an impolite salute. "The foam is going to want to float, so you need to start at the ceiling and work your way down. Start at the back of the cabin or deck and work your way back to the porthole where you're going to exit."

"We don't want anyone getting trapped inside the hold because they filled up their exit," Kal said.

"That would be pretty stupid," Catie said with a giggle.

"Yes, but we all manage to do stupid things," Marc said.

"One person controls the nozzle while the other manages the hose. The second person has to keep the hose from getting kinked and limit how much is lying around on the deck," Blake continued.

"Okay," Marc said. "Blake and I will start filling the gundeck with foam. If we come up with any problems, we'll meet again to discuss them; otherwise we'll stick with the rotation."

"Got it," Liz said.

It took them an hour to hook the hose back up to the Lynx and get the foam mixture correct, then they started spraying the foam into the gundeck. Everyone had had a chance on the nozzle when they finally took a break for lunch.

"I liked it better when we just had to move the hose around," Liz said. "This nozzle thing is a lot of work."

"But you get to see more stuff," Catie said. "You're right there in the ship when it's filling."

"I've mostly seen casks and trunks," Liz said. "Nothing exactly earthshaking."

"We've just started," Catie said. "We're working on the gundeck now."

"That's right," Liz said. "Hey Marc, where are all the cannons?"

"We're going to start looking for them tomorrow. When one of us cycles off the hose, they get to backtrack along the current line and see if they can find any cannons," Marc said. "Take a few lift bags, and if you find one, deploy the lift bag on it. We'll try to bring them up and put them on the ship before we raise it."

"Are you crazy?" Catie asked. "They'll make it heavier."

"We can always toss them over the side, but it would be nice to at least gather them up for the Portuguese," Marc said. "They are paying us to retrieve all of the Chagas."

"Where are we going to put them?" Catie asked. "We're filling the gundeck with foam."

"We can put them on the main deck," Marc replied. "There's plenty of room. And we can spray foam around them to secure them in place, and that will lighten the ship up even more."

"We need to tell Fred to get the foam base loaded," Blake said. "We're going through it pretty fast. I think we'll need a refill on Thursday unless we're going to take Friday off."

Marc gave Catie a questioning look. "He's right, we might even run out on Thursday if we keep going through it at this rate," she said.

"Okay, call Fred and tell him to load up some more foam," Marc said. "Plan on rendezvousing two hours earlier on Thursday since we'll need to set things up to pump."

"Got it," Catie gave Marc a quick salute.

By Tuesday afternoon, everyone was hating having to run the foam nozzle. It wasn't hard work, but it was continuous and tedious.

Liz was managing the hose for Blake as he was filling the last section of the first deck of the forecastle. She was anxious for him to finish because then they would get to explore the forecastle, and she thought it would have some more interesting artifacts to see.

She was moving the excess hose out of the room he was in when she saw him drop the nozzle. She stopped pulling on the hose and waited for him to pick it up. Blake moved around to get behind the nozzle so it wouldn't spray on him. He tried to pick it up, but it was partially jammed between two warped deck boards. He twisted it to free it, but when he did, the control went all the way to full stream. The force of the stream knocked the nozzle from his hands, and before he could get control of it, it had filled the room with him in it.

Liz rushed out to signal the Lynx that they had a major problem; she was glad they'd worked out the hand signals for all possibilities.

Catie was keeping watch when she saw Liz signal *disaster*. She killed the pumps, pinged Marc, who was resting, and then waited for an explanation.

Marc rushed out of the main cabin, grabbed a Seabob, and jetted over to Liz. After a few minutes, they both came back without Blake. Marc signaled for Catie to follow them into the main cabin.

"What happened?" Catie gasped after she cycled out of the airlock.

"Blake is trapped," Liz said.

"How?"

"He dropped the nozzle," Liz said. "When he picked it up, it got jammed on full. It filled the space he was in so fast he couldn't get himself out. He's stuck in the foam."

"What, he'll suffocate!" Catie screeched.

"Settle down," Marc said. "His rebreather will keep him supplied with air. We just need to figure out how to dig him out."

"We'll need to cut the foam away from him," Catie said.

"But how do we do that without cutting him?" Marc asked. "We don't know where he is exactly."

"It'd be nice if we could just heat the foam up and let it melt," Catie said.

"I don't think that's going to happen with the whole ocean acting as a heat sink," Marc said.

"If we can figure out exactly where he is, we can safely cut away the foam," Catie said. "When we get close enough, we can break him loose by hand."

"But how do we find out where he is?" Liz asked. "I kind of know where he is, but not well enough to go using a saw."

"I've got it," Catie yelped. She had been furiously texting with ADI on options. "We can use hydrogen and nitrogen," she said. "It'll produce ammonia in an exothermic reaction. The ammonia will dissolve into the water. It should get hot enough to melt the foam and not so hot that it will burn Uncle Blake, at least if we go slowly."

"Do we have hydrogen?" Liz asked.

"If we don't, we can make it," Marc said.

"We should have enough, Catie said." "We just need to run another small hose out there and change the nozzle. We have a smaller one we brought before we were sure about which size to use for the foam. If we just drill holes, we can figure out where it's safe to use the saw."

"Okay, let's get the hose run," Marc said. "I'm sure your uncle is getting a little impatient."

They were unrolling the small hose when Kal came back from finding cannons. Marc signaled him to go into the Lynx and get an update from Catie. He swam over to her and touched helmets.

"What's going on?" he asked.

"Uncle Blake got trapped in the foam," Catie said. "We're running another hose out so we can mix hydrogen and nitrogen to make ammonia. It will generate heat so we can drill holes in the foam and figure out how to cut him out."

"We can't just leave him there and let the Portuguese dig him out later?" Kal joked.

"No!" Catie squeaked and punched Kal in the shoulder. "Now go help. Take the saws with you."

It took them two hours to dig Blake out. He swam directly back to the Lynx and cycled into the main cabin without saying or signaling anything. Catie followed him in.

"Are you okay, Uncle Blake?" she asked as he came out of the bathroom.

"Just peachy," he said with a sullen tone.

"Hey, Liz said it wasn't your fault," Catie said. "Don't be mad. We got you out as fast as we could."

"I'm sure you did," Blake said. "But couldn't you find a way to let me know what was going on?"

"We didn't think about that," Catie said. "Once we figured out how to get you out, that's all we thought about. I'm sorry."

"Don't be," Blake said. "I guess I would have done the same thing."

"Hey, Mister Foamy," Kal said after he cycled into the main cabin.

"Don't you start," Blake snarled.

"Too soon," Kal said with a laugh.

"I think a couple of years too soon," Catie said as she patted her uncle on the back.

"Maybe two weeks," Kal said. "I think I can hold off for that long."

"Well, it's your life," Catie said as she punched Kal.

On Thursday, the team started at 1:00 a.m. Blake was in a marginally better mood. He seemed to have made it a personal mission to use all the foam up before the end of the day. When he had the nozzle, whoever got stuck handling hose was scrambling to keep up with his mad pace.

"Cer Catie, I have an emergency message from Cer Fred," ADI said.

"Put it through," Catie said as she swam to the airlock to cycle into the main cabin. "What's up, Fred?" she asked.

"We've got a Portuguese cutter hanging out past the marina; based on surveillance from ADI and our best guess, they plan to do an inspection."

"Oh no," Catie gasped.

"Right, they'll be surprised to find just three of us," Fred said.

"Can you go back to the slip?" Catie asked.

"We're almost to the exit," Fred said. "We're kind of committed, turning back now will raise questions. Can you ask your dad what we should do?"

"ADI, signal an emergency recall," Catie said.

"Give me a map of the area and where the cutter is," Catie ordered. The map came up on her HUD. "How fast is the cutter moving, and how far is it from the marina entrance?"

"Ten knots, and one nautical mile," ADI replied.

"Okay Fred, I want you to stall for two or three minutes, check fuel lines, slow down to a crawl, anything to buy a little time. Then I want you to head west as soon as you exit the marina, take her up to max speed. When the cutter is within a quarter-mile, swing around so you're bows on, and act like you've just launched the Seabobs. Then stall when the cutter gets to you. We're all diving, just a normal day for all of us."

"Then what?"

"We'll be there," Catie said.

"How can you, you're almost three hundred miles away."

"Don't worry, I've got a plan! And Dad can always change it once he gets here, but you have to start now!"

"We're on it. Slowing to a crawl," Fred said.

"ADI, plot a course to an intercept point where the Mea Huli will likely come to a stop. Make sure the sky is clear where we come up and fly. Assume constant acceleration, deceleration profile; get us there in ten minutes. Ping me when everyone is aboard."

"The captain is entering the cargo hold now," ADI said.

"Seal the hold, start pumping it down," Catie ordered. "Are the hoses free?"

"Yes, the captain followed protocol and disengaged them," ADI replied.

"What is the acceleration profile, max velocity?"

"Acceleration is 0.25Gs, max V is five hundred forty-three meters-per-second."

"Engage along plotted course, what's the speed in Mach?"

"Mach 1.5."

"ADI, emergency decompression starting now!"

"What's going on, Catie?" Marc's voice came over the comm now that he was in the Lynx.

"The Mea Huli is about to be boarded for inspection by the Portuguese," Catie said.

"Shit!"

"I have Fred stalling, then doing a bit of a high-speed chase to buy time. I have a plan that gets us there, but our friends are going to know this is more than a sub."

"Keep executing your plan. Blake's coming up to confer with you."

"Alright, everyone needs to be strapped in," Catie said. "You've got one hundred twenty seconds."

"Copy," Marc replied.

A minute later, Blake cycled through the airlock to the bridge. "What up?"

"You heard what I told Daddy?"

"Yes, so what's the plan?"

"We go airborne," Catie said. "Maintain a quarter-G acceleration, drop back into the water, close the rest of the distance, then get on the Seabobs, and pretend we've been off for a morning romp."

"We can't come up four hundred meters that fast," Blake gasped.

"We're using the emergency decompression the Paraxeans developed."

"What's that?"

"Decompress two atmospheres, hold for five seconds, then compress up one and hold for twenty seconds, repeat."

"That works?"

"According to ADI. If we start having the bends, we'll abort."

"What's the max speed we get to?"

"Mach 1.5."

"Big shock wave," Blake said.

"Nuh-uh," Catie said. "No shockwave. Didn't you see that in the specs?"

"Oh yeah, I did," Blake said. "Then I got distracted with sunken treasure ships and didn't get a chance to read up on it."

"Something about the shape of the hull and some things sticking up," Catie said, "prevents a shock wave from forming."

"Okay, stick to the plan."

"Hold on," Catie yelled, "we're going to pitch up out of the water."

"Yeah, how is that going to work?"

"Watch," Catie pointed to his HUD. "ADI put simulation of the flight up on our HUDS."

As the LX9 approached thirty knots, Catie pitched her up to 20 degrees. Two seconds later, her nose exited the water, and she started gliding along the surface. The engines were now taking in air instead of water; they superheated the air, and it came boiling out behind the LX9 as it really started to accelerate. Soon the LX9 was traveling well above her takeoff speed, and Catie pulled the yoke back and sent her into the sky. Five seconds later, Catie leveled her off and brought her back down to the deck. Now she was accelerating right above the ocean surface.

"I assume ADI is stop-gapping you," Blake said nervously.

"Yes, I get to fly unless I exceed one of the safety limits," Catie said. "If I hit one of the limits, ADI takes over and keeps us safe, but she can't be as aggressive as I can."

"Good to know," Blake gasped.

"What's going on up there?" Marc yelled over the intercom.

"You all were strapped in, weren't you?" Catie gasped.

"Thankfully, yes," Marc said. "How long do we have?"

"We'll be level for another eight minutes," Catie said, "then we'll have to land on the water again, and it'll get bumpy until we slow down enough to sink."

"Okay, we'll just stay strapped in," Marc said. "Blake, you good?"

"She's got a good plan, just hang in there."

"Copy."

"How do we approach the Mea Huli?" Blake asked.

"We'll drop down into the water about one mile out," Catie said. "We're too low for radar, and with the hull absorbing light and EM, we'll be practically invisible. Then we drop down to twenty meters and go diving."

"Okay."

"ADI, status on the Mea Huli?" Catie asked.

"Cer Catie, the Mea Huli has started accelerating away from the marina."

"Time to intercept?"

"The cutter is just turning toward the Mea Huli now," ADI said. "Researching online, I have found that its top speed is specified at thirty-two knots, but I have also found references to a top speed of thirty-five knots."

"Use the thirty-five knots!"

"That would give you fifteen minutes before Fred would need to execute the stop maneuver as instructed."

"Okay, give me Fred."

"Hey, they're just starting to chase us. What's the plan?" Fred asked.

"Same as before," Catie said. "ADI will transmit the coordinates where we want to meet, but essentially just keep heading southwest until you have to stop. We'll adjust on our end as we get close."

"How are you getting here so fast?"

"Later, Fred," Blake cut in. "Let's just let Catie's plan play out."

"Okay, we've got about fifteen minutes on our end," Fred replied.

"That's what we're calculating as well," Catie took back control of the conversation.

The LX9 continued to accelerate until it reached the halfway point.

"We're going to decelerate now, everyone, hold on," Catie announced over the comm. Then she extended the XJ9's flaps and pitched its nose up 10 degrees to force the deceleration necessary to get slow enough to enter the water. As they slowed below the LX9's 120-knot max surface speed, Catie set her down on the water. She let the LX9 skip along the surface of the water. It took ninety seconds before it slowed down enough to sink below the surface.

"Okay, folks, we're back to normal cruising speeds," Catie announced. "We'll be rendezvousing with the Mea Huli in four minutes. Did you copy, Fred?"

"We copy," Fred announced. "We're just about to shut her down and turn as instructed. They're getting close."

"You just need to stall them for a couple of minutes," Catie said. "Tell them I challenged everyone to a race. They'll expect that of a twelve-year-old."

"Yeah, as long as they don't know you, they will," Fred replied.

"ADI, start flooding the cargo bay again."

"Yes, Cer Catie," ADI said.

"Okay, Uncle Blake. Let's go back and get geared up. I've got the autopilot set to bring us to within half a mile of the Mea Huli. We'll have to do the rest on the Seabobs."

"That'll only take us a couple of minutes," Blake said. "So, we have to chase you?"

"Yeah," Catie said. She slapped Blake on the chest and yelled, "You're it." She ran to the airlock and cycled through it. She ran through the cabin so she'd be the first through the second airlock to the cargo hold. "Liz, stall Uncle Blake for me, will you? Everyone, we're doing a race on the Seabobs back to the Mea Huli. We should be stopping in about two minutes." With that, she donned her rebreather and cycled through the lock.

"Where's that brat?" Blake snapped when he finally got through the airlock from the bridge. Catie had used her command override to put it in a self-test cycle just as she exited it. It had taken Blake a couple of minutes to figure out what she'd done and reset the airlock.

"She's probably on her Seabob heading out by now," Liz said as she waited her turn at the airlock. Kal and Marc had already followed Catie into the hold, and the airlock was just about to open to admit Liz. Blake grabbed the handle to the airlock. "Hey, wait your turn," Liz snapped, slapping his hand. "I'm next."

"That brat trapped me in the cockpit," Blake complained.

"So, she's smarter than you," Liz teased.

"But I'm bigger," Blake retorted. "Wait until I catch her."

"Why have you boarded us?" Fred demanded of the officer from the Portuguese cutter.

"I am Segundo-tenente Santoro. We are just doing a quick check to make sure everything is alright," he said. "Tell me where Dr. McCormack is?"

"I told you he is diving with his daughter. They're doing some kind of race."

"Where is everyone else?"

"Walter and Fatima are down below showering," Fred said. "The others are all in the race."

"We did not see you …"

"I win!" Catie yelled as she yanked her rebreather off and steered her Seabob over to the dive deck of the Mea Huli.

"You cheated," Blake shouted back as he pulled up beside her.

"I did not, I just used tactics," Catie shouted back.

"Ah, here they are now," Fred said.

Marc, Liz, and Kal arrived at the dive platform at a more sedate pace, bringing their Seabobs to rest without bumping the Mea Huli.

"We have guests," Fred yelled down to Marc.

"Oh," Marc said. "Give me a minute, and I'll be up." He secured his Seabob with a line and then made his way up the ladder to the main deck. "To what do we owe this pleasure?"

"Minister Sampalo was curious as to how you are doing," the segundo-tenente said.

"And you are?" Marc asked.

"I am Segundo-tenente Santoro, of the Portuguese patrol boat, Guadiana," he replied.

"I'm happy to meet you, but Minister Sampalo assured me that the Portuguese government would not interfere with our efforts."

"We are not interfering," the tenente said. "We are just checking in. The minister had indicated that he thought you would be very busy right now. Not racing and playing games."

"We're still doing training and prep work," Marc replied. "We gave the minister a two-year timeline. I'm surprised that he is so impatient."

"He is not impatient," the tenente said. "Just curious and maybe a little anxious. Well, I will let him know that you are still training."

"Please do."

With that, the tenente boarded the small launch that had brought him and his aide over to the Mea Huli. They sped off back to his cutter.

"I didn't like that," Blake said as he came up behind Marc.

"I didn't either. I'm wondering why anyone else is aware of what we're doing," Marc said. "Do you think they have another leak?"

"You can count on it," Kal said. "There is just too much money on the table, or ocean floor to be precise."

"I suspect you're right," Marc said. "We'll need to do some planning."

"Yes, we will," Blake agreed.

"Okay," Fred interrupted. "How the hell did you guys get here so fast?"

"Top secret," Marc said. "Suffice it to say, Catie likes to go fast and is willing to actually study to make sure she can take any opportunity that presents itself."

"Is that really all you're going to tell us," Kal demanded.

"Unless there is a reason you need to know more," Marc said. "Are you still on the team?"

"Sure, sure," Kal said. "Even more so. I want to stay with you, so I get a chance to see how fast Catie can really go."

"Same here," Liz said. "Nothing's changed, except we have a lot more capability than we thought we had."

"Thanks, guys," Marc said. "We'll find a time to share more when it's appropriate."

"Alright, we've got an extra four hours to indulge ourselves. I say we go back to the marina and have a nice meal at the most expensive restaurant we can find. Catie's buying."

"Why am I buying?" Catie squawked.

"You won the privilege with all your tactics," Blake shot back.

"Okay, just as long as you admit, I won."

◆ ◆ ◆

It was Tuesday the next week when the Chagas finally moved. *"Wow!"* Blake thought to himself as the big ship shifted. He turned the nozzle off and waved everyone away from the ship.

Kal pumped his fist as he pushed himself off toward Liz. They did a high five when they met up.

"What's up with them?" Catie texted her father, touching her helmet to his so they could communicate. They were in the cargo hold waiting to rotate in.

"I think she moved," Marc texted back.

"Woohoo," Catie texted.

Blake signaled for Willie to be sent out. They had been using Willie to scout out areas of the interior of the Chagas before sending someone in to spray foam. As Marc got Willie out of the hold and sent him off toward Blake, Liz and Kal made their way over to the LX9. Once Blake ensured that Willie's tether was free and he could survey the area around the Chagas, he made his way back to the LX9 and cycled into the main cabin.

"So, she moved," Marc said when Blake exited the airlock.

"She sure did," Blake responded.

"Why stop?" Catie asked. "Seems to me that we should get her floating by the end of the day."

"Hold your horses, Missy," Blake said. "There's a lot of suction where she's settled into the silt. If we kept spraying foam in her, she might just pop free and pop to the surface before we could do anything."

"Ohh."

"We need to see if we can rock her free," Blake continued. "Let's get a couple of lines on her and use the LX9 to see if we can get her loose from the bottom. Then we can figure out how to balance her out."

"We've got lots of cannons to do that," Catie said. The crew had collected fifteen cannons that had been strewn in the Chagas's wake as she was sinking to the ocean floor.

"I'm sure they'll help," Blake said. "I say we all rest for a couple of hours while we use Willie to look around her. Then we'll go out and run a couple of lines and nudge her a bit."

"You're the engineer," Marc said. "Everyone, you heard him. Get some rest, we have some hard work ahead."

After two hours of rest, they all headed out and strung the lines to the Chagas. It took two hours to get the three lines in place the way Blake wanted them. Then Catie went to the bridge of the LX9 to do the nudging. They had strung a fiber-optic cable to Blake so he could maintain constant communication while they were trying to spring the Chagas free.

"Okay, Catie," Blake texted. *"Just give the LX9 some buoyancy and see if we can gently nudge her."*

Catie pumped some water out of the cargo hold to give the LX9 some lift. As it floated up, the line became taut, and the LX9 started to drift over toward the Chagas.

"Let her keep drifting over," Blake texted. *"Just keep adding to the lift."*

Catie continued to expel water from the hold. Soon the LX9 was directly over the Chagas, and the lines were tight.

"Now apply the engines," Blake continued to instruct Catie. *"Keep the LX9 level, she's going to want to sink a bit as you apply thrust, just let her. We're not in any hurry here."*

"Understood," Catie replied as she started to apply thrust.

"A little more… more… Cut!" Blake added.

The Chagas lifted out of the silt and righted itself. She had about 30 degrees of list as her keel settled back on the bottom. *"Alright,"* Blake texted, *"shut her down and don't let the cables get tangled."*

Catie set the LX9 down, backing off from the Chagas so the cables were straight, but not taut. Blake signaled everyone to re-board the LX9 as he made his way back over to it.

"Okay, another survey with Willie," Blake said once everyone was in the main cabin. "We'll check out the main cargo holds now." Up to this time, the crew had been adding foam in the gundeck, in some of the cabins, and in the bilge. They had been avoiding the main cargo hold.

"Now we get to see what's up with the cargo," Blake said. "A lot of it might have settled back into place. We'll add foam as we need to, but it would be nice if we could get her to a natural balance."

"We don't want to be shifting the cargo around," Marc said. "That could be dangerous."

"I know," Blake replied. "Let's just see what we have, might be able to do a little pushing with Willie to get things settled in. That's it for the day. I'll work with Willie for a while, but we won't be going back out until tomorrow."

"Should we skip the rendezvous with the Mea Huli for tonight?" Marc asked.

"I think so," Blake replied. "We don't want to have to undo the cables. And I'd like to keep a watch on her in case something shifts around on its own."

"Good plan. I'll let Fred know."

Everybody was buzzing, hovering around Blake to watch the video feed from Willie. "Guys give me some room," Blake snapped, frustrated at the constant hovering.

"Hey, if you put your view up on the net, we can all watch from our own HUDs," Catie told Blake.

"Good idea," he replied, giving the necessary commands.

"He should have done that earlier," Liz said as she settled on her seat. "This is much more comfortable."

"Yes, it is," Kal agreed, "very inconsiderate of him."

"Enough from the peanut gallery," Blake snapped back.

"And so disagreeable," Catie added with a giggle.

"Do you think he still has foam in his ears? Maybe it's causing him to be irritated all the time," Liz whispered. She had to duck a punch from Catie, who was still a little protective of her uncle about the foam accident.

"I heard that," Blake said. "Just you remember, paybacks are hell."

Blake continued to operate Willie for four hours. He managed to shift some casks that were piled up against the side of the hull. They rolled down to settle in the bottom of the cargo space. There were a few other shifts in the Chagas, and by the time Blake was ready to call it a day, the Chagas was only listing at 10 degrees.

"Great," Blake declared. "Tomorrow, we put foam in the main cargo space until she's floating. Then we'll add cannon or two on the deck to get the list out of her. She should be ready to raise by Friday morning if all goes well."

"That's nice," Marc said as he bit his lip and nodded his head. "Friday morning."

"Do you have a plan for our navy friends?" Blake asked.

"I think so," Marc said. "We'll have to see how it plays out. For now, let's eat and then get some sleep so we can get that baby ready to float."

It was Kal's turn to cook, and he decided to go big as a celebration. He whipped up some pork BBQ and Hawaiian fried rice. Everyone was surprised when he produced a couple of bottles of wine to go with the meal.

After dinner, Marc called Minister Sampalo. "Minister, I'm glad I caught you in your office. I was afraid you might have gone home."

"Not to worry, this is still early for me. I don't usually leave the office until after seven," Minister Sampalo said.

"Long days."

"Not really, I just like to start a little late, then meet my wife here in the city for dinner. To what do I owe the pleasure of your call?"

"We're getting ready to raise the Chagas," Marc said.

"Oh, so you're ready to start work on her. That's good to hear."

"No, I mean, we're ready to raise her," Marc corrected. "We'll need our escort tomorrow."

"Tomorrow! That is certainly a surprise. A delightful surprise," Minister Sampalo said.

"I'm happy to hear that. Will you be able to have our escort ready?" Marc asked.

"I'm sure I will. Admiral Santoro has assured me that it can be in your area within twelve hours. So, what time would you like it, and where would you want it to be?"

"We'd like the escort to meet us at 14:30 hours at 38°01'02" N 22°11'58" W. We're looking forward to having the Chagas on the surface. She is looking beautiful now," Marc said.

"And we are looking forward to seeing her as well," the minister said. "I will be meeting you at Port Delgada on Friday, then."

"We look forward to seeing you," Marc said. "Good day."

"So, you're setting them up to tip their hand early," Blake asked.

"Right," Marc said. "I want to see who shows up at the rendezvous coordinates and where the Portuguese navy winds up."

The next day the crew drove several corkscrew anchors into the ocean floor. They then anchored the Chagas to them to keep her from floating away. Then Blake, had them add the cannons. Each cannon was anchored with foam to stop it from rolling around. Then they added foam in the hold with each cannon until they reached neutral buoyancy. It took them all day to get the fifteen cannons loaded on the ship. By the time they were done, the main cargo hold was almost full of foam, and the Chagas was pulling at the lines holding her to the ocean floor. At 4:00 a.m., just before their regular break, Blake called a halt to the foaming efforts. He had the crew roll up all the hoses and return them to the LX9's cargo hold. During the break, he explained the next phase of the operation.

"She's pretty buoyant now," Blake said. "But as she rises, the density of the water will go down, and she'll lose buoyancy. So, after the break, we'll be spreading the canvas under her hull. Each side will be held up with lift bags (as he indicated using a napkin), just like a diaper. Then we'll keep inflating the lift bags until she breaks the surface. Once she's floating, she'll be more buoyant since there won't be any water on her upper deck, and the upper cabins will spill all their water as well."

"Oh joy," Kal said, "that canvas must weigh a ton."

"Not quite," Blake said. "It's two hundred fifty pounds per strip, and we have ten strips to deploy, and that doesn't count the lift bags. So, rest up, me mateys."

Everyone groaned as they grabbed a sandwich and settled down on their couch to rest. They were already tired from wrestling all the hose back into the cargo hold, so nobody was looking forward to having to wrestle all that canvas. The two hours of rest that Blake had allowed them went by fast.

"Okay, boys and girls, time to go back to work. I want each person to drag one strip of canvas over to the Chagas. Put a lift bag on it before you leave the LX9, inflate it until it's neutral, and then guide it over. Make sure you don't get it moving too fast, and it shouldn't be too hard."

Marc elected Catie to stay with the ship. This time she didn't argue too much. She'd had her fill of schlepping heavy stuff around and didn't mind being excluded due to age and size. She watched as the others made two trips each to get the strips out to the Chagas. Then while Liz and Kal started unrolling them, Blake and Marc made a third trip to get the last two strips.

Liz and Kal unrolled the 8-foot-wide strip of canvas and dragged one end under the Chagas. Then they attached another lift bag to that end and filled it up until the canvas was snug against the Chagas's hull. It took them three hours to repeat the process nine more times. Marc and Kal ferried lift bags and air canisters to them as needed. Finally, all ten strips of canvas were deployed. The lift bags on each end were about half the distance up the Chagas's hull, just below what Blake was setting for the waterline.

"We're ready," Blake declared as he cycled into the main cabin behind the others. "By the way, Marc, aren't we approaching the appointed time?"

"We are at that. I moved one of our satellites into position; it's waiting over our coordinates. ADI says she's been tracking a group of naval vessels from Portugal, but they've settled in at a set of coordinates that are one hundred miles north of the target location."

"Interesting," Blake said.

"Anything approaching the coordinates?"

"Not for sure, but we have a likely group of five vessels. They left Port Delgada early this morning. Ostensibly they're on a fishing trip, but they've been staying close together and inching toward the coordinates. They're a little over four hours away at twenty knots."

"Well they had better hurry, or they'll be late," Blake said.

"Maybe it's not them," Catie said.

"I have a feeling," Marc said. "And we have a winner! They've changed course and are heading that way at full speed."

"Do we know who they are?"

"No, ADI traced the registration. They're all rentals, so no trace on who's doing the renting. Apparently, they paid cash and left a cash deposit."

"No wonder you had a feeling," Kal said. "What size are they?"

"They're all about twenty meters, so pretty big boys as far as fishing boats go," Marc added. "ADI says they have a top speed of about twenty-five knots, so plenty of juice there."

"I wonder what they're carrying," Kal said.

"We'll see once they get close."

"Where's the Mea Huli?"

"She is all the way on the north side of the island, actually kind of close to the Navy boys. What say you? Should we go meet up with the Mea Huli and go talk to the Navy guys?"

"How long will it take us to get there?"

"I think Catie can get us to a rendezvous about ten miles from the Navy, where we can meet up with the Mea Huli and then take a nice leisurely cruise over to say hi."

"Alright," Catie pumped her fist as she made her way to the cockpit. "Everyone, strap in. It won't be too bumpy, but I don't want to dump anyone on their ass."

"Catie!" Marc hollered.

"Give it a break, Marc," Blake said. "She's been hanging out with all of us; you can't expect her to stay a little girl."

"I know that, but her mother might not," Marc said.

"Well then, she'll have to watch herself around her mother. We certainly did around ours."

Marc laughed, "I guess we did. And especially around Gran. Man, could she make you regret a misspoken word."

"She still can," Blake laughed with his brother. "My ass still hurts thinking about it."

Catie cycled onto the bridge and settled into the pilot's chair. "Ship, seal the cargo bay, start pumping out the water. ADI, give me a course to a location within ten miles of the Navy flotilla that the Mea Huli can reach in two hours."

"Plotted," ADI said.

"Fred," Catie said, "we're going to be meeting you at these coordinates," Catie pushed the coordinates to Fred via her HUD. "We'll meet you there in two hours."

"I heard, thanks for the coordinates," Fred replied. "See you there."

Catie brought the LX9 around and headed along the vector. She had it depressurize using their standard routine, and started rising up toward the ocean surface. This time instead of trying to get airborne, she would simply bring the LX9 up onto the surface where it could do 120 knots. They would be a little early to the rendezvous, but she figured she should test out the LX9's max surface speed, just *because*.

"Captain," Marc greeted the Portuguese Navy captain as he came aboard the Mea Huli.

"Dr. McCormack," the captain returned the greeting. "I'm pleased to meet you, but I was led to understand you would have another ship sailing with you."

"That was the plan," Marc said. "Let me introduce my crew first, then I'll explain."

"Of course."

"This is my brother, Blake; my daughter, Catie; and our colleagues, Kal Kealoha, Elizabeth Farmer, Fred Linton, Walter Williams, and Fatima Cartwright."

"I'm pleased to meet you. I'm Captain Nunes of the Frigate Corte-Real, and this is my aide, Commander Reza." The captain and the commander exchanged handshakes with everyone.

"Now that we know each other," Marc said, "let me explain."

"Please do," the captain said; he was obviously not pleased with the situation.

"These are the coordinates we gave the minister for the rendezvous," Marc said as he handed the captain a slip of paper.

"What? Why this is almost two hundred kilometers from here."

"Yes, hence my surprise when we identified your flotilla via satellite," Marc said. "We couldn't see any other naval flotilla in the general area, so we decided to come visit you. Now here is a satellite image of the area around the coordinates where we were supposed to meet." Marc handed the captain a picture that ADI had pulled from one of the many satellites now available to commercial ventures. It showed a reasonably good picture of five large cruisers approaching the target area.

"Who are these people?" the captain asked.

"We don't know, but we were pretty sure that the Portuguese government would not be sending a few large fishing charters out to escort us to Port Delgada."

"Certainly not," the captain said. He turned to his aide and instructed him in Portuguese to contact Port Delgada and ask them to intercept the five fishing boats there. "We shall find out," the captain said once the commander had moved to their launch to communicate the orders.

"I wonder if it might have anything to do with Segundo-tenente Santoro, who stopped us a little over a week ago. We were surprised to have someone from your Navy show interest in us before we called. Our agreement with the minister was to minimize the knowledge of our activities."

"That is Admiral Santoro's nephew. I am surprised as well. The minister's instructions to me were to minimize any knowledge of the activity. I am the only one in my command who knows that the Chagas is supposed to be here, and I only found out the specifics of it two hours ago. Before that, all I knew was that we were to rendezvous here with an important ally of the Portuguese government. But Admiral Santoro has been taking an uncommon interest in my activities for the last three weeks."

"I'm happy to hear that the minister has been taking precautions," Marc said.

"While my aide makes sure we discover what is going on with these pirates," the captain said, "may I ask where your companion vessel is?"

"Of course," Marc said. "She's about three hundred miles from here, resting on the bottom and waiting for us to let her rise to the surface."

"She is still at the bottom?" the captain gasped.

"Yes, but she has been filled with foam and sealed up. She's floating about two meters up and just needs to be released from the anchors, and some additional gas injected into the lift bags, and she will surface like a porpoise," Marc said. "Would you and your command like to escort us to her? We just need to make the final dive to bring her up."

"I would be most delighted to do so," the captain said. "Would you like to bring your gear aboard our ship so we may make better time?"

"The Mea Huli can do thirty-two knots," Marc said, "and we have quite a bit of equipment. We'd probably lose the time that more speed would give us, just shifting the equipment."

"An impressive speed for such a craft," the captain said, obviously impressed. "We should make way now. We have fifteen hours of sailing ahead of us. I guess we should not hurry, it will be very early in the morning when we arrive."

"That will not be a problem," Marc said.

"You will dive in the dark to raise her?"

"I think that might be best," Marc said.

"I think you may be right," the captain agreed. "Might I invite you and your daughter to dine with me tonight? We could accommodate two other members of your crew as well. Possibly Ms. Farmer and your brother?"

"We would be happy to join you for dinner," Marc said as he glanced at Liz. Liz nodded her head with a smile.

"Very good, we'll send the launch. When we get underway, please lead us at twenty-four knots," the captain said. "We do want my patrol boats to keep up with us."

Catie was happy that Liz had talked her into wearing a dress. Everybody at the table was dressed in their dress uniforms; Marc and Blake had wisely elected to wear suits.

"And you wanted to wear capri pants," Liz teased.

"How was I to know?"

"Dr. McCormack and Commander McCormack and ladies, welcome."

"It's just Mr. McCormack," Blake said.

"Ah, but I disagree. My commander assures me that I would bring disgrace on the Portuguese Navy if I did not refer to the winner of the Navy Cross by his true rank," the captain said. "Please come in, and I'll introduce my officers. You have met my commander. This is Primeiro-tenente Da Cruz, who commands our patrol boat, Dragão." The tenente snapped to attention and gave a slight bow. "And this is Subtenente Peixoto, our communication officer." The subtenente snapped to attention and gave a slight bow also. "Gentlemen, may I present, Dr. McCormack, Commander McCormack, the doctor's daughter, Catie, and Ms. Elizabeth Farmer, who I understand was also in your military, a captain."

"You are correct," Liz said, "but that is behind me now. Ms. or senhorita works just fine."

"Of course," the captain said. "Gentlemen, if you would escort the ladies to their seats, we may begin our evening."

Subtenente Peixoto extended an arm for Catie, and Primeiro-tenente Da Cruz extended an arm for Liz. They led them to the table and seated them, then took a seat on each side.

The captain motioned for the steward to pour the champagne. Catie looked at Marc, and he gave her a nod to let her know she could have some.

"Let me offer a toast," the captain said. "To Las Cinque Chagas!"

"To Las Cinque Chagas!"

The steward then brought out the soup for the first course. The meal was leisurely, and the food was outstanding. The meal consisted of caldo verde, a kale soup, followed by posta mirandesa, a tenderloin beefsteak with new potatoes. At the end, the steward brought out leite crème, a Portuguese version of crème brulée.

After the dessert was finished, the captain leaned back and signaled for the steward to serve coffee. "Dr. McCormack, might I ask how you became a treasure ship hunter?"

"Of course," Marc said. "It was actually Catie's idea. I had developed a new sonar design that I sold to the U.S. Navy. It gives a much clearer picture of the ocean floor. Once I sold it, we were talking about what we should do next, and Catie suggested searching for sunken treasures."

"A bold move."

"Yes, we did a lot of online research, looking for possibilities," Marc continued. "We decided that if we found one, it would be great, if not, we would have a great time cruising around the world in the Mea Huli."

"Why do you think Las Cinque Chagas has not been found before?"

"Several reasons," Marc said. "One, the survivors said it blew up, so one wouldn't be looking for a whole ship."

"Why would they say that?"

"As we told Minister Sampalo, it looks like the ship broached and capsized. I'm sure it sank very quickly. A ship on fire disappears suddenly. *It blew up* sounds better than it disappeared."

"Ah, possibly, it would be better to say that than to have everyone wonder who was able to sail it away."

"Yes," Marc said. "Then two, the way it sank, it actually floated a long way before it hit the bottom. We recovered cannon for over one hundred kilometers. So, the location was very inaccurate. And given the depth of four hundred meters and silt covering the ship, it was very difficult to find."

"But your new sonar was able to find it."

"Yes, we got some very clear imagery of a vessel. The Chagas is a very impressive ship, and even with much of the top structure destroyed by fire, it's still massive."

"Do you think the fire affected the treasure?"

"The main cargo hold seemed to be unaffected. There were quite a few holes in the stern, but they mostly affect the gundeck."

"Most fortuitous. And how did you come by your Mea Huli?"

"I bought it from the government," Marc said. "It was seized in a major drug bust that I was a consultant on. We wanted something comfortable to sail and also so Blake could run charters while I developed the sonar."

"Yes, that is a very fine vessel," the captain said. "Very impressive speed and far more comfortable than my frigate."

"I don't know," Marc said. "This looks pretty comfortable to me."

"Well, there are certain accommodations that a captain has," the captain said. "But we don't have a sundeck, nor the leisure of diving or swimming off our stern."

"I guess the work part does get in the way of the cruising," Marc said.

"We will be arriving at 01:00. What time will you be diving?" the captain asked.

"I think we'll target 02:00," Marc said. "That will give us time to prepare our equipment and time for you to ensure we don't have any uninvited guests."

"Speaking of uninvited guests," Blake said, "do you know what happened with the five fishing boats?"

"We had an aircraft sent to herd them in. One of our patrol boats from Port Delgada met them and brought them back to the port. They tried to throw their weapons overboard, but the patrol boat managed to discourage them," the captain said. "Of course, they deny everything, claiming they were just out to have fun and fire off the weapons in the open waters."

"Not very believable," Blake said.

"No, we will have to see what happens. The possession of such weapons is a serious crime. They may decide to talk once they understand how much trouble they are in."

"And Admiral Santoro?" Blake asked.

"It seems that the admiral has taken a vacation trip with his wife and children to Brazil, where he has some family."

"Interesting timing, when did he leave?" Marc asked.

"He left yesterday, right after we received our instructions to meet you," the captain said. "Now, I think we shall end our evening. Until tomorrow, early though it may be."

"Until tomorrow."

"Well guys, what do you think?" Marc asked once they were back on the Mea Huli with the others.

"I think we can trust the captain," Blake said, "and I'm happy to have them patrolling above us."

"Yeah, but it means we can't use the LX9," Catie said. "We're going to have to dive down the hard way."

"It won't be too hard. But we will need to ride those nitrogen canisters down," Blake said. "We'll put a lift bag on each, and then someone needs to guide it down, releasing the gas as they go."

"So, one hour down," Marc said. "We deploy around the Chagas, each of us next to one of the big lift bags we placed there yesterday. Then we ease her back up."

"What about the anchors?" Kal asked.

"We detach the lines and pull them up," Blake said. "We can put them aboard the Chagas. But that adds another hour."

"So, a three-hour dive," Liz said. "Not such a bad way to earn 2.6 billion dollars."

"We did most of the earning over the last month," Kal said.

"Okay everybody, go rest up," Marc said. "I'll have Fred wake us when we arrive at the site."

The next day was anticlimactic. They just followed the script. Catie filmed the effort since they couldn't use the LX9 as a base with its external cameras. Marc had given Captain Nunes and Fred a wide, keep-out area so that the Chagas didn't come up underneath one of the ships.

Then they dove down. Handling the nitrogen canisters was difficult, and they were happy that they'd done so many practice dives with them. Once the lines were cut, the Chagas rose another ten meters before it reached equilibrium. Marc, Blake, and Kal removed the six corkscrew anchors, while Liz positioned the canisters next to each of the main lift bags.

Two hours in, and it was time to start going up. They set a steady pace, stopping every fifty meters. Blake wanted to make sure that the foam had enough time to outgas and that the divers would be fully equalized before progressing upwards. Although they didn't have to worry about nitrogen narcosis, they still had to avoid the bends. The compressed air in their bodies needed time to expand and release. Although the pace of their climb was supposed to take care of that, Blake was taking extra precautions. He wanted them to pause and stretch and move about to encourage their bodies to reach equilibrium with the reduced pressure.

They paused again at fifty meters, giving Catie a chance to circle the entire ship with the camera. They switched over to nitrox while they waited. After their air had time to exchange fully, Catie went up to ten meters to film the last part of the climb. Aboard the Mea Huli, Fatima had a camera trained on the target point of emergence. Blake gave the signal that he was ready to start the final climb. Once he had a thumbs up from everyone, he released a lift bag to mark the likely point of emergence for Fatima and the Portuguese.

They started the last part of the ascent; when the Chagas reached ten meters, they slowed the assent way down. They wanted the Chagas to emerge in dramatic fashion, slowly rising up from the sea. Blake had

Marc and Liz on the bow increase their lifts so the Chagas would rise up, bow first, and then they took her up to two meters. They each shot the rest of their gas into the bag, detached their canisters, and pushed away from the Chagas to let her rise up the rest of the way on her own.

Las Cinque Chagas emerged from the water, her bow leading the way. She gracefully continued up until her entire upper deck was clear. Slowly she continued to rise until the gundeck was also above water. The lift bags were just below the surface, giving the illusion that the Chagas was floating on her own. When she first broke the surface, the Portuguese Navy started a twenty-one-gun salute. The cannons continued to boom as the Chagas rose above the water, and it ended just after she settled with her decks entirely above the water.

The crew swam over to the Mea Huli and pulled off their gear. They each took a quick shower and changed into their clothes, then they all got in the tender and went over to the Chagas. They climbed the rope ladder they had attached to the sides and waited.

Captain Nunes and Commander Reza were being brought over on their launch. As Captain Nunes led the way up the ladder, Liz blew a whistle that piped him aboard.

The captain was surprised and obviously pleased by the addition of the whistle. "Captain Nunes," Marc said. "I formally hand command of Las Cinque Chagas over to you and the Portuguese Navy."

"I accept," Captain Nunes said. He looked around the deck in awe. "Even with the fire damage, she is an impressive ship."

"I assume you will be towing her to Port Delgada?"

"Yes, one of my patrol boats is making ready to extend a tow," the captain said. "Will you come out to join us when we sail her into the harbor?"

"We would be happy to. Just tell us where to take up station," Marc said. "We'll wait for you at Vila Franco Do Campo."

"Yes, we'll have to sail at ten knots," the captain said. "It will take us two days to get there. We don't want to tow her at night."

"Then we'll come out and meet you when you're a few hours out," Marc said.

"Excellent. Until we meet again."

"Things are going to be hectic for the next few days," Marc said. He'd gathered the members of MacKenzie Discoveries in the lower salon where they would have some privacy. "We should talk about future plans now."

"Sure," Kal said. "I'm up for anything."

"We're not going after the Spanish galleon?" Liz asked.

"I think that would be risky," Marc said. "With all this exposure, and as we've seen no lack of people willing to kill and bribe their way into wresting it from us, I think we should shelve that for a while, if not forever."

"You're probably right," Liz said. "We're rich; we're all alive; we should probably count our blessings."

"Right," Marc said. "Now yours and Kal's share of the Chagas is forty-eight million each. We don't have the money yet; it'll probably take a few weeks for the escrow to clear, but I can advance you each one million, so you have some flexibility."

"What are you going to give Fred and crew?" Catie asked.

"I was thinking one million each would be fair," Marc said.

"Wow," Blake exclaimed. "More than generous."

"Well, it was a bit more hazardous than we expected," Marc said.

"I agree," Catie said.

"Okay, so our plans are to sail the Mea Huli to Lisbon and put her in storage for a while. Then, after all the parties and ceremonies are over, we're going to go looking for an island to buy."

"An island! Why in the world would you want to buy an island?" Liz asked.

"We have some additional technology like the LX9 that we're planning on commercializing. We want to do it from a base that we can control. Someplace remote enough that it will be difficult for various governments or corporations to interfere."

"You mean, steal your technology," Liz said.

"Steal, interfere, various things," Marc said. "Anyway, we want to be as autonomous as we can be."

"Where is this island?" Kal asked.

"We're thinking one of the Cook Islands," Marc said.

"Geez, where are they?" Kal asked.

"About three thousand miles due east of Australia," replied Marc. "Actually, they are almost due south of Hawaii. Hawaii is twenty degrees north; the Cook Islands are about twenty-one degrees south."

"Sounds really nice," Kal said. "It would be just like home."

"So, if we wanted to stay with you, what would our roles be?" Liz asked.

"We'll still need security, even more so now. We'd want you two to head up our security force; hire and train the right people to protect the technology and us. There will probably be other duties as we expand and learn what we need."

"What's the pay?" Kal asked.

"Not as generous as this was, but let's say 0.5 percent of profits on top of a base salary of three hundred thousand," Marc said. "Profits will start out small, but should ramp up into the billions if we're successful."

"I could go for that. Build a nice beach house, take some kick-ass vacations," Liz said. "What do you think, Kal?"

"Hey, I'm in. I'm not cut out to be a playboy."

They reached the marina a little after 5:00 P.M. Marc took the team out to dinner and announced the bonus package for Fred, Fatima, and Walter. The three of them were ecstatic. Fred said he wanted to keep flying for Marc and company, especially when Marc said he would be extending the lease on the G650. Walter said he'd use his money to start a small charter company in his home state of Wyoming. Fatima was torn, but she said it was time for her to start a family. She and her husband had been waiting until they could afford for Fatima to quit work while the children were little. Both Fatima and Walter agreed to stay with them until Fred found replacements.

After dinner, everyone retired to their hotel rooms. When they entered their suite, Marc looked at Catie. "Okay, spill it. What have you been bursting to talk about?"

"You could tell?"

"Of course."

"I've been working with ADI, with all that time on the LX9 just sitting around."

"I'm glad you made use of the time. Did you get any schoolwork done?"

"Yes, but that's not what this is about."

"Okay, what is this about?"

"I felt real bad for Kal. He worked hard, and his prosthetic legs didn't really help that much. He had to work twice as hard as anyone else because he couldn't get any power from his legs."

"Yes, I think we all admired him for his courage and refusal to let it hold him back."

"Me too. So, I asked ADI what kind of prosthetics Dr. Metra's people had for people when they lost their legs. ADI said they didn't use prosthetics. I was shocked. How could they be so cruel that they just let people go around with no legs," Catie looked sheepish. "But then ADI said that they didn't use prosthetics because they just made them new legs."

"Wow," Marc said. "As in biological legs?"

"Yeah, they print them up on a three-D printer using the patient's own DNA to design them. Then they attach them to the patient, and after a couple of days, it's just like they never lost their legs."

"So can ADI do this for us, or help us design the printers?"

"She can help with the printers, but all of that information and the process is in their medical computer, and ADI doesn't have access to it."

"That's strange. ADI, why don't you have access to the medical computer?" Marc asked.

"Captain," ADI answered, "it is for security reasons. The captain of the ship has control of me; if he had control of the medical computer as well, it would be impossible to control him if he were to become ill or insane. The medical officer is the only one who can access the medical computer."

"Okay, what happens if the medical officer is killed?"

"There is a chain of command," ADI replied. "However, our medical officer is not dead, she is in stasis."

"Can we just wake her up?"

"No, the current medical situation on the ship has a very strict protocol that must be followed."

"Daddy wait, I'm not finished," Catie said.

"Okay, what else?"

"Well, when I realized how advanced their medical science was, I asked ADI about other diseases. I asked about Alzheimer's."

"I see," Marc said.

"ADI says that Dr. Metra was very interested in Alzheimer's and dementia because her people suffered from the same type of diseases. She actually did some experiments and determined that a similar treatment to the one they use would work on humans."

"What kind of experiments?"

"She gave the treatment to actual people," Catie said. "I guess some alien abduction did go on in the seventies. Anyway, she treated them, then let them go. They never knew they were abducted. But they all got better."

"That is significant."

"Yes, we could help Grandpa Pa and Grandma Ma," Catie pleaded. "But we have to hurry. They're getting really bad."

"I know. Your mother told me the last time we talked," Marc said.

"Can you figure out how to get Metra out of stasis?"

"I'll work on it."

"Promise?"

"I love your mom's grandparents, too," Marc said. "I'll figure a way."

"Thanks, Daddy!"

◆ ◆ ◆

"Prime Minister Marsters will see you now," the beautiful Polynesian secretary told Marc.

Marc led the way into the office with Catie following. Marc thought that having Catie along had smoothed the negotiations with the Portuguese; it was difficult to play hardball with a twelve-year-old girl watching.

"Thank you for seeing us," Marc said. "My daughter, Catie."

"I am pleased to meet you, Dr. McCormack," Minister Marsters said, "and your daughter as well. Please, how may I be of assistance?"

"I run a new company, MacKenzie Discoveries," Marc said.

"I have heard of you. You were the ones that found the Las Cinque Chagas last month," the minister said. "I'm sorry to tell you, but we don't have any treasure ships around here."

Marc laughed, "We're not looking for treasure ships now. That was a way to increase our startup capital. We're looking to buy a location where we can headquarter our business."

"If you are not seeking treasure, what is your business?"

"We have several advanced technologies we are looking to commercialize. We're looking for a friendly place where we can develop and manufacture them."

"We are very ecologically conscious here," the prime minister said.

"As are we," Marc replied. "We promise to develop and manufacture our products with a minimal impact on the environment. In fact, many of our technologies are intended to improve the environment."

"Please tell me more," the prime minister said as he leaned forward in his chair.

"We have developed a new battery technology, which has five times the power density of the lithium-ion battery. We've also developed fuel cell technology, which is extremely efficient. We believe between the two of them, they will revolutionize the trucking industry."

229

"Very interesting," the prime minister said, "but we don't have very many natural resources here. Why our islands?"

"Our biggest concern is industrial espionage," Marc said. "We want a remote and secure location where we can manufacture the key components. Then we can ship the parts to industrial countries where they will be integrated into final assemblies."

"Interesting, but again I ask, why our islands?"

"You are remote, we like your weather, you're independent of any large industrial power," Marc said, "and we actually would like to buy an island."

"To buy one of our islands?"

"Yes, Manuae, to be precise," Marc said.

"Manuae is a sensitive nature preserve," the prime minister gasped.

"I know," Marc said. "We guarantee we will preserve that essence. We need a small, ground footprint, but we plan to build floating offshore structures to house much of our facilities."

"And how much would you have to invest?" the prime minister asked.

"I'm sure you know that," Marc smiled. "We have approximately two-billion dollars to invest."

"And what, besides your money, would my people get?"

"Several things," Marc said. "One, jobs; two, an advanced medical facility; three, educational opportunities."

"Jobs, I can understand; however, you should know that employing Polynesians does come with some unique issues."

"I am aware of that. One of our partners is Hawaiian. He assures me that he can develop a set of work rules that allow Polynesians to both enjoy the benefits of employment as well as the benefits of living in Polynesia," Marc said. "He tells me that he won't give up the opportunity to go fishing or sailing just for a job."

"Ah, I see he does understand. *And*?"

"We will guarantee any Cook Islander free access to the advanced health care of our medical facility. We cannot afford to provide basic health care to everyone in the islands, but as we develop cures for diseases and advanced treatments, we will provide those to your people, even things such as prosthetics."

"And to gain all this, what do you want?"

"As I said, we wish to have control of Manuae. We will pay you a negotiated sum for the rights to the island for fifty years. After that time, we will restore the island to its original condition. We also would like to negotiate a favorable tax rate for our company."

"Ah, you don't want to pay taxes."

"We're happy to pay taxes. We just want to simplify the process. We think that fifteen percent of gross sales should cover all our tax liability. Of course, we expect to pay social security and other employment taxes for our employees."

"You are willing to have your taxes based on gross sales?" the prime minister asked.

"Yes," Marc said. "It eliminates all the accounting dances that most corporations play. We want to invent, develop, and manufacture technology, not become accountants."

"I am greatly intrigued," the prime minister said. "I will discuss this with my cabinet and the legislature. I believe we have room to negotiate."

"Thank you," Marc said.

"And may I ask how you fit into all this young lady?"

"I'm one of his partners," Catie said. "My mother is a doctor, and I'm interested in the medical facility."

"It's due to Catie's insistence that the medical facility is one of the first capital investments that we plan to make. We already have some promising treatments that we would like to make available to the world. Of course, for many of those treatments, the patient would need to come to the Cook Islands."

"Our hotels and tourism industries would be pleased to accommodate their families," the prime minister said. "As I said, I will discuss your proposal and get back to you. Let us say two weeks."

"We look forward to continuing our negotiations," Marc said.

The team settled into the Pacific Resort in Rarotonga. Marc wanted to be close to the government offices while they negotiated their deal, and it was one of the nicest places available.

"You know, none of us has ever negotiated this kind of deal," Blake said. "Aren't you nervous?"

"Sure, I'm nervous," Marc replied. "That's why I'm bringing Samantha Newman in."

"Samantha Newman?" Blake gave Marc a confused look.

"She's the one who handled the papers on the Mea Huli."

"So, a boat lawyer is what you have."

"She's more than a boat lawyer. She handled the deal on the Mea Huli as a favor to our DEA friend. She's a senior partner in a firm that concentrates on international law and trade agreements."

"So, you hired her firm?"

"No, she's taking a leave of absence," Marc said. "I offered her twenty million dollars and the job as our legal counsel if she makes this work."

"She should be motivated."

"Yep, and if you remember, she was beyond tenacious. Dale, our DEA friend, his wife, works as her paralegal. She says Samantha scares the crap out of the other side when she's negotiating treaties."

"That's what we need here," Blake said.

"Hey, I'm going to be gone for a while. I need you to find us a hospital ship to use while we build a new clinic. Figure a twenty-million-dollar budget."

"You want me to find what? Where are you going?"

"Can't tell you yet," Marc said. "Don't worry, Samantha will be here next week; she'll help you."

"You know I'm the sail and fly around the world kind of guy, not really a businessman," Blake said.

"Then it'll be a good growth opportunity for you," Marc quipped. "And I need you to watch Catie for me."

"No!" Blake howled. "You can't saddle me with a child. I'm finally getting some action. The women here think scars are cool, the sign of a warrior. I'm finally sexy again."

"Liz will help you," Marc said. "Catie just needs to know her Uncle Blake has her back."

"You are asking a lot," Blake said.

"You can handle it."

Chapter 15   For The Ones I Love

"Why can't I come with you?" Catie asked.

"Because I will be in meetings, and I can't afford to leave you unprotected. We need Liz and Kal here to start up our security service."

"But..."

"But nothing. It will only be a few weeks," Marc said. "Just behave yourself and focus on your studies."

"Okay," Catie said. "But call me."

"I will."

Marc boarded their jet, greeting Fatima at the hatch. This would be her and Walter's last trip. Fred had located two replacements and would be picking them up in Hawaii.

"Welcome aboard, Marc," Fatima said.

"Hello," Fred said from the cockpit. "Six hours to Oahu. I hope you brought something to entertain yourself."

"I have."

Once in the air, Marc took advantage of the privacy being the only passenger on the flight afforded him. He needed to have a serious discussion with ADI.

"ADI, please restrict all information about my location and movements as well as access to the queries I will be making."

"Yes, Captain."

"I want to discuss the situation with the medical officer. Explain under what circumstances she can be brought out of stasis early."

"The medical officer may be brought out of stasis if the medical quarantine is declared over," ADI said.

"How would it be defined as over?"

"A qualified medical officer would have to decide the emergency was under control."

"Define qualified medical officer."

"Any senior medical officer of the Paraxean fleet would qualify."

"How does one become a senior medical officer of the Paraxean fleet?"

"The doctor would have to serve aboard a Paraxean ship under a senior medical officer for five years," ADI replied.

"Okay, what other circumstances would allow you to bring the medical officer out of stasis?"

"A medical emergency," ADI said.

"Define a medical emergency."

"Any medical threat to a member of the crew that could not be handled by the normal medical bots."

"What are the medical bots?"

"They are small, you would call them robots, that have an AI and are capable of handling small medical issues."

"What types of medical issues are they not qualified to handle?"

"Serious life-threatening issues, medical conditions like a stroke which might result in permanent impairment, serious infections from unknown sources."

"What would be a life-threatening issue? Ignore infections, list injuries that would require the doctor."

"Brain trauma, a heart attack, a spinal fracture, kidney, and liver disease, although they would likely be handled by the medical bot. Wounds to the heart, lungs, liver, intestines."

"You are aware of our weapons and the damage they can do."

"Yes, Captain, I have observed the use of weapons by your team."

"Specifically, a 9mm Beretta."

"Yes, Captain."

"Would a gunshot from that weapon into the leg qualify as such an emergency?"

"No, Captain, the medical bots would be able to handle such a simple wound."

"A gunshot to the shoulder?"

"No, Captain, the medical bots would be able to handle that as well."

"What if it impacted the joint?"

"They would, with an eighty percent certainty, be able to handle such a wound."

"A gunshot into the gut?"

"Captain, please define gut."

"A bullet right below the navel."

"There is a ninety percent probability that the medical bots would not be able to handle such a wound. There are too many complications that they would not be able to handle."

"If a crewmember were to sustain such a wound, what would happen?" Marc asked.

"The medical bots would be called to assess the wound and stabilize the victim. The doctor's stasis pod would start to bring her out of stasis. If the bots determined that the wound required the doctor, they would move the victim to the medical bay if possible. There the patient would be put into stasis until the doctor fully woke from her stasis pod."

"How long would that take?"

"It would take approximately four hours," ADI said. "The time varies based on the individual."

"Once the patient was taken care of, what happens to the doctor."

"Normal procedure would be for the doctor to reenter stasis."

"Can that procedure be overridden?"

"Yes. In the current emergency, the doctor can declare the medical quarantine is over. That would start the process to release all the crew from stasis."

"What else?"

"The captain can rule that the medical officer is vital and cannot return to stasis."

"Am I authorized to make that ruling?"

"Yes. You are the captain."

"Thank you, ADI."

It was late at night when Marc took the wave runner out to sea from the marina at Grand Hyatt Kauai Resort and Spa. He had purchased it the day before and had it delivered to the hotel's small marina. In only a few minutes, he was out of sight of anyone on land.

"ADI, have the LX9 surface one hundred meters in front of me. Once it has surfaced, have it open its cargo bay."

"Yes, Captain."

Marc could barely make out the LX9 as it surfaced and opened the cargo bay. Only the light of the cargo bay gave him any indication that it truly was there and not just a shadow from the moon and clouds. He drove the wave runner up into the cargo bay and shut it down.

"Ship, close the cargo bay and submerge twenty meters."

Marc made his way to the cockpit of the ship. "ADI, have the LX9 return to the Sakira."

"Yes, Captain."

It only took two hours until the LX9 entered the flight bay of the Sakira. Marc had to wait an additional twenty minutes while the water was purged from the bay. Then he exited the LX9.

"ADI, show me how to get to the bridge."

"Follow the guide on your HUD," ADI said. "It will show a green line along the path you should walk."

"Thank you, ADI." Marc made his way to the bridge. The path included some kind of elevator that took him sideways as well as up. When he exited it, he was clearly on the bridge. There was a huge display and two pilot chairs in the forward section. The center of the room held a large chair with a smaller chair next to it. There were several consoles around the side of the room with chairs for the crewmembers. It reminded Marc of the bridge of the Stennis when Blake had given him a tour.

"ADI, please guide me to the medical bay."

Marc followed the green line to the medical bay. It was just a few floors below the bridge, and the elevator took him most of the way.

The medical bay looked much like a hospital emergency room. There were small alcoves with treatment beds on them, a laboratory off to one side. Some exotic-looking equipment was spread around the exterior, mounted to the ceiling.

"ADI, I forgot that I had my Beretta on me," Marc said as he pulled the weapon from the holster on his back. "I probably should have secured the weapon when I came on board."

"The captain is entitled to carry a sidearm," ADI said. "The preferred weapon on board the ship is a laser pistol, but your weapon will not be too dangerous."

"Thank you, I should make sure the safety is on," Marc said. He held the weapon pointing sideways and looked at the safety. His finger was on the trigger, and it twitched. The gun fired, shooting a bullet at a 10-degree angle to the side of his navel. "Oops."

"Medical emergency! Medical emergency in the Medical Bay!" blared over the ship's speakers.

Afterword

Thanks for reading **Starship Sakira**!

I hope you've enjoyed the first book in the *Delphi in Space* series. As a self-published author, the one thing you can do that will help the most is to leave a review on Goodreads and Amazon.

The next book in our series is **Delphi City**.

The McCormacks have a starship, now they need a safe place to start harvesting the technology. They're starting with a place in the Cook Islands, but to succeed they have to avoid spies, figure out how to manufacture the new technology using Earth-based tools, and then introduce it without getting into too much trouble with the governments and big corporations of Earth.

Come read along as they build their team from the initial five to enough to run and protect a city. They're preparing to take the human race into space, but will they succeed before someone manages to take over their spaceship and technology? And can they finish before the Paraxeans come looking for their spaceship?

Acknowledgments

It is impossible to say how much I am indebted to my beta readers and copy editors. Without them, you would not be able to read my books due to all the grammar and spelling errors. I have always subscribed to Andrew Jackson's opinion that "It is a damn poor mind that can think of only one way to spell a word."

So special thanks to:

My copy editor, Ann Clark, who also happens to be my wife.

My beta reader and editor, Theresa Holmes.

My beta reader and cheerleader, Roger Blanton, who happens to be my brother.

Also important to a book author is the cover art for their book. I'm especially thankful to Momir Borocki for the exceptional covers he has produced for my books. It is amazing what he can do with the strange PowerPoint drawings I give him; and how he makes sense of my suggestions, I'll never know.

If you need a cover, he can be reached at momir.borocki@gmail.com.

Also by Bob Blanton

Delphi in Space
Starship Sakira
Delphi City
Delphi Station
Delphi Nation
Delphi Alliance
Delphi Federation
Delphi Exploration
Delphi Colony
Delphi Challenge
Delphi League – coming in April 2021

Stone Series
Matthew and the Stone
Stone Ranger
Stone Undercover

Made in the USA
Middletown, DE
26 July 2021